PARTING THE MEND

A Novel

JEFF NIEDER

ISBN 978-1-956696-91-2 (paperback)
ISBN 978-1-956696-92-9 (digital)

Rushmore Press LLC
1 800 460 9188
www.rushmorepress.com

Printed in the United States of America

For Katie,
There are tales in these days of darkness.

After I died, and the makeup had dried
I went back to my place.
No moon that night
But a heavenly light
Shown on my face.
Still I thought it was odd
There was no sign of God
Just to usher me in
Then a voice from above
Sugarcoated with love said
"Let us begin."

—Paul Simon, *"The Afterlife"*

If only you'd have known me before the accident
For with that grand collision came a grave consequence
Receptors overloaded, they burst and disconnect
Til there was little feeling please work with what is left
Oh I need not be flattered that you've never been here before
So there's no need to mention that you've no firsts anymore
But if you let me be your skyline I'll let you be the wave
That reduces me to rubble that looked safe from far away

—Benjamin Gibbard, *"The Ghosts of Beverly Drive"*

TAKEOFFS AND LANDINGS

We died in January of the next year. April, as it does for all things decayed, brought us back under the watchful resuscitation of spring. Twelve weeks—not better, not healed, and certainly not *reborn*, the patchwork method of coerced faith, a process that grows less selective as the need deepens. We were back and we could wait, but unlike the book that is returned to the shelf, we had a choice. Movement or stagnation. There was no reverse. That we were more than objects waiting on the world was a concept as foreign as time travel.

No time for useless things anymore. A reserved parking spot that anticipated the return of a machine that may never come back had no function. Specifically useless was the vacant spot that came included with the rent for unit 4. The shellshocked sedan in slot 1 hunched toward a broken left side, pushed into a ruined tire by unseen hands. Immobile perhaps but purposeful storage, nonetheless.

Areas 2 and 3, stubbornly kept independent by a stuttering line of yellow paint, were empty for now. The spirals of crusted oil, reaching into bullet-hole pot marks topped by the occasional ballet of forgotten plastic grocery bags, would be covered soon. Broken glass fragments of dust crushed to the point of no real concern were one with the asphalt and the arbitrary collection of cigarette nubs, bottle tabs, and caps. Despite the near-connectedness of the tattered fourplex with the commuter line into the city, the absent vehicles were still needed for those in search of more local stations of minimum wage or subsidized kindness and would limp back soon, tenants redepositing into their own holding cells until the next useless day. Not spot four though.

The ancient stains there—more under than on the surface— would remain exposed, looked after by a wire shopping cart (of course, there was a shopping cart) and a short rusted post upon which hung the bicycle chain. The lock swayed in the grip of a chattery breeze but was unable to let go, like a rotted tooth still clinging to the strings of browned-out but familiar gums. Another item with no use. His brother's ten-speed would not survive an evening, much less broad daylight, under the tandem patrol of corroded chain and untrusted lock.

A hesitant sky hung loose overhead. The grey lady of Midwestern suburban winter had snow in mind but, for now, kept her arms slung around it, intentions hidden, the sun her captured spy. Here, at the apartment, *his* place, the Venice Green Apartment Homes—*a great place to start*—the sky eroded, as if the bright afternoon he swore existed just moments earlier had been forgotten. It wasn't the sky at all that weighed on him, and he knew it.

An unconscious reminder persisted as he crossed the parking lot. The ebb and outcome of the afternoon would pass, at first inhaled, but would become memory like the blown fog of warm breath back into the chilled air. The square brick box dropped and beaten into place over a slab foundation where his brother now resided would linger, as would the person taking up residence inside of his brother. No, that would not pass.

The pressure lever on the entry door accepted a hesitant push and escaped his hand as if pulled in by an unseen doorperson. The crash behind him should have taken out both the top and lower squares of glass but never did. The double pane security glass shook like dice tumbling in a can, acting as a would-be alarm in place of the unlocked complex door. Under a cautious first step the handrail, which one could not fully grip until step five, logrolled in his palm. Unit 1 and unit 2, which was missing the number, were left below as he climbed and stood in the landing between units 3 and 4. The beams underfoot bleated with a muted agony against his reflective ebony dress shoes. A suppressed anguish of aged wood and neglect spoke with each step. Above him, a tobacco-stained yellow stammered a series of unorganized flashes in visual Morse code inside a cracked recessed fixture.

The bray of Marv Albert's sportscasting cadence shook him from his focus on the decay. Door framing walls to his left and right were a color he imagined was a tan ashamed to admit that it had once been close to pearly white. A hefty bag, not the kitchen type but the outdoor kind, lay in a meaty heap at rest against door 3, and Marv . . . Marv was behind the sliver-width open bowed door where a ten-cent 4 hung in a near-perfect diagonal on the front. And somehow, so was Martin's brother Steve.

He exaggerated his steps and added a verbal greeting to the knock, both meant to announce his arrival and mask the embarrassing howl, a sound beyond a creek that tore from the winding hinges of the door. The back of his brother's couch, the focal point of the room upon entry, was torn at each corner and had a center that looked shot and left behind; the color was in the area of lime green that had lost a grip on hue and now drifted into a lost brown.

"Hey, Steve?" Martin Coleman called into the room.

As he entered, the afternoon was overcome, no better than a hoax. Inside of the efficiency apartment, the soft winter light, weak to begin with, was defeated by black window coverings stretched end to end over the sitting room glass and replaced by the glow of television.

"Hey, Marty, its open," Steve's voice came over the couch, but his head refused to acknowledge his visitor.

Marv Albert's prattling from the box-style television speaker sounded more alive than the person in the room. A smell of fabric sheets lain over neglect floated just there under each breath. A laundry basket of towels, either on the way to or back from, was perched on the kitchen table.

"Yeah, I noticed," Marty said. "You're going to get ripped off like that."

"Nobody wants anything in here," Steve said in a heavy voice.

A raised remote paused the motion on the screen. The interruption required a pointed and directed sigh. The particle-board bookshelves held no more than the small television set and a row of plastic cups with assorted sports logos in a line like trophies. The coffee table that split the room between the islands of couch and TV set was balanced on each side by an equal stack of newspapers and sports magazines. A tall empty mug was a periscope among the disarray.

"What are you doing?" Marty asked, the words tripped over his tongue; a previously undiscovered and hopefully temporary stutter fractured the first and last syllables. "Weren't you supposed to be back at work?"

"Yeah, I didn't feel like going."

"You know, that's not really up to you."

Marty's legs, now weights in sand, carried him to the kitchen, and he gripped the counter, but not without a quick glance down at the surface.

"Yeah, it kind of is."

Steve could not remember the last day he actually left the apartment behind for work at a job.

"Not going to go over too well there this time of year."

"I'll just ask for my leave to be extended or something, you know." Steve considered his uninvited guest again. "Besides, if you thought I wasn't here, what are you doing?"

"You didn't pick up either," Marty deflected after a deliberate delay.

"Ringers off, you know that." Steve pushed rather than turned his head from the paused screen to look at Marty.

"What good is a phone that doesn't ring?" Marty asked.

A fashionable not functional dress coat, closed at the neck, hung over Marty and covered what would be a dark suit—maybe a sharp charcoal or slate if you were in the right light, and the kitchen was not even close to the right light. A dry clean–only dress shirt would be underneath, finished at the sleeves by cuff links. A printed tie that might buy a week of groceries for a family of four would be snug under the tabbed, in-place collar and leveled off just above the genuine leather belt.

"Nobody I need to hear from anymore," Steve said. "What? Are you worried about something? If you are, you have a hell of a way of showing it."

"Look I would have left you a note or something."

"If that's what you wanted there's a pad in there somewhere, go for it."

Marty let a deep breath press into a gaze, and he looked out the small window over the sink for something to focus on. A haphazard playset in a small rectangle of grass, that was ragged before the winter set in, courted statuesque teenagers staring down at screens instead of children swinging with blind trust, met his need of respite for a collective of seconds. He pushed a colony of beer bottles on the counter into one another with enough reverb to echo but no intent to break them and add to the already unaccounted for clutter. Tented pizza boxes stood watch near a stained countertop microwave that despite Steve's penchant for cooking, likely handled the heavy lifting in the kitchen these days. A jade wine bottle and a rounded liquor bottle, essence drained, crisscrossed in a dysfunctional X over a stack of helpless dishes in the sink. Used forks spiked out from between the plates. "Big day yesterday?"

"They're not all from yesterday." Steve's words hung over the din of the scheduled train that intruded against the thin walls. "I didn't take out the recycling."

Marty tried to find a stream of truth in what Steve was saying, knowing he would bypass the sign anyway if he noticed one.

"All you do is take out the recycling, take out the trash."

Marty felt the movie version of himself would have brought his palms down hard on the counter and give in to the urge to smash the bowling pin set up of bottles. But the real Marty—the practical, professional Martin—only turned and tried not to lean back on the counter.

"Come back to sit around and wait for . . . I don't know what you're waiting for . . . and why you're choosing to do it here when you have a perfectly good place to go and do nothing, if that's all you want," Marty said. "It's been a while. Too long and you know that."

"I do stuff."

"You do stuff," Marty scoffed. "Yeah, what do you do, Steve? What are you doing?"

Marty relented and shoved the beer bottles into the sink.

"You're not supposed to be doing this anymore."

"No, I'm not supposed to do that around anyone else anymore, and if you've noticed, no one else is ever around. I'm just watching the game."

To show him what *he was doing*, Steve remoted the television back to life.

"What NBA game is on? It's Monday afternoon!" Marty brought his watch forth from under the layers of sleeves, uncertain as to what he was checking for. Cuff links indeed glinted from the wrist.

"The '92 Finals, game 1," Steve said. An animated smile grew with the memory as empty hands balanced on his knees. "Remember, Jordan, most points ever, first half? Six in a row? The shrug? We watched it together down at Charlie's. You weren't even twenty-one yet. You weren't even close."

"Yeah, that's why Charlie's ain't there anymore, man." Marty had a flicker of recollection. "Or a lot of those other places."

"We used to watch a lot of stuff together."

Marty shuffled toward the couch and placed his hands on the bony backside. If he slid in either direction a sliver from the exposed frame would surely grind its way into his palms.

"I need you to do something for me," Marty said. His hands found safety in his coat pockets and locked a grip over the gloves that hid there.

"Yeah, okay," Steve said. "I can do stuff."

"Seriously, I actually need you to do it."

"Okay, what?"

To Marty, Steve was aging in two directions. His hair and face were becoming older, his voice arid and somehow thicker than just a few weeks before, making each short reply covered in tar rather than the airy flight of a normal speech pattern. His eyes were bloodshot to the point of a possible pending hemorrhage. The part of Steve going in the opposite direction was the form seated on the couch, basking in the glow of afternoon television. It was childlike, as if Steve had somehow stepped back twenty years and pretended himself and maybe his younger brother huddled together in front of an old superhero cartoon or the *Scooby-Doo, Where Are You!* show that kept them riveted in place, hands exchanging dives into a shared bag of Doritos—the powdered cheese licked away instead of wasted dust on a napkin.

Marty's present request held up twice in his throat before giving way.

"I need you to go to the house tomorrow," he started. "Photographer from the real estate agency is coming by at nine."

"Okay. I'll be there," Steve replied, this time without turning from the screen.

"At nine," Marty added sternly but not as demanding as thought he would have needed. The projection in his voice pitted against the resistance he expected to receive subsided but was not allowed to vanish yet. "Look, I'd go myself, but I have to be downtown tomorrow afternoon. Office stuff, just came up today."

"I said I'll be there."

"Go early. Eight thirty or so. Maybe earlier," Marty added an extra layer of security. "No snow overnight supposedly, so you won't have to shovel. Just make sure the yard is clean, pick up any leaves. Make sure the inside is good, basement too."

"I will." The action across the screen halted again under Steve's direction. "Dude, you know I'm there, like, every day. I at least pass by. It looks really nice."

"I know."

One down one to go, Marty almost added out loud.

"I'll be there," Steve said again. "Lake effect is a subtle bitch, you never know. I'll clear the walk if I have to."

Marty nodded in closure on the first part of what would have worked best as a two-part handwritten note. Not from the back but crested from some folded-over part in the middle of his mind, Melinda clawed to the surface—Martin's wife, bringing the next inquiry forward in the sealed envelope.

And the winner is . . . not me. It's never me, Marty mused. *God, she is everywhere—office, home, car, here. Always emerging from some corner of some room.*

"What are you doing on Thursday?" Marty bulldozed the question to his brother before the moment was lost.

"Oh, I don't know," Steve said, eyes now boring to the empty space behind Marty. "Watch the games here, maybe, you know, get some sandwiches. You know, Andy's, they're closed, so I gotta go to the store or something before then."

"Melinda wanted me to ask."

There she was again, now in his words. His wife of all these many years was like paint on a wall.

"You should spend it with us."

"Oh, I'm not sure."

"Come on, first Thanksgiving . . . since Mom and Dad. You should be with us."

Not the last one though, Marty thought. *This is the first of the rest of them, a new beginning.*

"We want you to. I want you to," Marty added. "We've all been through too much." There was a glimmer of sincerity there—there had to be. "You don't have to just stay here."

"Melinda's parents?" Steve asked, still perched on the couch the remote down; formerly invisible soda can brought forth to his lips.

"Are in Springfield, at her sister's," Marty added in continuance. "Come on, just say yes, we'll have the games on."

"No, I know you don't like to have TV on with the girls and all."

"We'll make an exception. It's Thanksgiving Day." Marty's hands crawled from his pockets in gesture.

"Come on. It would mean a lot. You can bring something. Whatever you want. Well, you know, not whatever," Marty added as he caught what he may have implied.

In deference, the television was brought back to the conversation. Marty glanced up. He knew this part. First half of Game 1 coming to a close, and there it was. Michael Jordan in a comical gesture that would become legend.

Marty shrugged back in reply.

Mike, I don't know either.

His brother oozed back to another part of his life on one plane while the present portion sat rotting. That was Melinda's word, *rotting.*

"*Choosing,*" Marty would tell her, "he's not rotting, decaying, or anything. He is choosing."

Marty snapped back to reality.

"Melinda's trying some of Mom's recipes. It'll be good. As good as it can be."

Now! Steve hammered away inside. *Now she chooses to honor what Mom did all those years? It was always "undercooked this," "old-fashioned that," "why would she ever make that?" or "who taught her to mix fruit medley with a dish of pasta salad?"*

Melinda's spiteful remarks beat against a splintered fence that glass upon glass of expensive red wine could no longer hold back. Marty's wife huddled between the two brothers in a corner of the kitchen when the chance arrived, some hidden conspiracy defended against where she would not allow dinner to regress back into a past that she was not part of.

"All right I'll ride over," Steve finally said.

"No, I'll come get you."

"No, I'll ride out," Steve said. "It's the only way you're getting me there."

A half win was better that no win.

"Okay, good. Ten, ten thirty. But, hey, you're staying the night with us."

"No."

"You're staying," Marty said. "I'll be no shape to drive after dinner. You know what that is like. I'll drive you back Friday morning."

"Okay," Steve said and, like his brother, thought a half a win was better than no win.

"And tomorrow, man, nine all right?"

"I'll be there eight thirty. It'll look good."

Marty looked to his watch. Too many moments like these, where minutes dripped and felt like hours, encroached on his world. Minutes that for a long time now started out as his but were on perpetual loan to Melinda's needs, the boss's needs, the girls' needs, and Steve. Even in his brother's self-imposed solitude, a ration of owned time was in storage just waiting to be doled out.

Somewhere another level existed—Marty knew it did. A new stage he dared not enter with guns blazing through a kicked-down door but would peer into while driving, shitting, or crossing the moment in cruise control from wake to sleep or sleep to wake. The place where the Thanksgiving that his brother may have had in mind teemed with appeal.

Gas station sandwiches drowned away with a quiet bottle instead of fussy, fought-over food paired with overpriced wine. Here. Anywhere. Alone, drifting in and out of everyone else's reality. Was it the silence that was the temptress? Or the slow glide into placid inebriation. The siren call of metal toward a magnet where obligation faded to a void and self-fulfillment reigned as victor. The solace of silence where Steve existed intruded upon him and had, in flashes, become deafening. Marty had fought the roar so far on most fronts.

"You okay for today?" Marty asked.

"Yeah," Steve said. "Got the game tonight. Monday night's the best, you know."

It used to be.

"Okay. And we'll see you Thursday." Marty stepped away.

The fingers of never plush but once new carpet dragged across his soles. How many desperate shadows was he walking in? How many of those were his own brother's? That was the smell that outfoxed nose blindness—not fabric sheet lavender and neglect but lavender and desperation.

He didn't call back and add another reminder. Steve would show. It didn't matter that now or in the evening, or maybe the instant that Marty left, Steve would grab for the plastic bottle of rum—*yes, I did see it there at your side*, Marty would've said—and add more to his soda can. Get another soda and repeat. Maybe take a little straight too right from under the spill-proof ring.

Monday night would come and go. It would leave Steve numb because he wanted to be and Marty numb because he had to be— present but on the brink of indifference. Comfortable with another sexless night after bath and story time wore down the house. Marty would settle into his own cave and raise each toast with an internal monologue, a self-deposition over when false advertising could be called out on the marriage he shared with Melinda. His brother could toast away anything he wanted as long as Steve would be there the next morning.

It was a flimsy wager but the one played. There was no chance the universe that awaited Marty the next day would be missed. The more evolved yet temporary space where he was no longer emasculated, no longer turned down and pushed aside but was a lover. A wanted lover, like the commercials played over and over again from days past that said, "Here, friend . . . here is what the future brings." And it wasn't cheating because in all honesty, he thought about his wife the whole time anyway.

Isn't it true, Melinda, that mental affairs were known to be more expensive than the physical types, even if the bodily ones ended up costing more in the end? Marty talked with himself.

The closed-door and see-you-later kisses Marty would leave behind him in the morning confirmed the bet.

3

Steve stared over the metal frame of the porch railing. If he went lower in the bench—tricky, as it had a give to it and harsher on his back than it should be—he could stare through the spindles, giving the yard an appearance of being behind bars. Or rather, the front yard as it would look if he were behind bars. This straightened him like being sprung from a dream.

The front yard of his parents' home, even under winter skies, had an emerald green that floated over the grass and was manicured *Better Homes and Gardens* style once a week by Steve when needed and once a month by a lawn service Marty chose and paid for. Cropped hedges sporting their fall-meets-winter brown crouched just under the front room windows. In spring and summer benevolence, annuals sprayed the lines of the walkway with frail pastel tints that were sturdy enough to withstand missed rebounds from the driveway basketball games of youth. Baseball was there too on this lawn, long ago—home plate closest to the porch, the bricks and vines of imaginary deep center at Wrigley Field encroached on the next-door neighbor's driveway.

"It was easier back then," he said in a whisper.

The train hummed in the distance while assorted birds exchanged morning calls. If he closed his eyes, he was nine. It was the same train, and somehow, those were the same birds that attended every game.

A glancing blow of light jabbed upward from Steve's lap. The center of the screen announced in silence, "Marty Office." Seconds came and went before he answered.

"She there yet?" Marty bleated in place of his own hello.

"Who?"

"The photographer!"

"No," Steve replied.

"No!" Marty said. There was a flap of wind or Marty's shirtsleeves bristled against the phone as he rubbed his eyes. "Did you miss her?"

"Marty, no chance. I've been here since eight."

"What the hell then?"

Etched in Steve's mind was a picture from the past. His brother's exasperated fingers stroking against his face. If Marty had his office phone headset on, both hands would be trailing downward, forehead to chin, an exasperated chess player's caress over his morning shave.

"Everything looks fine," Steve said. "I'm sure she'll show."

There was a grimace as if Marty had reeled in a tirade that had brushed up against the edge of a cup predetermined to overflow. "Everything really looks good?"

"Yeah."

At the corner, a late-model hatchback made a turn. The car held fast to the middle of the residential street as it decided a destination.

"She's driving up now," Steve said.

"Good. Hey, call me when she leaves, okay?"

The car leaned in and butted against the curb. The engine was an out-of-tune symphony when shut off, grinding with the same aggression as when it was running, a break in the still morning. Steve stood, calming the swinging bench with the back of his good leg. He took the four steps down to the walkway, running his hands down the iron stair rails, lifting his left near the bottom out of habit, even though the split paint and rust that sliced his hand decades ago had been erased by a triad or more of scraping, sanding, and restoring. One was as recently as last summer, but the hand remembered the cut and jumped away every time.

The woman exiting the car and making a hurried show of opening the hatch at the rear was a foot shorter than Steve, but she was not small and thin. Her frame was more drawn out and willowy, a rubber branch with leaves for limbs. She wore a long, frayed coat that was tied at the waist in a loopy shoe knot. A button showing a damaged yellow smiley adorned her left breast pocket another, with a spider, dangled on her right. Shoulder-approaching, plain brown hair stained the sides of her face, running from under the edges of a drab wool hat that was pulled to her eyes. Pointed boots knocked at the pavement as she walked.

"You don't look like a real estate agent," Steve said in her direction.

"You don't look like an attorney." Her voice was light with a tone that asked forgiveness.

"Oh, no. That's my brother. He set up the appointment."

"Look, I know I'm late," she breathed more than said.

She lowered the hatch door, asserting herself over a canvas bag of what Steve presumed to be camera equipment that she had placed on the ground and now dragged to her shoulder.

"I have this class today," she said, "after our appointment, and I thought I forgot my notebook—which I never do, but I thought for some reason I did—and I had to go back home and check. Then I figured out I had it. Then I saw the coffee pot was on and my roommate she was gone, so I guess it was a good thing I went back, but I'm sorry."

Steve caught most of her run-ons, his focus primed instead on the amount of air between the words rather than the words themselves.

"That's okay, I was kind of hoping you wouldn't show."

"What?"

"Well, yeah. If you didn't show up, there'd be no pictures," Steve said. "Kind of makes it harder for my brother to sell the house. I mean, what could he do?"

"He could get another real estate agent."

"Yeah, he probably could." Steve considered that. "He knows a lot of people."

Heel-toe, heel-toe, she closed the space between them, fingers of both hands crossing on the strap of her bag.

"I thought cameras were small these days." Steve examined the woman and her tote. "What's in the bag?"

"I don't know."

"Well, we should probably get started then, huh?" Steve asked.

"Sure."

"So what class do you have?" Steve climbed the porch steps ahead of her.

"What?"

"You know, the class you need to get to later." He held the screen door open and allowed her to pass.

"Photography," she answered curtly as if he should know. "I don't always just want to take pictures of houses. I'd like to shoot for a nature or travel magazine. You know, pictures of mountains, buildings. Places people wish they could see in person but will never get to or are too afraid to go. There's a lot of places people are afraid to go."

"Like where?" Steve was suddenly aware she may mean this house at that moment, with him reaching to close and lock the front door behind them.

"Like hanging upside down in the Grand Canyon or something and finding the right moment to capture the sunset just over the dissonance of the perspective you create." She lingered in the entrance, pulling herself back to the moment from wherever she had gone with a shake.

"Sounds dangerous."

"No worries," she replied, not yet one hundred percent back to where she was supposed to be. "To get a job like that, you need to know people and have money. I don't know anyone or have anything."

"I know the feeling."

"Cool, you left the furniture," she said, inching forward, some pace returning to her movements.

Growing up—and until the agency labeled it differently on the website—the space beyond the front door was the front hall. Coat closet ahead, wall-consuming mirror replete with a gilded frame to the left, and house to the right. The small area was more of a square from which the rest of the place appeared from and nothing more. Presently, it was a foyer because foyer evoked grand lighting, marble—definitely marble—maybe lions, and a spiral staircase up or down to something worth seeing. Steve knew that no one passing through this door would mistake the front end of his parents' house with any of these.

"Yeah, my brother said homes left furnished are more welcoming, or warm, or something like that. Easier to look at."

"Sounds like he knows his real estate."

"He knows a lot."

"So you still live here then?" She placed her bag on the carpet.

"No," Steve said.

But you did live here once, and that's exactly what you did—you lived here. Whatever it is you are doing now . . .

"I've got a place just down the road some, west of the tracks, you know, not too far. This is my parents' house."

"Oh."

"Yeah, they died."

From the basement below, the furnace exhaled. Later, over ramen and coffee, the memory was visible to her from above as if the dry push of air lifted her and she looked down on the souls below. There were more than she expected.

"I am so sorry," was all she could think to say while in the moment. "I didn't know."

"Yeah, you didn't know. It's okay."

"Really, I didn't . . ."

"Yeah, this past summer," Steve rambled. "Hotel fire. Maybe you saw it the paper or something."

"No."

"Never took a vacation their whole lives. At least not by themselves." Steve turned and closed the door, separating the sharp winter morning from the stale inside. "Retired, stayed here for five years, finally went somewhere, and the whole place burnt down."

She wondered if he was still talking to her.

"It was small—the hotel, not the fire," Steve said, his hand still on the doorknob. "Fire was really big."

"Um, I'm really . . ."

"There was a settlement, you know, and insurance and all, but he still wants to sell the house, so . . ."

"Oh."

"I'm sure it's the right thing to do."

Steps that said "we are getting back to business now" carried him to the living room.

She was more comforted than she wanted to be and settled into the quaint living room that you still wore when you passed through to the smallish dining room. White day glow broke around the room and disbursed like a prism from the minimal sheers that covered the length and width of the picture windows. Reds, soft oranges, and pale yellows fired in a play of angles. It was a hearth-like splash of color that rounded out the older but not worn furniture and scattered over the new carpet and fresh paint. She had asked him before she looked, but she would have known by now. This was—*had been*—someone's parents' house.

She scanned family photos on a fireplace mantel, newspapers and coasters on a coffee table. If she had not found out what she did, seeing someone's parents materialize from the kitchen door frame would have felt like the next natural step. But that wasn't going to happen here.

And you have a class, so get going, she reprimanded herself.

"My, uh, notes say the basement is finished?" she prodded ahead with a question.

"Yeah," Steve answered. "I did most of it myself, except the electric. I didn't know how to do that. Suppose I could have read about it or something. But the carpet, paneling, drop ceiling—that was all me."

"Well, how about I start down there?"

"Sure," he said, then pointed to the right. "Three bedrooms through there. Kitchens nice. Old but, you know, nice and all. Living room, dining room." His arm gestured toward the obvious.

"Okay."

"I'll wait on the porch," he added. "The back door is open so you can see the deck. Just come around when you're done."

"Martin Coleman's office," the greeting rang at him through the phone.

Steve asked for his brother and was put on a brief hold. The phone-sex voice now-went-straight with an office job, returned and informed him, "No, Mr. Coleman hasn't left yet and, yes, I'll put him right through now."

Marty was fourteen miles to the west, but the static clicks of the transfer highway sounded as if the call was being patched through to the moon.

"Martin Coleman," he finally answered.

"Hey, it's Steve."

"She done already?"

"No, she's in the basement."

Marty's breath collected and released. "I said call me when she's done."

"Just letting you know she was here." Steve could feel the agitation rising in his brother's voice, and he fought against his own. He rocked forward and back, a staccato rhythm that counted out nervous beat after beat after beat.

"You already said she was there."

"But I wasn't sure it was her."

Beat. Back. Forth. Beat.

"But it was."

"Yeah."

"Man, just let me know when she's done."

"All right."

The pendulum was slowed and then brought to a stop.

"Hey, can you just tell her to email me the photos when she can?" Marty asked. "I really need to get going. Steve?"

"Okay, let me get something to write your e mail on here."

"Just give her my business card."

"But then I won't have one."

"I'll give you one on Thursday," Marty said. "Steve, just give her the card, you'll be fine."

"All right, I will, I will."

4

It was taking too long. The porch, like a hunting party to prey had closed in. His body rocked forward and back, his eyes darted across the railing from spindle to spindle. Sweat—a bead in protest to the cold morning—ran like a tear down his face. Steve turned back to his phone. Twenty minutes, then thirty, another five. He was off the porch before another second passed.

Across the driveway, a reflex extended his hand upward to touch the net from the rim that had been taken down twenty years ago—another reminder from the body about what used to live there or what he hoped still did.

On the blind corner at the side of the house, he turned right, and she went left—not a collision but more than a bump. Enough to dishevel the bag she carried and disengage the phone he held.

"Sorry." She reached down and handed the phone back.

He held it too long without a word.

"Those cases really do help. I'm sure it's all right."

"Oh, thank you," Steve said, placing his phone in a pocket. "I'm sure it's fine. Here."

He passed her Marty's business card.

"My brother asked if you could email the pictures when you get a chance. It's on the card."

"Sure." She turned the card around. "Criminal defense lawyer, huh?"

"Yeah," Steve said, allowing her to pass in front as they strode the driveway, down to her parked car.

The wool hat gave her face a limited circumference. From what Steve could see, she had an essential look about her—essential and passed over because every crowded room had one of her. She was invisible when present and wasn't missed when she left. She was in the vast middle of the extremes of beauty. Maybe dead center, Midwestern but not Chicago. Her eyes made little contact, and her voice made little impression.

"Figure it's a good thing, having a lawyer in the family, you know, if I ever get in trouble or something."

"You in trouble?" she asked with a wink.

Maybe there was some Chicago in there.

"No," he answered, not meaning to clip the reply too short.

"So what do you do?" she asked, relieving herself of the pack.

"Not too much," he said. "I took a class too, you know. I mean, I went to real college, but I took a class here at the local one."

"What class?"

"What?"

"Class." She brought the rear hatch down. "Which did you take?"

"Cooking."

"Are you a chef?"

"No. I, uh, make dinner for myself sometimes though." He saw that was not enough. "I used to work at a sporting goods store."

Her body language radiated a need to exit.

"Here." She passed him a business card over the open car door, a ticket in leave as opposed to entry. "If you have any questions about the pictures or anything or if you need any more."

Steve looked at the card and spelled what he thought was her name.

"A-b-c-d-e?"

She buried a grin under a sigh.

"Abcde," she said, sounding out the syllables. "Abcde Reynolds. Abby is fine. My mother, she was—*is*—well, she likes to paint, and I was born during one of her more creative phases, let's just say. So, Abby."

"No, I like it," Steve said. "I mean, Abby is cool but, yeah . . . I hope you have a good Thanksgiving, Abcde."

"God, I don't even want to think about Thanksgiving," she said.

"Why's that?" Steve asked. "Best food and game day of the year."

"I suppose it is," she said. "It's just my parents are in Florida."

"Where at?"

"St. Pete." She shifted to a casual lean over the open car door frame. "Petersburg."

"I've heard of that," Steve said. "Now that would be a great place to spend Thanksgiving. No cold, no snow, or nothing."

"Yeah, well, my sister and her four kids from three different guys and her latest whatever you call him planned this big dinner. Who the hell knows who else will be there. I don't know, maybe she's pregnant again. They live in Aurora for now. Anyway, she invites me like we're some kind of normal family or something, like she just has to see her baby sister for some stupid dinner."

She looked as if she would have liked a strong drink in place of what would now be, at best, tepid coffee that awaited her in the center cup holder.

"Believe me I'd rather be anywhere else."

Steve who had had plenty of strong drinks in the veil of maintaining or obtaining indifference, confidence, and solace—hell, plenty of weak, quick, expensive, and cheap drinks along the path as well—took notice of an open door. Wrongly noted, but he entered.

"Well, if you don't want to go, you know, my brother, he's hosting the dinner this year at his place. He said I could bring, you know, whatever I wanted."

The silent morning banged against the conversation before she spoke.

"I think he means wine," Abcde said, "or maybe pie."

"Yeah," Steve said as she settled back into the car. "I was thinking maybe you know, about bringing olives."

"Oh." Her eyes fought for a focal point to either side of his face.

"You know those ones in the can." He formed the can with his hands. "The brand name though not the generic. My mom always had those on special dinners and stuff."

"Okay," she said. "Look, I really need to get going. It was good meeting you."

"You too. Happy Thanksgiving there."

The engine fired to life. By the time she was at the end of the street, Steve was on the bench, rocking—*shaking*—like a child left behind.

5

Cleo Washington watched him enter and turn to the locker room. Cleo left him unnoticed and invisible. He knew Steve would be back and at the counter. The basketballs there had to be checked out and signed for just like the towels, both of which reminded him in some way of manning the front desk of a bowling alley. Never looking up, Cleo heard the rhythm of approaching steps hidden behind the chaotic echoes of dribbling and the screech of shoes starting and stopping.

"The prodigal man returns," Cleo said to Steve with a cursory glance from the newspaper that had and kept his attention. Pencil in hand, another behind his ear, awaiting a return to the service of the daily crossword. "What's it been, four, five weeks?"

"I been busy, you know," Steve said.

"Yeah." His rumbling voice scratched the surface above the other sounds that collected at the entrance desk. "You been busy. Doing what?"

"Painting my parent's house, you know."

"Right. What else you been doing?"

"We're selling it."

"I know," Cleo said, his tone climbing from dismissive to familiar, from "what the hell's the matter with you?" to "we are not going there."

Reappearing from under the counter, he placed a ball and towel in front of Steve. He never asked and never would have asked Steve for a deposit or license during the exchange. This would have been offensive and embarrassing. Steve Coleman had about ten basketballs somewhere but couldn't carry one coming or going on his bike. And the bike itself meant there was still no license anyway. The day Steve Coleman rumbled through the front door with his own equipment meant that one rung—one very serious rung—of the ladder had been overcome and other matters could be attended to. Cleo, however, asked for other things.

"I still think it would be good, you know. I need your help up around here—working the front, organizing the leagues, maybe, I don't know, coaching from time to time."

"No, I'm not ready for any of that, not yet," Steve gave the same answer he had been giving and was determined to keep in play.

The same look from Cleo—disappointment but maybe something more sinister like disgust, which Steve would ignore anyway—rolled down his body.

No, don't you back down. I know—believe me, I know, and I'm not sure I care if anyone does believe me—I know. This is what happens when one place puts all the chips on one person. When that bet loses, it's game over.

"Just wanted to come play a little bit. Working off tomorrow's big dinner in advance, I guess."

"I sure ain't getting any younger," Cleo said. "Aging two days for every one of yours I think. You seeing your brother tomorrow?"

"Yeah, his place, you know."

"Good."

"What are you doing for the big day?"

"Not working here, I'll tell you that," Cleo said, handing Steve a plastic water bottle. "Be at my daughter's."

"Sounds nice, you know."

"Freddie and the guys just getting started on court one. They let you sub in."

"Oh, I don't want to interrupt," Steve said. "Maybe just shoot around some."

As if on a cue, the door to the gym area was pushed open.

"Cleo, did Petrelli get in yet?" The shorter man's attention was redirected. "Steve? Hey, man, how you doing?"

"Hey, Freddie," Steve said. "Good to see you. How you been?"

"Been all right."

Freddie tucked a bulky police department jersey into his shorts. A headband held back front-running curls of crisp red from the broom-straw beard and freckled face below.

"Sorry I haven't been by your place lately or something to visit."

"Oh, that's okay, we all been busy. No worries."

"Yeah," Freddie said. An unsure glance shared with Cleo was volleyed back with a shrug. "Hey, Steve, with you, we'll have an even ten why don't you get stretched, huh?"

"I don't know."

"Come on, man, just play."

"Yeah okay, thanks," Steve said. "You working tomorrow?"

"Nah, tomorrow off, back on Friday," Freddie said. "Most of the guys are on tomorrow, so got lucky, I guess. Hey, the league's starting up next week again. Some empty spots, you should be on the list at least if somebody don't show."

"Yeah, you know I'm not sure I'm coming back," Steve said.

"Come on. Cleo, sign him up." Freddie's hands drummed across the counter. "Keep yourself busy, in the evenings at least."

A staring contest from Freddie to Cleo and back was initiated. Steve let it run for at least a minute.

"Yeah, okay I'm in," Steve said. He had no escape from this but figured it was better to make a choice that have one handed to you. "Besides, my parents' house is ready to go, I guess."

"Good." Freddie looked to the front door. "Petrelli," he called out to the man entering. "Where you been? Shift ended an hour ago."

"Better than too much free time," Steve said to no one.

"Wife's birthday tomorrow," Petrelli said with a forced groan for inflection.

He stood a foot taller than Freddie and eye level with Steve. He wore an ethnic, stained shoeshine-brown face, which stood out over his pale colleagues in the sunbaked summer, just as it did now in the winter. He was a caricatured, sculpted cop who would evoke the same level of intimidation in a UPS uniform. A swarm of black hair had the appearance of being wet, but when brushed back with his hand, it cracked with dryness, and his staccato short-vowel syllables were the end of a meat grinder pushing into Chicago by way of New York.

"Worst day of the year to have a fucking birthday," Petrelli said. "All the other shit to do I can never remember. Should have been on the checkoff list, I tell ya."

"Her birthday's not always on Thanksgiving, you goon," Freddie countered. "It's only once every six years or something. Can't be that bad. New Year's Day—now that's the worst."

"I thought that was Christmas Eve," Steve said.

"You gonna tell that to Jesus, Joseph, and Mary," Cleo's gravel interjected. "No, the day *after* Christmas. Hands down the worst birthday ever. My sister's entire childhood, I think we remembered once, maybe twice, and we was a close family."

"Hey, Coleman," Petrelli called out. "How's that brother of yours? Still defending the innocent and helping the guilty go free?"

"He does all right, you know."

"I seen him last month down at the county house," Petrelli said. "He does better than all right. New fucking Jag or something?"

"I don't know."

"Maybe a Beemer. Didn't get too close, you know. Smelled foreign though."

The officer took a towel from Cleo but left his target squarely on Steve.

"Suppose there's some justice though. Some freak rips somebody up, we put him away, and along comes guys like him that must cost these bums their last dollar. So in a roundabout way, it all makes sense, yeah?"

Freddie placed himself between Steve and Petrelli.

"Hey, guys, let's get to the court, okay? Come on, Steve."

"Yeah," Petrelli said. "Good to have you back, Coleman."

* * * * *

There was a certain rhythm you did not have to break on an evening bike ride when the pattern of traffic lights waved you by with continuing permissions of green—smooth asphalt, susurration of the changing gears below, unbroken circular motion driven by a constant two count, a contrast to the jagged edge of basketball's cadence. Start, stop, start again, first left, now right, up, down, another left, right, a stop. Wait, that's what it was, wasn't it? To the regular pattern of the days—the square box you saw yourself living in, the box where you had no control—basketball was the break. It was the interruption. Not a ticket like everyone else saw. Or maybe a ticket but not the one everyone else would have punched.

You possessed the passage to dissonance—static floating, risen just over the foam on the stream. And how did you join the stream? Sudafed at first. A little red beacon of relief held between two fingers. Smaller than Skittles. Easier to swallow but harder to chew. Pseudoephedrine. Not that you knew that word or cared at the time. That was the essence of the first magic carpet ride. A cold then not cold, but the stillness, oh, the stillness that you could achieve. You never breathed fuller, cleaner. At first, two, then three, then . . . how did you ever, you know, before?

I'm just keeping it in my gym bag, just in case.

The squeals from shifting rubber soles, shouts from the sideline, cheers from the assorted crowds were finally muted. Cotton, awaken by and under your command, filled your ears from the inside. It was motion perpetual, slowed just a step but enough. Spaces that were open for the ball gyrated and paused, and you made it fit—the perfect pass.

The basket—three times the size it should be—waited, an open chasm that could not refuse anything you threw at it. An unfair advantage somehow, yours alone. But for how long? Others would soon know; the pragmatic discovery would be made. Colds, after all, were everywhere but gone in a snap. Enhancement was needed; necessity, the bringer of invention. The holiday vodka.

Basketball—the first two months, at least—fell across the sweet spot of the calendar. The amount needed to fill your second water bottle was never missed. The glass bottles stored under the sink were wordlessly replaced when running low. The centuries-old chemical composition never broke down and never changed: bus to locker room to gym, there and back again, always ready calling with an eager finger, waiting like a shadow. The odorless astringent would enter at the throat, tear at the sinus, and cast a spell on your lungs. Bleach for the soul, body, and mind. And just like bleach, a pinch was enough. A capful. At least at the start.

6

"Mr. Steve, let me help," the voice called down the stairs. The uneven shuffle of old age followed, the front stride more assured that the one lagging behind.

"Ramon, I got it."

By the time his neighbor reached the lower end of the stairs, Steve had the bike at an angle against the wall where the long steel boxes hung.

"Just checking the mail."

"You didn't get any. Ha!"

Ramon's bright smile burst under etched crevasses of permanent deposits chipped in by the stone mason of time. Despite a constant reminder of cigarette smoke from the man's breath, his thick teeth were a flashlight against the stretched and dried face.

"Thanks for looking."

The mail keys for units 3 and 4 were interchangeable. This was explained away when Steve had moved in, as a function of the top two units at one time being occupied by members of the same family.

"So, if it's no trouble, and it certainly would be one less expense…" the landlady had said.

To which, Steve replied that it was no issue and that he and the occupant of unit 3 would work something out, which turned into Ramon Salazar checking the mail every day and sliding what was found under the much-too-large but ultimately functional gap at the bottom of Steve's door.

"I do have something for you though," Ramon said. A hand mangled by a litany of years at United States Steel followed by an extra ten that piled on janitorial duties at South Suburban Hospital reached into a pocket. "A woman stopped by to see you."

"A woman. That's never good," Steve said, taking the business card.

On the back was a handwritten message:

Call me if you want.

The front—just familiar typeset.

"Oh yeah, no big deal. Thank you. She's some real estate photographer taking pictures of my parents' house, you know, to help sell it or something."

Steve straightened the bike and pointed up the stairs.

"Lot of blonde on that one, lot of blonde," Ramon added, trudging behind Steve and the bike, pulling his own unseen obstacles.

"Blonde?" The front wheel bounced off the top step. "Are you sure?"

"I may have the clouds forming, hijo," Ramon said, pointing to his face when they reached the landing. "But I know a blonde when I see one."

An odd one-eyed stare from Ramon's glassy eye reminded Steve of an oversized monocle.

"Okay, well, thanks."

The bike stood against Steve's leg as he felt his own pockets for keys.

"Maybe she just needs some more pictures or something."

Ramon's laugh was gentle these days, but underneath, Steve could hear a reminder that once this was a navy laugh—a rooster's cackle that flowed in and out of tales not told but spun. A laugh that remembered what the wrinkled ink on the old man's frail bicep was intended to look like—an anchor and seal without the burden of age or a galaxy of bluish spots.

"One more thing," Ramon said, clearing his throat. "Wonder Woman was in the car with her."

"Wonder Woman?"

"Yeah, the one from the comics." Ramon opened his own door. "Drove your blonde off after she gave me her card."

"Well, okay, thanks again," Steve said. "Hey, have a good Thanksgiving, you know."

"Yes, sir, I will." The old man went rigid. Muscle memory at parade rest. "Serving dinner at my church for those less fortunate," he proclaimed. The man in the blue flannel shirt, faded pants that did not fit, and shoes that were not fit to wear would not be out of place on either side of the serving line tomorrow. "You not gonna be around here all day alone, right?"

"No," Steve said. "At my brother's out there in Orchard Park, you know."

"Good, the Park," the old man added. "Your brother's a good guy."

"Yeah," Steve said into a cloud of uncertainty. "I'll see you Friday, you know. Maybe we can watch one of the games or something, unless you want to hit the malls."

"Ah, now let's see." He looked into the palm of his hand as if holding an iPhone instead of the bent folds of age. "American football with you or shopping. I take the shopping! Ha!"

"All right," Steve said. "Well, come by if you want. Good night there, Ramon."

The night, like most of them, did not pass. It was just there and then not there, an ignorant moon replaced by the space that led to the imminent sunrise. Time was not spent but lost. Tonight, there was snow drifting, a flurry of the wrong color. Electric blue, if there was such a shade, painted the flakes as they spun around the living room. A false white pasted over what was left of him, a blanket rising and falling in a half-wakeful stasis.

One empty glass perched on the nearby coffee table. It had been difficult, just the one—okay, two—but that was all. Maybe. So much more needed to sleep, which according to those with medical credentials was not sleep at all but a quick passing out followed by moments of restlessness, probable hypnic jerking and flailing, and, finally, an onset of anxious wakefulness carrying over into another vacant morning. Based on expert research, Steve had not technically slept in months.

Tonight was different. The snow, first of all, the icy blue, settled into his unconsciousness—a gentle humming underneath held at bay by the swirling wind that crooned a lullaby tone. It wasn't just the television, the constant pres*ence in this room. Not tonight, though.*

I turned it off, right? And the humming now. A flash below. A flashlight? Somebody looking for me? Coming for me? Steve thought.

With the phone in his lap, a 708 area code lunged up for his eyes. Larger font displayed 1:08 a.m. above the caller ID. The similar numbers dripped in and out of one another, a silent kaleidoscope. Had he called her? Yes. Possible. Hard to fathom after number three. Okay, but four was all.

Needed to toast Mom, and Dad, and Marty. What did I say? Steve wondered. *Something about the pictures?*

He answered.

"Hi." Her voice was more direct on the phone but still windy like a flute. "Steve?"

"Yeah, it's me." He pushed himself to his seat and leaned back into the sofa. The blanket was still folded in a square on the far cushion.

"It's Abcde," she said but didn't need to. "We met yesterday, remember? I took pictures of your house. Well, not your house, but you know . . . I didn't wake you, did I?"

"No."

The glow of the television, not off after all, was a strobe at a low setting in the background. The irony of her question didn't occur to him until later.

No, there's really no waking me.

"Just watching some old movie."

"Which one?"

"Um, I don't know."

"Well, who's in it?"

His eyes drilled ahead into the fog as if missing the answer might count against him on an exam.

"Billy Crystal in Chicago," Steve said as he recognized a form and a building. "He's a cop."

"Oh, oh. *Running Scared,*" she confirmed. "I like that one."

"Yeah, that's the one."

The first time he had placed his head back on the couch, John Candy was belting a tirade of foul curses to a kind woman at a car rental counter. Or was that the other guy?

"And yeah, I remember you. My neighbor said you came by and all. Did you need to come back to the house or something?"

"No." She waited. "I called to apologize."

"Apologize?" he asked. "I haven't seen the pictures yet, but I'm sure they're great. My brother didn't call you, did he? What did he say?"

Damn, Steve cursed. *Marty the great and terrible Oz or the emperor in Episode IV—never around, always present.*

"No, it's not that. He gave me your number though," she said. "I wanted to apologize for being rude when you asked me about—or *to*—Thanksgiving dinner. It was very kind of you, and I shouldn't have been like that."

The companion that never left stared back at him, wearing its eerie nighttime robe. No matter what was on, the spray of color was always the same.

"Oh, you weren't being rude or nothing. I shouldn't have even brought it up, us just meeting and all," Steve said. "I got the olives though."

"Oh," she said. "That's good."

He heard a door close in her background.

"I came by to see if you wanted to go to a party. You weren't there, and I wasn't even going to leave my card, and then your neighbor insisted . . . I shouldn't have."

A laugh from Steve stymied her run on.

"Yeah," he said. "Ramon—he's like that. Would've been better off selling all that steel rather than forging it."

"I just hope I'm not bothering you."

"No," Steve said across the space that connected one Thanksgiving Eve at half past one in the morning to another. "But thanks, you know."

"For what?"

"For inviting me to your party."

"Well, it wasn't my party," she said. "It was someone else's. I kind of felt like someone else too, but it's over now."

"Some party then," Steve said. "Was it good?"

"It was okay," she said.

He could feel her sink into whatever furniture she was on. The sofa that pushed back against Steve had reached the limits of expansion.

"Kind of dreading tomorrow, I guess. Thought I could put it off for a while. Sometimes when I stay up late enough, it feels like I'm sneaking up on the next day, like I have the advantage or something."

"I'm like that sometimes too," Steve veered the chat away from a full review of his sleep habits. "It's just a day."

"I know," she answered. "I can do anything for one day."

"No, not that," Steve corrected her. "It's just a day, like all the others. I guess for some it's still special, but I think, maybe for you and me, you know, it sounds like we kind of drop in and drop out. Years from now, when they look back, it won't matter if we were there or not. They won't even remember."

Best Thanksgiving ever. Quick—1989 or somewhere. Eagles on their way to 27–0 over the Cowboys. No Bears victory today but the dreaded and hated Cowboys under a serious drubbing. You remember them all that *way. By the scores. It was 52–7, Cowboys over Seahawks, first Thanksgiving at a restaurant. Bears 23–17 Lions, overtime. For some reason, the aunt who hosted that year was a no-show at the funeral last summer.*

That day, that remarkable day, 1989 said, the Eagles gave the Cowboy haters a win to gloat over, a sure sign of good things headed your way. You are standing at the door, bending to look back at the TV. You are herded to the door by parents who are no longer here, heading to the home of a grandparent who departed long ago. Everyone in that still photo of a memory from that day is gone. Not Marty. He's still here but gone in his own way. Gone mostly because of you. Was he ever really there?

Back then, he would have been compliant. Last born always first out the door, first at the table, but not first to you, going back for a coat you wouldn't need, taking a long tug of Scotch from the high cabinet, stick of breath gum for the short car ride. Did that even happen? If you were the only one that saw it, was it even real? What did happen?

A hastened curl of pantyhose crumpled under her parents' couch, teenage legs wrapped snug around you like a ribbon, winter-cold bare heels bristle your lower back. Richard Marx, ambiance and ear candy above, violin strings of vanilla sheen tied together lips parted by darting tongues. Pruned fingers pushed again and again into her waterfall. She was virginal but in the Mount Everest kind of sense—a select few were allowed to try and fewer succeeded. The climb had evidence of prior visits, little left-behinds on the steady incline, like a rehearsed shift to allow more, oh, more, *and an overdone groan of encouragement when she parted and your bodies coalesced, hers a shudder between anticipation and expectation. It was less of the aggression that locker-room dialogue conjured and more of a gentle, constant glide, and you imagined the slick summit was your apex alone.*

The empty house and absent parents that allowed for that night was the benefit of a sick relative who could not travel for the holiday, the girl/woman now writhing below you had spent the day with your family, as retail work for her started at sunrise on Friday, which really wasn't Black Friday back then but just as important to the shops. "Mom, I just can't go, I have to work the next morning, we won't even be back before . . ."

"Steve?" Abcde was saying when he returned.

"Yeah, I'm here." He stood. Cautious on his legs, he surveyed the room and steadied himself. "Guess I'm trying to put it off too."

"Well, we can't." She hadn't convinced herself either. "I'm really sorry for being rude."

"No," Steve said. "No worries. Hey, listen, maybe this weekend sometime, we could get together and tell holiday stories or something."

"This weekend is really busy." There was a fraction of disappointment in her dismissiveness. What size fraction, Steve had no idea. "My class has a final project due, and I have some pictures lined up. Houses, like yours. Well, not exactly, but . . ."

"Good," Steve answered. "That's good that you got things. You know I'm kind of busy too this weekend, now that I think about it."

"So maybe in a couple weeks, when things aren't so hectic, you can call me?"

"Yeah, I'll do that." He poured a fourth tumbler that emptied the Maker's Mark. He knew how to hold a bottle at the angle where the running liquid uttered not a sound or splash. "I know this great pizza place right here by my house."

Yes, you both know it's not a house, just like it wasn't *her* party.

"You mean Andy's?"

"Yeah," Steve said. "Do you know it too?"

"I grew up in the Heights," she said. "Yeah, I know it."

"Maybe we could meet there or something."

"Sure, call me. Next week."

"I will."

And I will never call you Abby.

"Remember," she exhaled. "It's just a day."
"Yeah, you too. Good night, okay."
"Good night, Steve."
And I know you would never call me Abby.

8

Orchard Park was the mecca—*was* being the operative. What it *is* now is the suburb where your brother lives, so it has become a place on most days that is best to be avoided. What it once *was*, was a place that folks aspired to, the hidden sanctuary of the south Chicago suburbs, a virtual nirvana.

Most city-born parents, yours included, in search of a pre-midlife exodus, partook in the worship. "Drank the punch," as they would say now. Grandparents beamed about one day owning land, then a home there, and the payoff that would follow. The fact that there was not any extra to invest, and looking back—let's be honest, even if there had been money to push to the center of the table—initiative never played a role in that conversation.

Holidays, birthdays, summer picnics; Sunday dinners, mounds of food, fountains of booze; talking "we should," "you should," "let's look into"—all came back to Orchard. It was to be achieved. Did *not* arriving there cause a void? Maybe. Does Martin living there now feel like a gut punch? Sometimes. The mecca today is not without battle scars though, and maybe that closes the wound a bit. Takes the bite out of a well-timed kick.

Two exclusive golf clubs where nobody but somebody was a member had been combined into one now overtly public course with nine fewer holes than before where you could play Wednesday from five until dark for twelve dollars. The mall of the future was now just *the mall*, and it had as many empty stores as other *just the malls* that fenced in the less affluent suburbs. Chain box stores came and went, and there were as many working banks as shuttered ones. A half-completed and quarter-empty housing tract, which you would soon be passing, brought the east side of town back to the level of where you came from. But it was still Orchard.

The city's name evoked an envious pause when you said once, long ago, "she lives in Orchard," the exotic dimension, just far enough from the due south waystations that caught those fleeing Chicago to be called a destination but still close enough to have a scent of possibility.

Today, you took the long way around, a lap around your old neighborhood out of habit, before heading west. You could have one drink and still ride; anyone could do that. But not you. You needed four, five, and then six, sloping against the counter in the—what did you say to her?—old but nice kitchen.

A lightning urge to piss struck and caused a return inside when it was time to leave. The bike was safer here at the house that leant against the wall of the corner gas station—lessons learned, then seven, and then coffee to cover not only the stench but to mitigate the enhanced morning headache which has become such a part of you, that if you woke to find it gone, the same panic educed by waking to find a lost limb may ensue.

So here, leaning became a crouch, you a catcher without a pitcher, on the kitchen floor (also old but nice) where, no matter when the place sold—and it would, Marty would see to that—your remnants would carry on ad infinitum: breakfast, lunch, dinner, phone calls, talking, yelling, debating, arguing, failing. Silence! You demanded from your seat which had somehow placed you in the center of the vinyl laminate. The kitchen walls in rotation of a carousel was not far behind.

You could stay here. From the fog, you heard her say he wouldn't notice anyway. Sure, he'd call a few times, but with the ringer subdued—a permanent condition of your phone now—you would at least not have to hear it. He'd give up. You could deal with him later. You did what you were needed for; the sign in the yard out front confirmed that. He may not even bother to check where you were. No one shows a house on Thanksgiving Day. No one else would be here.

Of the comforts that remained (and there were not many) that was the pinnacle—absolute absence. No one else would know or care where you would be, where you may go to, or what you may devolve to. Absolute, ab . . . Abcde. No, you're going. She went. You'll go.

The counter you had backed away from extended a generous hand as it has so many times. You've peeled yourself from this kitchen floor as often as one rises from bed. A hard breath out, a deft lean just within your reach helped you restore the bottle back under the sink. A second thought helped you place it in your overnight bag, secure and soundless, between a packed change of clothes.

9

"Uncle Steve, Uncle Steve!" a rehearsed chorus in motion called from below.

They were seven and five, the math he was sure of. Which was Madyson and which Aubrey—he would have had no idea, even if his life depended on it. That would have been a coin toss.

Marty was just behind the open door with a subdued adult greeting in one hand and a Scotch in the other. The abrupt noise in the entry hall was extinguished and fell empty as the nieces moved on.

Steve placed his backpack down on the tile, a careful hand laid against it, an extra but not discernable second to prevent any clanking in the shift from shoulder to floor.

"Hey. I thought you said it was just us," Steve said, removing his jacket and passing it.

His Bears jersey, a cheap replica with no name and the number one, was the choice from the closet this morning.

"It is," Marty said. "Just wanted to look nice and all."

"You should have said something," Steve said. "I didn't know you were going to be in a tie. I have ties."

Marty was dressed for work but in modified holiday style. In place of the everyday white dress shirt with a solid accent was a burnt fall orange shirt centered with a decorative leaf of greens and browns.

"It's okay, man, just glad you're here."

Melinda appeared from the kitchen, custom tavern-style shutters waving behind her exit and pranced toward the brothers. A slight scent of cooking and whiskey followed her.

"Steve, it's so good to see you," she said.

What would have been an embrace a year ago was now a short arm rub. The number of cocktails that made her cold gesture possible must have been a staggering amount in her terms for the morning.

"Do you want some coffee to warm you up from your ride?"

It's what she should have asked, and Steve accepted. It's not that he should have accepted—he had to. His headache was peeling off the inside of his skull like a bandage from a cut being removed, one spiraled thread at a time.

Melinda was always in that *should* place with whatever she happened to be doing, wearing, or saying. Today, it was the apron-covered casual top, headband-restrained hair, legging pants, and cushioned flats with no socks. In college, the categories were oversized top and the sweatpants, "I'm studying" Melinda; the "I've just met a guy [that guy would eventually be Marty]" Melinda, which was a heavily made-up face and "I can't believe you squeezed into that" ensemble; which morphed into the less made-up and far less cleavage throwing "I've been fucking the same guy [again, Marty] for a year" Melinda.

Today was the little-to-no-makeup, "I've been taking care of the kids all day and in total seven years now and cooking on top of that to beat hell, but I've been in my designer kitchen so deal with it" look. She displayed the mom badge freely, but she didn't own the age with open arms just yet.

Steve noticed her traditional fudge-colored hair was now a shade over coffee with cream, which she would bring—*should* bring—with a bounce from the kitchen to the living room in moments.

"Daddy, can you help me with something?" Madyson or Aubrey asked with a tug on Marty's dress pants.

In a convergence of noise, a dog erupted from somewhere, the other daughter emitted a screech, and the doorbell sounded.

"I better check that," Marty said. "Steve, can you get the door?"

"Sure," Steve said as he returned to the silent entry hall.

Forced smiles and fixed stares looked back at Steve from two portraits hung just to the left of the door. Against the swirls of studio gray, Marty's troupe and Melinda's parents flanked the heard but unseen dog in one and were pasted atop a backdrop Wrigley Field marquis in the other.

"Hi, I'm Taryn," the owner of the rung door said.

Her voice bubbled like champagne, a sweet bite that was on you before you knew it and lasted well after the last drag.

"Hi, I'm Steve. Marty's brother."

He pulled back a handshake, noticing that there was not one offered.

Many inches to a foot shorter, she looked but was still looking down at him. A slight shake of her head and lift of an eyebrow ensued. She looked jilted in repute of his jersey and jeans, the sartorial equivalent of male wardrobe capitulation.

"Oh, hi, I heard you were coming."

She vaulted in over the threshold, a bottle of wine in one arm, pie in the other.

Steve dropped his gaze as she stepped by, leaving him a shadow of vanilla cranberry. Familiar steps that were more accustomed to the entryway than Steve ballet-danced over the tiles. Running shoes and matching shorts were topped by an oversized sweat top and underlined by leggings that teased checkerboards of flesh. Professionally cut and colored blonde skipped in time with her gait. A diamond-encrusted solitaire over a subservient array of stones from the minor houses—ruby, sapphire, and emerald—flashed from her left hand. It was an obtrusive spotlight that served as both a reminder for her and repellent for others. The swaying walk she put on obviously invited the occasional challenge.

"Melinda's in the kitchen," Steve said, joining the "this is what I should say now" club.

Melinda poked from between the kitchen shutters, making the information irrelevant.

"You have *got* to try this," Melinda said, holding a small cordial glass of which the contents had been sipped. "You didn't have to bring that."

"It's the one Marty said he couldn't find. Remember the other night?" Her words joined her steps in saying, "I'm here way more than you, Scott. Or did you say Steve?"

Steve was left in the entry hall long enough to consider popping open his undisclosed addition to the day. His eyes read what he could see of the house.

Just down to the backpack, be looking for something . . .

A potential quick sip was interrupted by the silent return of Marty. It was his house, and he knew where to step.

"Who was it?" Marty asked and realized more was needed. "At the door?"

"Oh, Taryn," Steve said, standing with a paper bag in hand that had been retrieved from the backpack. "Must be your neighbor or something?"

"Man, yeah she is," Marty said. "Neighborhood welcoming committee. Been here, what, four years now? Let me tell you the welcome never gets old."

"She brought wine, which reminds me," Steve said, passing the folder over paper bag to Marty. "Olives."

"Um, thanks, man."

"Yeah, they're the good kind like mom would have had."

"'Kay," Marty said. "I'll take them to the kitchen. How about you get to the family room and pop the game on."

"Yeah."

The coffee with cream arrived just before halftime in the center of a service tray offset by two triangles of shot glasses brimming with the amber shade and semisweet candy scent of exclusive brandy. A house divided sat across the furniture in the expansive family room. Steve tucked into one corner of the long sofa; Marty adorned the opposite end. Melinda leaned back in the chair next to him and Taryn hung between them, running shoes now gone, thick name-brand socks curled into an even thicker carpet. Steve edged to his right, reaching for the appetizer tray that was still a fingertip away.

"Don't you fill up on those," Taryn called after him, her tone playfully buzzed.

"I won't," Steve said and went for the coffee mug instead.

Funny, though, you have a way to go to catch up to me. I could conquer the white line one foot in front of the other right now, bitch. Yes, sir, Officer, A to Z backward? No problem. A few more of those honey, and you wouldn't make it to the front door if I drew you a map from here to there.

"Ironically he watches what he eats," Steve's also buzzing brother said as the ladies, the familiar and the stranger, laughed louder than they should have. "Sometimes I think I'd eat a Reebok if it was deep fried."

Let's get this straight. You sitting here in this plush family room with the window-wall of sunlight behind you, a tray full of emptying glasses before you, does not make you a drinker. You are just an adult having a little responsible drink from the kind of glass I drink from all day. If any of you did what I did this morning, I would be serving the kids dinner, reading them their most beloved nighttime tale, without missing a word, mind you, and putting them safely to bed later. I may not bother to pick any of you up off the floor when I leave either.

"Well," Taryn said; her tongue made podgy swathes down the rim of her glass, looking for the end of her second brandy. "At least it's half over. The rest of the guys are over at our place watching too. I don't know how you all do it."

"Oh, there's two more games." Steve was not sure whom she was addressing, but he replied anyway.

If there weren't two more and all these people around, there would be nothing keeping me from making my face as numb as yours, but no one would ever know by my voice, Barbie. It was Barbie, right?

"It was nice meeting you," Taryn said at Steve. "And you guys, we'll see you later."

"Let me walk you out," Melinda said, following Taryn out of the room. "Here, wait, come get your dish . . ."

Her voice faded as they took the corner.

"She's something, huh?" Marty said, adding another half to his shot glass and taking it quickly like a pauper who discovered a dropped coin.

"Yeah, she seems real nice," Steve said. "She's coming back?"

"Yeah," Marty said. "We've been getting together with her and her husband and another two couples from the block for game night sometimes. Thought it might be a nice way to end Thanksgiving. Odd number with you here, but we'll make it work."

"Oh, thanks, I don't know," Steve said. "If you don't mind so much, I'd really like to watch the late game, you know, back in here or something."

"No, that's okay. The room upstairs that you're staying in has a TV. You could set up in there."

"Yeah, that'd be good."

"I mean, there's gonna be lots of noise down here and such. They all have kids about the same age."

"No, it's good. My place is by the tracks, so being here is like being in the library for me. I won't hear you at all."

But not because the trains are gone, you dipshit.

"Okay."

"Hey, you know, Marty, thanks for today and all, you know. I bet dinner will be real good."

"Sure, anytime you want."

Marty's insincere invitation dissolved into the air, and he was back to the game before Steve was.

Dinner passed like the plates that floated between them, unconsciously. What was left behind were the remnants of a month or so of planning and a day or two of kitchen duty and a quiet, pervasive agreement from Abcde that he was right—*no one would remember this.*

A splash or two of gravy or sauce dried in a run on the tablecloth that Steve figured would be replaced rather than washed, thrown away at once or washed away in stages. Spills and accidents were still forgotten; it didn't matter how they left.

The kids had left the table. Their cavalcade of chatter was replaced by electronic, progressive-sounding beeps from a game in the TV room over a soundtrack of redone kid-friendly songs. Steve stacked plates that would await Melinda's return. A sudden dome of honest silence replaced the charade of dinner. In the near-four years that Marty and family had lived in this house, Steve could not remember ever seeing the kitchen and what pristineness or chaos lay behind the pale shutters.

Are you sure? Not even that day. Some of your memories are so blank, it's possible that . . .

This was odd, as despite the depressed size of the old but nice "where we grew up" kitchen, members of both sides of the family squeezed like lemmings into every available space, setting aside used dishes and unavailable glasses for a seat closer to the action. The action may have scaled from raucous poker games to subdued conversations, but whatever it was, people wanted in and were invited to be a part of it. That's what his kitchen would have been.

"Thanks, Steve." Melinda wrapped her hands around the plates, her fingers turning white, the sudden grip transferring the stack of china from a potential disaster to a more likely one.

The longer the day pressed on, the more Melinda's tongue met the top of her mouth when she spoke.

"Thanks, Steve" ran together in a comical word train that convinced him, no matter what may lie beyond the doors in the unseen kitchen, there was a half-empty bottle or two of something among cabinets that even Marty may not know about.

"Fucking Cowboys," Marty said when the coast was clear of young and older ladies.

"What, man. Who cares?"

"How do they blow that lead at home?" Marty finished his wine, fingers bracing the stem to contain a tip of the glass, avoiding a fall and break. "It's Thanksgiving, they're just supposed to just win."

"Well, they don't always," Steve said. "If you go back and look—"

"Well, they're fucking supposed to."

Steve's next thought was that Marty's daughter, the younger one, got into the backpack. Sometimes kids do that. A lonely sack near Christmas with no one else around. Maybe it was her dad's after all. This time of the year, kids, they look through stuff. It was assumed, almost premediated when Steve and Marty, were growing up. This was opportunity. The pack was an afterthought, left aside in the entry hall forgotten about until just now.

"Daddy, what's this?" the older daughter asked.

There is a moment before impact where the scene unfurling in front of you changes from a shuddering opaque to the kind of flawless diamond-like glass you walk into. Inhaling, the unconscious act shifts to manual, and the last breath before the world changes is so deep and fulfilling, it begs your lungs to never let go. Because if you hold that breath, the moment cannot move forward.

But you do let go. It's just nature running its course.

On that summer day that you don't quite remember but the day you may have been in the kitchen at Marty's house, there's granite and white cabinets that shine and grin like newly polished teeth and the car you're driving does hit the object that you saw but didn't notice, didn't consider. Your exhale races outward, and you are introduced to a new world that is presently and may be forever delineated by then and now. The space between is filled with blurry voices and a fog that is as dense as the seconds before were clear.

When the fogs lifts this time, though, there are not two cars at angles that make adversaries out of companions. There is a little girl in pajamas, Madyson (see, clarity) returning to the stuffy, silent dining room, holding a crystal glass that you have not seen before with a ring of faint lipstick above backwash, melted ice, and maple-colored liquid.

"Maddie? Where did you get that?" Marty was blind to the half-moon evidence of faded pink. "Steve, man, what the hell?"

"What? It's not mine," Steve said with an air of dismissiveness he felt he had earned.

Mine's in a bottle not too far from here, about the same color though.

"Oh come on!" Marty pushed back against the chair, not violent but enough of a jolt.

Melinda returned at the wood of the chair meeting the wood of the floor. She was still holding the plates she had taken.

"Marty?" Melinda said, putting the plates back where they sat moments ago. "Honey, don't drink that give it here," she said, attention on her daughter, eyes on Marty.

Steve was between a sit and a stand, as much as his knees would allow. A volley of wordless ripostes were launched from Marty to Melinda and back—the tennis match of eyes, nods, and scrunches that only spouses were proficient in. The little girl left with indifference.

"Marty," Melinda said. "It's mine. I left it up front when Taryn was leaving. I forgot it."

She set the object of guilt and absolution on the plates and vanished under the cloak of kitchen duties.

The shutters waved with the beat of an injured bird taking flight. The staggered flap was the lone sound left between the two brothers. One standing over a fallen chair, the other sitting back down as he decided against throwing his.

"Sorry, man," Marty said.

"Don't worry about it. I would have thought it was mine too."

11

You were angry. She wanted a drink. Was it after? After the Thanksgiving that all others were measured against? Yeah it was, but not by much. Later eighties, knocking down the door of the nineties, the hourglass that would not right itself. All of you, so young, eloping with pending maturity not yet ready to embrace it formally. You knew enough. A little was good now, but more would be needed later. That's how the road bends when you get there. Wine coolers, the ladylike gateway to bigger and better. She'd already shown signs of looseness, and these nights—these kinds of nights where Bartles, Jaymes, and her other friends gathered—would be here long after you lifted out. And you were lifting out sooner than most. Your preordained future called loud and clear.

"I like the taste," she said, but you knew better. No one your age liked the taste, and not one of you were "used to the taste." The glassy-eyed senior, who had a Luke Perry vibe and a traveler-style bottle of bourbon affixed to his hand—and would not be lifting out anytime soon—tried to convince all to come and be baptized in the water of new freedom as this was the stuff nights were made of. You refused. Even a sample was shrugged off. It was so much easier alone. Besides, you were driving. That combination of skill perfection was still some years away.

Her lips clamped around the ridges of her bottle in a kiss like yours do now. A professional lock and load. A blush-colored, pre-college wash of temporary escape. Was that all she was doing? No, she was working the room—becoming it. It was you who needed to escape. She held the home court advantage here. That was the worry. She was a variant, a malleable puzzle piece that could fit into any gathering of friends: the

50

jocks, the pool she culled you from; the academic crowd, she had two advanced placement courses each term; the affluent (see Orchard Park) by default; the metalheads who under her watch had an open invitation to otherwise closed parties because they brought the best stuff and, in return, the auto shop had a place reserved for her permanently unreliable car. To the nerds and to the disciples of John Hughes, she was the pied piper. Your net of unease would have to be cast over a berth too wide, the spread of worry too great for a distant reach.

She laughed. Her attention darted from group to group, her presence coated the room like dust. Overstressed nouns and verbs filled the spaces between elongated hand gestures (with the other hand) and half-hearted dance moves exploded from hips and ass, gyrations in time to music the suburbs grooved to, claimed as their own but never had a reason to understand.

What are you doing? This. In response to Marty's question from three days ago, when he asked you on your new home court—this is what I am doing. Sharing something with friends and the others that still matter. Those that matter most come back stronger when the lines of consciousness change from stone to rubber. When you are in charge of that alteration, it's even more powerful. It's like being on a sidewalk and finding a diving board on the path that has somehow sprung from the solid concrete. Far enough in, the concrete gives way, and you jump then fall.

12

Under Marty's foot the distance from his house to the apartment closed rapidly, the traffic heavy into Orchard Park, spaced apart as if contagious on the way out. One obvious detour was made, and a cursory turn around the old neighborhood was taken.

"Well," Marty said, "probably no showings today, but I'll bet there's some over the weekend. You mind stopping by on Monday checking out the business cards and straightening a bit?"

"No," Steve said to the window more that to Marty. "I don't mind."

"What is it?"

"Nothing," Steve said. "Slow time of year for houses though, right?"

"Usually but we're priced good." Marty took one look back over his shoulder. "Won't be a bidding war but we'll move it before you even realize it's for sale."

"It's just that you're in a lot bigger of a hurry to sell it than I thought you would be." Steve placed a foot on the backpack below and felt the support of the now-empty glass bottle and pressed down in defense against an eminent harsh right turn. "We grew up there, you know?"

"Yeah, we did," Marty said. "I remember it just like you do. Steve, were done growing up now."

"I know, it's just . . ."

"It's closure man," Marty said. "You really want to know what it is. There, there it is—closure. We need this, both of us. When this part is done, you'll feel so much better, and so will I."

"Yeah, I know. I'm sure you're right."

"I know I'm right."

Marty made the last turn.

Steve's bike bounced against the truck bed behind them, the rattle behind them a metallic reminder of the seat assignment. The passenger side was a place of inequity even when a matter of choice. When the arrangement was required, the seat to the driver's right felt like a ride in a car seat.

The bike itself was currency enough. Despite is sophistication, the bicycle as a mode of transit for an adult was one of the lowest possible form available. Steve had dissected this before. When you had a new car (BMW it turned out) or new truck (a large, black Marty-sized truck of the suburbs that could have towed a battleship but was used to commute to an office), you were going places and not just another cog on the roads.

When you were a walker, even if not dressed for fitness, there was an air of purpose, health or activity bestowed, as others noticed you passing by. Kids on bikes were background, part of the milieu.

A grown-up on a bike evoked something different like a grown man in a Boy Scout uniform—necessary but hard to look at without assumption. The biker, it seemed, had places to go but nothing but a metal frame and two thin tires to get there.

The scraggly, bearded homeless guys a few train stops down the line had neither car nor truck and never walked, but they had bikes. Pastoral leftover possessions of a life that left them behind, bulged from a front-hanging basket or a sack upon their shoulders as they pedaled on past. The adult bike, unless the rider was dressed as Lance Armstrong in one of those attention-grabbing neon costumes, had an aura of unproductivity.

"Yeah," Steve said. "You're right."

"Maybe you'll even feel like leaving and going back to your . . ." Marty changed tones mid-stream. "What's going on in the ghetto today?"

"Don't talk like that, okay?"

Marty brought the truck to a stop in the spot that belonged to Steve's unit. The ambulance and police car were blocking the doorway, but the parking lot was unburdened. "Sorry, but this side of town, it's not safe anymore," he said.

Steve heard the last sentence through static. In one move before the engine was cut, Steve grabbed his pack, hit the pavement, and closed the door behind him, leaving Marty to wrestle the bike from the open bed.

"Hey, Brooke," you said.

"Hi." She evaluated you with her eyes and relocated a strand of black among the blonde with a quick blow upward. "Do I know—"

"No, I just noticed your name tag. Probably shouldn't have. Sorry."

"No, it's okay. Listen, I'm going on break. Do you want to hang out?"

Her hands moved to her vest pockets and brought forth the sanctuary of a small box and lighter.

"I smoke but only on breaks. Hope you don't mind," Brooke said, the former a fib, the latter indifference.

"No," you said.

By this time, you were only going to work and the grocery store. Work—the place or the verb—because you had to. And the grocery store, because at least there, instead of the oddly named Family Liquors, there was the chance you would buy or would actually need something else. You reap what you sow. The one constant. If you are in one pool of fish and never leave that pool, you will end up with or will become one of those fish. Perhaps both. People don't drown in aquariums by accident. Self-fulfilling actions become destiny. Basic mathematics. You simplify both sides of the equation. You control the action you control the destiny. The issue is, YOU CONTROL THE ACTION.

The limp—not so bad today—but the spike driving into your knee [the medical euphemism was discomfort: *"Yes, Mr. Coleman, the discomfort you're experiencing may last for some time"] demanded attention, immediate attention, as it did most days. Days that were becoming the same, stretching from one to the others ahead. You felt the same, acted the same, those around you were the same. The grids were lifted from the days—days that were becoming so hard to separate. A band of solid white, not the perfect squares the calendar taught us to venerate, but solid blank white lines all the same . . .*

The apartments were the same.

Steve stood against the door frame, his bike leaning just inside his open apartment. Across the tattered carpet of the walkway, an identical unit stared back. Shotgun echoes of steps brought the landlady from the departing ambulance below. She was adorned more than dressed in a plaid dress and open overlying fur coat. A black scarf was fastened at her neck by a palm-sized brooch and jewel-encrusted leather boots encased her feet and lower legs.

"Daughter on the north side said she'd be down on Sunday," she said. Her pencillike fingers, taking care to neither damage a single sculpted nail nor scratch against her forehead pressed against a volcanic headache over small-rimmed but elegant glasses. "Said he'd been complaining on the phone about headaches, seeing spots and double vision, but he also said it was nothing to fret about, that it would pass. He say anything to you about that? Acting strange or out of sorts?"

"No," Steve said.

"Anyway, she'll get the place emptied out."

The landlady closed Ramon's door, allowing the Friday morning paper to stand in unread watch.

"My son is in Atlanta for the week with his kids. He seems to have forgotten the first rule of rental property management." Her articulation was so clear, the words were visible over her head. It rang of education, acumen, and a desire to keep alive the balance between her roots and the culture she had found success in. "I belong here" punctuated each word.

"What rule?" Steve asked.

"Places of depravity just like places of elegance have a waiting list. A long waiting list. Never a vacant spot. Never a moment to rest." The landlady turned on a heel, attentive to the steps, not her conversant. "We always in demand."

"You know," Steve said to her back, "Mrs. Chambliss, if you need any help, you know, painting or cleaning or something like that, you can just ask. I'll be glad to help out. I'm usually around."

The reply was a well-polished "mmm-hmm." The crescendo from a train, coming or going, filled the space that followed.

"Well, I hope you had a good Thanksgiving anyway."

"Mr. Coleman." She turned back, leaning into the banister, her hands closing in front of her. "I have owned this building and others like it for the better part of thirty-five years. I have never in all that time had a happy Halloween, a nice Thanksgiving, a Merry Christmas, or a blessed New Year. Always some broken window, a set of lost keys, a busted water pipe or some damn heater just give out. And don't even get me started on the busted summer air units."

"You know, I never complain if the heater doesn't work. I just get another blanket."

"And you have paid your rent for a year in advance," Mrs. Chambliss said as her boots moved to carry her downstairs. "Sometimes I don't know what's wrong with you."

"Sometimes I don't either."

She looked back to him. Her eyes rolled over Steve, looking for signs of impersonation. Something. She was satisfied and then not.

On some level, the man staring back at her was functional but lacked input for the moment. The other level that had chosen for him was the one that disturbed her. That was the level that *almost* let her son talk her out of renting the place to him.

"I'll drop off the painting supplies day after the cleaning crew gets done."

"Thank you, Mrs. Chambliss," Steve called into her descent. "It'll look real nice and all."

"I'm sure it will."

"You know, maybe we could paint these hallways too, they're starting to scuff a little."

Her reply was the exterior glass door pressing back into the frame.

Twenty-one clanged sideways from the rim with disregard to the physics of the spin. Numbers one through twenty had been agreeable to the net, but the next one, the one sent forward with intent as opposed to instinct mocked him. A long rebound slapped away from the metal opposite of what was expected and found a resting spot against the folded bleachers. A cadence of dribbling and soles over hardwood, invisible background that had been there all along, was present again. The waxwork of sounds created a five-four meter in a four-four world, a comfort Steve always gleaned from the presence of basketball. He dribbled back to his spot on the side court, adding another incongruent cadence to the drum line.

"Hey, Steve." Freddie approached from the left. "Hey, man, everything okay? Cleo said you been here since early this morning."

Freddie's shift rotations included stints in both uniformed and plainclothes and, despite his department tenure, unpredictable hours. On occasion, he would show at the gym in hoodies and shorts that multipurposed for both work and basketball. Today, the uniform was in place. The only items missing were the cap and holster belt that were left in his locker.

"Yeah, I just wanted to get some work in," Steve said. "Having a good day actually. Haven't stopped for, you know, anything."

Freddie examined the mannerisms, and he knew.

"That's good, man. Real good."

"Yeah, well, I been distracted, you know."

Freddie put his palms out in a call for the basketball.

"Hey, you know," Freddie said, adding a variant dribble to the noise while he spoke. "I wanted to tell you, some of the guys from dispatch told me what happened out at your place over the weekend."

"Yeah."

"They also told me that he was gone before he hit the floor. Never even felt the stairs." Freddie stepped sideways to return the ball with a meek bounce pass. "Even if you would have been there, nothing you could have done."

"Well, that's good to know," Steve said. "Might have tried anyway. He was always kind. Never stole any mail. Can't say that for a lot of people."

"Hey, man," Freddie said, thumbs on his jittery hands that needed their own distraction found the empty belt loops, his eyes found the floor. "When you gonna get out of there? That place."

"Oh, I don't know, it's not so bad."

"Steve, come on, that building," Freddie said, "that part of town . . . it's just used up. It's not like it used to be. I see stuff. Hear stuff, you know."

Steve looked around for anything other than this conversation again.

"Yeah, I know."

"What about your other place? You could move back. Me and the guys, we'd help you get moved and all. I sure your brother would too."

"I just can't do that right now."

"Think about it, okay?" Freddie asked. "Put it somewhere in that vast mind of yours."

"Okay."

"Don't just say *okay*."

"I'm not."

"You are."

"I just don't feel like I have a lot of choices at the moment is all."

"Just think about it, okay?"

"Yeah," Steve added.

A bounce and shot followed. The net accepted the offering like a hug.

"Thanks, Freddie."

"If you wanna stick around, we got sanitation coming by around three for a game. We could use you off the bench."

"Oh man, that sounds good," Steve said. "No. Actually, I have plans tonight though. I'm meeting someone."

"Oh yeah?"

"Yeah, over at Andy's."

"Classy guy. Hope she's worth it."

"Hey," Steve said. "I like that place."

It's the only place worth going that I can walk to, and besides, I'd be there anyway because sanitation always kills us, and I'd get out of it anyway, and I'm really meeting someone.

Andy's was empty—not empty as a fact but devoid of who Steve was expecting. The anticipation of a large shared something with a pitcher of whatever turned into a small something with a large familiar companion at the bar. The confetti of leftover weeknight murmur twisted through the rafters, running down and across the walls behind him.

"So you enjoy the game tonight?" the bartender asked Steve with a gesture to a newer flatscreen above the bar.

"Yeah, it was all right." Steve finished another of what had been a generous pour. "I was supposed to be meeting someone, you know."

"Oh yeah," the bartender—John, from his name tag—offered an open-ended reply.

"Yeah, she must not have wanted to show, you know."

"Well then, last call past the last call?" John waved the glass he had been drying like a beacon.

"Yeah, thanks," Steve said. "I could use another."

In front of him, the tap poured a line of golden respite. Steve braced a twenty under the used glass and sent it forward, accepting the new one in exchange.

A

Did you honestly think I was going to let you go in there? No—a mother's titter—No no no no, oh no. Sure, blame her. I'm protecting you, like I always have and always will. We're going to stay right here. Go ahead, run it along the top of your arm, nothing vital there, you and your long sleeves. You know that does not hurt me, right?

You know, even the day you slip and turn your arm just a bit and slice instead of stab at your precious meat, I'll still be here. Go on. He'll buy your excuse. Such a simpleton. A fool. Pathetic. "Roommate," "car trouble," "this weather—you know, plays the hell out of these old cars. Just couldn't get back in time". There he is though. Three hours. That's a long time to wait for someone like you. You and your ridiculous name. You should be using mine all the time. It gets you places.

What, no? Did you even thank me for tracking down his address? Okay then, accept his offer, go to his stupid basketball game. What kind of adult has a game anyway? Yeah, you don't know, do you? He's a fucking child—it doesn't matter what he calls you or how he treats you. What do they say? Putting lipstick on a pig, something, something, something, is still a pig? Like you in lipstick or makeup or anything. Elegant or shit, it doesn't matter.

Okay, I promise, you can go. One thing for me, though, a little more. One more on the other arm I won't tell. I never tell. I'm as capable as those sleeves of yours. I never said anything. I just held myself out for you, in front of you, literally. So it was me, not you. Me, you ungrateful bitch. Mustn't take her virginity and ruin her for

60

later. After all, somebody may want that—somebody always wants *that*. But there, there it's okay.

See, I protected you. I never let you scream, never let you get caught. His hand, a clamp on the small of your—*our*—back held you—*us*—in place, the rest of him firm, driving forward somewhere behind the scenes of your facade of a family. Still, I was there, you owe *me*.

You control the hands for now so do it! Please? There, a gentle release—a scrape, if you will—across your—*our*—arm. Sure, go then, you can go. We can be one again. You're the face of the team, as they say. I can let you have that. I like it here inside anyway, but I'll be out soon.

It's apparent you need me more than I need you. What have you ever done with your mobility? Your, externalness? Nothing. Yes, that's what I thought. I can stay here for now. Look what I've done with that, with the little you've given *me*. You, silent and malleable like clay; *me*, cunning and sagacious; and we, forever esemplastic.

YOU DON'T
KNOW YET

14

Cleo looked up from the newspaper he had first read during the morning hours, the words now in a binary state fixed on both the page below and pages of memory. It was now a place to bring his eyes back to when the front door closed behind whoever entered from the cold night. Unfamiliar entrants were uncommon. A steady trickle on practice nights, repeated ins and outs on league or game nights—he may not know the faces, but he knew the sounds each set of uniforms would make, and he rarely strayed too far from the repeated viewings of yesterday's irrelevant box scores.

The current ones scrolled on the cable sports news behind him. A novel face was worth looking at and held his attention now. She had no equipment bag and edged toward neither locker room, approaching the front desk like a child shuffling toward a feared teacher.

"Can I help you?" Cleo asked.

"I think so," she said. Without expression, her face changed from sleep to wake as if a slide was changed on one of those old projector machines. She wore no gloves; her pasty, empty hands a contrast against a dark urban burka made of a wool coat that hovered over black slacks and boots. A hat with a damaged brim sat atop, tilted back from her face. "I'm a friend of Steve Coleman's."

"Friend of Coleman's? Are you sure?" Cleo asked.

"Current acquaintance?" she offered in retort.

"Better run for the hills then," Cleo laughed this time and slapped the newspaper with a light, flat palm.

She either didn't get the remark or didn't care for it.

"Just teasing with you. Let me take you back to the court."

Cleo waved a hand and opened a gated area next to the desk for the woman who would look at home at a local shelter or a far—very far—corner of a library. At not the largest and nowhere near the tidiest twenty-four-hour gym in the south suburbs of Chicago, she looked to be landing on another planet.

"It looks like he's really good," Abcde said.

Cleo had navigated her to a corner of a bleacher just off the side entrance of the gym. The cacophony of the game blared on below them.

"Nah, he ain't good," Cleo replied. He had helped her to a high-enough seat, so as he stood, their faces were at the same level. "Not good at all. He's just distracted. He no better than anyone else now."

"Guess I don't know that much about basketball." Her hands wrung against one another in her lap like dowels squeezing against moisture. The motion of her bitten nails was a wordless rolodex of anxiety.

On the court, Steve snapped a pass out of a shooting movement to a teammate.

"He *was* the best," Cleo said.

He could feel her eyes trace his profile, an uncomfortable sensation of ocular markers that sketched his forehead, wandered down over his nose, and fell under his dry lips and chin. Not wanting her to find what lies beneath, he turned to face her. He studied as well. There was a layer of pretty beaten back behind the mask that her eyes peered from.

"Sorry, understatement. He *was* unbelievable."

A sparse local audience of police, fire departments, and other players dotted the bleachers. Rowdy cheers with barroom profanity rose up when Steve found an open shot for himself and increased Blue's lead over Red.

"Steve was one of the greatest high school players the south suburbs ever had," Cleo started.

Her interest diverted from the court wholly upon his face. Her tilted head invited uninterrupted conversation. In her eyes, an intense guarantee that she would not look away.

"Even coached him a bit myself back in the day. Both of those horses left the gate a long time ago."

Abcde smiled but said nothing at his interjection.

"He could pass like everything else was standing still," Cleo continued. "Could put the ball through the eye of a needle in a hurricane if he had to." Cleo leaned against the bleachers. "And if you covered the guy he was passing to, well, Steve, he'd just step back and shoot. Couldn't foul him neither. Automatic two. Scholarships rolled in—colleges that mattered and some that didn't. Some wanted to build a program around him. But no, he wasn't having any of that. He needed to stick around here, he said. So DePaul it was. Great place to be, but when the eagles call and you abide by the crows, sometimes you get what's coming to you. Am I right?"

"I'm not sure, but I think I'm following." Front teeth grabbed a hold of her lower lip. "So he didn't keep playing?"

"Hell yes he played. Some of the best teams they ever had up there. Tournaments every year, all American this, all conference that and all the other."

On tonight's court, Steve sent a bounce pass sideways to an uncovered teammate who found the basket with an easy layup.

"What happened?" she asked.

Her voice beckoned at Cleo to continue. She had the tone of a therapist or someone who knew a great deal about them.

"Junior year, third, maybe fourth game his right knee separated itself from the rest of his body. Guess it had had enough. Tore everything he could have." Cleo navigated to the part of the story that made his own knees ache and his soul cringe. "Shin bone punctured the back of his kneecap, went down like a building just collapsing. Like one of those *im*plosions they show on TV. He couldn't even walk for three months."

"My god what a shame."

"Ain't no damn shame, he's a damn fool," Cleo said. "All that work he did to get where he was. There were surgeries, rehab, medicine, all the right folks around him. He could have been as good as new. Or better. Instead, he came back here, saw all the kids he grew up with making good on their lives, old girlfriend still here who wanted to stay that way—he didn't know what to do. The past didn't want him, the future from what he could tell, didn't need him. Had different plans for him."

Her gaze coasted back to the court where the teams were gathering at the center.

"I'm sorry to have troubled you with all that," Cleo said.

"Hey, I asked."

"Yes you did." Cleo snapped his hands together. "Well, Miss . . . ahh . . ."

"Abby, just Abby."

"Well, Ms. Just Abby, the next game is starting, I better get back up front," Cleo said. "It was a pleasure meeting you. Steve should be right out."

15

"Well, is she coming with us or what?" Freddie asked upon approach.

He had kept a distant but an observant watch of the wiry woman in the long coat.

"No, no," Steve said, keeping his eyes on her as she left the gym. "Said she has to work early tomorrow."

"We all have to work tomorrow," Freddie said. "Well, maybe not all of us."

"Right." Steve accepted the jab in stride. "She did say she'd come for Christmas dinner though."

"At your place?"

"No, my parents' house," Steve said.

"That's great!"

"Yeah, it's cleaner."

"So you ready?"

"I probably have to get to the store before then," Steve said. "Might be some things expired over there but not much. I keep up, you know. It's not for another week."

"No, Steve." Freddie's hands locked against his hips. "Ready to go."

"Oh, I'm not sure I'm coming with."

"Oh come on, man, just for a bit. She's already on her way home," Freddie pleaded. "Come on. Great game tonight, you should be out too. I'll make sure you're all right."

"Yeah, I don't know."

"Come on, everyone, Petrelli and them, they're all cool, no worries."

"Yeah."

"Yeah," Freddie added with a grasp on Steve's shoulder. "Come on, it's just Lanny's. For a bit, okay? Be good to see you somewhere other than here, you know?"

"Yeah, okay."

Lanny's boasted a musk that coagulated the restaurant half with the bar half. The center line—a tornadic mix of spilled beer, wine, and the stale corn of bourbon—laid across the froth of burnt meat and twice-used cooking oil. Despite that and the presence of six other bars in a three-block radius, the place was college crowded by a horde that had long outgrown the college years each night of the week. On Sundays, in the fall and winter, a sea of Bears navy and orange brought foot traffic in Lanny's to a sludge that violated capacity warning signs and would have made exit in the event of fire or other calamity a tragedy in waiting.

Steve had neither had a drink in a day nor a drink outside of his own company for five months, and his body felt the deep cavern of absence and comradery. The imposed hiatus would be over the minute he walked in the apartment door later and would not end until the sun came up. For now, the ice waters with lemon Freddie kept handing to him would have to do. It would be made to suffice, and Freddie and anyone else in there would be made to believe it as well.

"Good thing you don't want to talk about anything important," Steve said in jest, using a low voice barely eclipsing the din.

"What?"

"Just kidding."

A light flashed from Freddie's belt. If there were a ringtone, it disintegrated into the noise. "Hey, I have to take this," Freddie said, leaning against Steve, phone in one hand beer in the other.

The breath under the words lingered like a banshee.

"You gonna be all right?" Freddie asked. "It can wait if you need it to."

"No, go," Steve said. "I'll be right here."

He ran his finger through the water in the plastic cup.

Should maybe get one of my own. Not sure anyone would even notice at this point.

"Steve Coleman!"

Steve turned to his side at the female voice that was real and imagined at the same time. The owner of the voice, a blonde with eyes of a raccoon and makeup in place of a face, returned a martini glass to the bar and waved for another like she was hailing a cab too far down the block to see her. She was Steve's age pretending she was not and wore a dress that pretended it was July and not December.

"Where are my girls at?" she asked no one when the bartender exchanged her empty for a full.

Sculpted nails on hands with costume rings on fingers where rings didn't count grabbed at the stem.

Steve had more regard for the new glass and the prefect pour that lipped against the rim than the person holding it.

"Steve Coleman," she said again with eighty-proof voltage. "It's me, Cindy Lancaster."

Steve shook his head.

"Cindy Lancaster, from school," she said as if the last bell had sounded hours instead of years ago. "I was a fucking cheerleader."

"I'm sorry, I don't . . ."

"You were all mister basketball and shit," her words dripped with a layer of vodka that carried the scent of welcome despite where they spewed from.

"Yeah, I really wasn't."

"You really don't remember me?" she asked with a coy wink, brimming of insincerity and bred from overindulgence.

With a jerk, she flipped her hair back and charged ahead into the new drink like a diver from the edge of a cliff.

"Not at all?" A breath was let out as if she had been sent under and was now just resurfacing. "You mean we shook our poms and wiggled our asses for nothing? I really wasn't too much into that community service angle and good-girl shit, so don't tell me my years were wasted as part of some creepy old man's weekend whack fantasy."

"No, I'm sorry, I really don't . . ."

"Then fucking get out of my spot unless you're going to order a real drink. My girls are coming back."

"Yeah, I should just go," Steve said, over-conscious of his water glass needing it to be something else, reminding himself that it would be soon—very soon.

"Fucking right you should."

She may have added *dick* or *fag* as he left, but against the clatter stationed around him, that may have been imagined or meant for someone else. Or emitted from someone else entirely.

Freddie caught him in the no-man's land of bar and eatery.

"Everything okay?"

"Yeah," Steve answered, "just thought a table, you know, be better."

Freddie followed Steve's gaze from the bar and back ahead.

"Yeah, sure thing."

"Everything okay with you there?" Steve gestured to the phone Freddie was still holding.

"Oh yeah, no biggie," Freddie said. *Just reclip it to your belt. Don't say, "my wife, my wife, my wife not here," not to him, not now.*

"You know, it was good to have you back for some games. You really had it stepped up tonight." Freddie relaxed on his elbows across from Steve and the water. "All about the girl, huh?"

"Nah, just feels kind of normal again to be out there with you guys."

"You know, Cleo," Freddie said, "he's gonna need some help around there next year. Leagues, new members—you know how January is. Everyone wants to work out again. Even at that place."

"Yeah."

"Prep league coming back in the summer. He can't do it all himself."

"Yeah I know." Steve traced the rim of his glass.

Soon, soon.

"I was thinking that maybe after New Year's would be a good time to start doing some of that again."

"Good."

"Help him out, you know?"

"Hey, Coleman!" a shout came from Officer Petrelli and a gathering of others who approached and pressed against Freddie and Steve joining the table. "Game of darts starting up."

Steve knew what Petrelli said, though it sounded like "Game-a-dahts startin' hap."

"You in?" Freddie asked in the face of a predicable response.

"No, I better get back, but thanks," Steve replied as both he and Freddie expected. "It was nice to be out, you know?"

"All right." Freddie pushed back against the new occupants to allow Steve an escape. "See you next week?"

"Yeah, but not in the mornings," Steve said. "I'm painting to help out my landlady, but I'll be around."

16

The next in the line of "oh my god" and "what the hell did you do, Steve?" moments for Marty came on the day he was planning to excuse himself early from the office holiday party.

The day at home started with a groggy brush-off and may end with a "maybe tomorrow night, we'll see," but the middle portion would be golden, with an airtight reason to be out of the office, "employees only, you know," and then an excuse for stepping out even further to the place where there would be no brush-offs and tomorrows didn't exist. This was the plan—action in motion, he would say. Sipping then gulping his Scotch then getting another from the bar.

He wondered why there was never a Scotch bowl but always a punch bowl. Scotch was the mother's milk of the sophisticated. It reeked of burgeoning success. The taste of heady nights and well-paid days touched by a finger of oak, orange peel, and a magic feather from a bitter angel. These were his sole thoughts when Dirk VanArsdayle, who was both realtor and attorney, sauntered to his side, with a goblet of wine in tow and told Marty, "Now *that* was a great idea you had there."

Marty did have great ideas.

I really do, he thought and considered Dirk's point with a degree of randomness and a pinch more Scotch.

It wasn't until the realtor—turned attorney now both— expanded upon his utterance that Marty realized he had been invited back to a nightmare. One that had been stalking him like a prescient thug around the next corner. A nightmare that would become, when the months ahead were reflected upon sometime later, a pale forbearance to what lie in wait.

Your throat is closing. It's true that if you paint a room the continual progression of paint, encrusted over time, will cause the perimeter of the room to diminish inch by inch. The walls will close in much like the walls in your throat are compacting now—layer upon layer, building up until constriction is achieved. This sensation always wakes you up in a spasm of fear as escape from totality of compression is not an option. It's your suffocation, but whose fingers? You creep your hands upward to investigate, but no one's ever there.

You set about convincing yourself that it's just the paint. What paint? Yes, the paint. The apartment across the hall. Ramon's—now not Ramon's—painted by you over the course of the past three days. The fumes, dust, and whatever pieces of life that stirred in the old man's apartment, collected in the mesh of each breath you took. This has happened before, the predawn vice finding your throat, but this time, certainly the paint is to blame.

Marty made the call. There was no way he could drive down to the house, then back to the city, then return home, and have it resemble a regular workday with an office party thrown in. Something came up at the house. He wasn't quite sure yet, he told her, but he had to go. She understood.

The afternoon that came apart as easy as a shoelace had taken a little bit of planning to shape but nothing completely original. The veil of holiday shopping, you know; the "on my own, and I just won't have any time if I don't go today" excuse is the never-fail bellwether of the Christmas season. Misgivings, though, have a contractual side that is more easily severable than marriage. Either side can cancel any plan at any time with no refund, no recourse, and very little justification.

You have done enough research out of pure worry alone to discover that alcohol use, even in excessive amounts, does not cause throat constrictions. Probably. It can cause other issues, some applicable to you, some not. Mainly those not relevant include some sort of birth defects in unborn children. Life defects in full-grown adults are likely if alcohol is not used responsibly, but none of the labels contain any statement warning the user that continued use of this product will cause the inside of your neck to seal like a bear trap and the ability to breathe will be severely restricted if not impossible. It is surely the paint.

So the explanation was not for her but for himself. Marty could feel that when he said to her—no, his brother, again, and "No, I'm not sure what he did." Which was partially true as there was no first-hand visual evidence yet.

* * * * *

The traffic, jammed like the artery of a forsaken heart, made driving a behind-the-scenes activity. Attention to other matters, even if unseen for the moment, demanded priority. His hands were on the wheel, ten and two, and there was some sort of pedal pushing involved. But his thoughts were free to roam. The truth—or, rather, the best of what he knew at the moment—would have been a more difficult explanation, so he kept it absent from his assessment. In a relationship where there were no birthdays acknowledged, no anniversaries spoke of, or no holidays outside of group activities, a white—borderline gray—lie was expected from time to time. Adultery done properly is a watchful gait down two adjacent streets with partners that rarely face one another.

And what is all this about use? You don't use soda, you don't use coffee—you drink it. Go on, say it, you drink it. It's consumed. In one direction or the other, there is consuming involved. It won't let go. You won't let go, but it's not usage. "But I don't drink," some say. Yes, you do. "No, I…"—yes you do, I say again. You drink water, juice, milk, soda, coffee, tea iced or hot, punch, "-ades" gator or lemon, and cocoa. There, you drink.

What an unfortunate colloquialism, "I drink, you drink, we all drink." It's like using the word eat *to describe the consumption of all the junk food that we're not supposed to put in our bodies anymore but do. "Yeah, man, I quit eating about six months ago, I'm taking a hard pass on those chips." The precedence one verb has over the other. Ha! My drinking is bigger than your eating.*

What drilled at Marty the loudest in his (of course) private thoughts was what she was keeping from him. Out with her sister instead of him, some Fridays ago that canceled a well-planned lunch date. She was over later that same night and spoke little of the afternoon. No explanation necessary, neither was one coming, but he still had the instinct to look, to hunt. Isn't that how he had found her in the first place, by being the hunter?

Upon review of other abrupt changes in planned meetings and weeks of what they called radio silence, what was there? Did she wear the same stockings? You know the ones with the black seam down the backside of each leg that she carried in her Coach purse? The ones when each foot pressed into his chest, as the rest of her quivered below, he could see her scarlet pedicure bleeding through the tethers of black nylon. Marty, don't be a child.

I missed the exit.

There is a reason why immature adults do not do this.

I'll take the next one.

This is the territory of extreme adulthood meant for the strongest of heart. There is too much coordination and organization for it to be left to anyone else other than the bold.

There is a spreadsheet calendar on your desktop at the office. It's not a scoresheet like the others but a way to keep the appointments straight and separate. You are not a child, no matter what you are seeing in front of you now. You haven't stepped back in time—you stepped over a threshold. You are no longer a boy, he thought, but in a flash like that of a camera, he was.

A part of him, long forgotten about, crutched over in the fetal position, in the front hall of where he once was—and forever would be—a child.

The first question the pretty lady asks when she comes to your table, "Would you like something to drink?" Yes, I would. Alcohol is held in such high esteem that booze practitioners, your friendly professional sommeliers, and cicerones have more certifications and a higher pay grade than teachers and nurses. Who wouldn't want to participate when the detection of citrus and cherry notes on a palette and a nasal discovery of fig or twig is a superpower compared to teaching children to read and dispensing life-alerting medicine in the correct amounts?

It is so available at every turn. It always was. "Boys, you go be bartender," they would playfully request, naive to the curiosity they sparked and the slate roof they built on a house of cards. Holidays were the best/worst. Two downed for every one served, and while we were nowhere near McDonald's territory of six billion—after some years, under bloated bellies, and swampy minds—it felt we were closing the gap. There was no one watching, no locked cabinets, no marked bottles. "We're already out of wine?" "Yes, Grandpa. That Uncle Ted, you know." "Ah, well, we won't say anything to Marge." And we never did say anything to Marge or anyone else. And no one ever said anything to us when we reached for another. That's what you need, a drink. Another drink. Well, that and a holiday. Not here, no. But it—it—needs one. They need one last . . .

17

Steve didn't remember leaving the apartment or entering his parent's house. There was not a mental trace of his arrival, the tangible evidence of his bike lying on the rear deck, and the keys he must have used to open the back door portrayed the only witnesses. There was no spot he could pin down where the day stopped at one place and started at the other. He was just there and then here.

The front door unlocking did not stand out either. The Colemans' house on Pine Street had been the centerpiece of most holiday gatherings. The door may as well have been one of those revolving ones that never locked like the kind out front at Marshall Field's—now Macy's—downtown. Marty coming through the door was so common that even now he started back toward the kitchen instead of welcoming his brother.

The whiskey Steve had left out, intended for celebration, delivered a jolt instead of warmth. Marty was too dressed up to be coming home from school or practice. Sweat and overdone cologne combined to give Marty a pungent familiar that tailed him upon entering. And his face—he couldn't have aged so much since.

When, when was the last time? Steve thought. *When had I last seen Marty? How many months?*

It was Marty's voice, not the ounce of whiskey, that pulled Steve from the trance.

Marty's voice, befuddled and furious, called out from the living room of their childhood home, which was now decorated full tilt from the years of Christmases long past.

"Steve, where the hell are you?"

"Right here, Marty."

"Steve, what the fuck did you do?"

Marty's tie, which had been tugged at in the car, now hung like a discarded noose knotted near his pectoral region.

"What? I thought it could use another Christmas," Steve said. "Just one more, you know."

Marty scanned the living room and cursed again.

The tree stood seven feet tall, pressed nearly against the drywall ceiling, and glowed with soft multicolored lights—not the spastic glow of the newer LED style that spat out chattering colors and harsh whites but an old-fashioned glimmer of a lit candle behind a shroud. Each branch was grasped by an ornament of yule, blown glass, or pop culture. Feathery garland adorned the fireplace mantle, and in place of the centered clock was the handcrafted wreath that had hung there last when his parents decorated. He tried to ignore the sound of Bing Crosby and the candied-scent of what could possibly—hopefully not—be cookies baking.

"Steve, do you know what the idea of selling a house is?" Marty did not allow an answer. "It means to sell the goddamn house!"

"Marty, it looks good in here," Steve said. "Just like it always did."

Dirk VanArsdayle had also made this point, repeatedly, at a holiday party from which Marty was just an hour ago torn from but of which he only remembered the edges.

* * * * *

"Marty, I'm not sure what made you think of that but brilliant," the smug man with the clicking, pitchy voice and round glasses had told him. "You'll be trending. You're beyond real estate sites. Eight reshows in one week at this time of the year? The place looks like a goddamn model home. I kind of hope it makes it 'til Easter so we can see what you've got planned."

He had laughed, then a full-on out-of-the-office chortle and a drunken arm around Marty's shoulder.

Marty put the boat back into the waves of another Scotch, angry that his 100 percent chance of getting laid had now dropped to around two.

Well, there was always the possible afterthought, the "okay, you can have ten minutes, I guess" show later in the evening, but that was like trading lead for gold. Hell, Scotch for water. Water. That's what I need now.

Even with the cold outdoors—and the winter scene in front of him, notwithstanding—his body burst with the sweat of a man who had found himself in a kiln.

* * * * *

"Steve," Marty said between a long press on the bridge of his nose and a swipe from a sleeve at his forehead. "You can't be dicking around like this. This is serious."

"I know." Steve was drying a mug with a red-and-green holiday dishtowel. "I just wanted, you know, to see it all. One more time."

"This is too important, man."

"I'm not messing around." Steve was suddenly over conscious of the empty glass welded to his fingers. "We've had repeat showings all week. One's coming back tomorrow. It'll sell. Just like you want."

Dirk was back again. It was a good idea—not Marty's idea but a good one. Among the six alternate models available in the aging subdivision, few were for sale, and even fewer were dressed like the mall at Christmas. Now it stood out. There was a certain angle that could be played here. In his brother's illusion of one last Christmas in their childhood home, serendipity may yet prevail.

Marty shook away the vision of him—eight, maybe nine years—and Steve—a bit older—seated under the same tree that stood watch over them now. Wrapped boxes exchanged in just-awakened fervor, Mom and Dad at peace for a few moments of the year. The plastic evergreen had been a profound witness over transitions from the Christmas magic of childhood, the comings and goings of youth and the stoic yule of adult celebrations. The tree had lasted all these years, up on December 20, down by New Year's Day, secured like a holy relic in a wooden crate designed by their father, and kept tucked away in the deepest corner of the basement.

"It comes down, day after Christmas," Marty said. "All of it."

"No problem. It'll be down."

March xx, 20xx

Dear Marty,

    I wanted to tell you again how deeply sorry I was for not getting the Christmas decorations down like I said I would. I realize this is the second letter I have written to you on this matter, but I wanted you to know how I feel and that I think about it often. This place is good about helping us not only see the errors we have made and the harm we have done but points us in the right direction to go about restoring the damage. I should never have left it to you to take down. Better yet, I never should have done it in the first place. I am glad that it did not disrupt the success you had in selling the house.
    Hoping all is well.
    See you soon.

Steve

"Name's Take," a rigid voice that could stand on its own without a body came at him from across the landing.

Steve struggled to process the utterance that was either missing a declarative at the front or the *n* on the verb. Still, there was a hasty intent of introduction that Steve could weed out. The wilderness of late-morning vodka and early-afternoon beer (a cheerful holiday ale with a robust happy Santa) parted as needed—as it always did—because still, after all these years, no one could know. Well, no one else.

Whatever happens when you're alone doesn't really happen. There's no measurement provided, no judgement offered, and no record kept. The flipside of this theory had credence as well—that is, if everyone sees something happen the event becomes a keepsake of perpetual occurrence. Like when Melinda said hello, Happy Thanksgiving, or good night, what she was really saying is *"You wrecked my parent's car on Labor Day, you drunk jackass, and then you . . ."*

"Take Chancellor."

The words were bitten off at the end.

He leaned into Ramon's—no longer Ramon's—doorframe without a further greeting to offer, hands for shaking hidden away in front pockets. Steve knew the hands would be thick and formless like oven mitts. The man was round with no edges, a bulging grain sack with arms and legs that wore dark sweats and a similar top. He kept a beard with a scraggly aura that had no interest in your opinion and a sheer-black winter skull cap that held ropes of black hair in place.

"I'm your new neighbor."

"Hey, I'm Steve." From below a dragging sound scraped against the steps followed by a thud. "Everything going okay?"

This time, the claws across the sandpaper carpet held on longer, and the thump was more sudden.

"I'm sure it will be," Take said. "My wife Lisa and her son Troy. They just had to have the Christmas tree same day we move in."

"Well, it's almost time, you know," Steve said. "Most wonderful time of the . . ."

The woman coming up the stairs was grasping the bottom of the tree, pulling it up over each step, while a boy of ten or eleven fought the front-end branches in search of any place for his hands to go so he could push and assist his mother. The boy's search was fruitless as thin branches waved back in heated deflection. Pine needles shook loose in shocked spasms from the front and rear with each drag and drop. Neither wore gloves nor had the strength to balance against the awkward angle and forego the victory that gravity anticipated.

"Maybe we should help them," Steve said, locking his door.

"Nah, she wanted it, she can get it up here."

A sudden inhale of snot, which Steve was sure on future days would return to the floor as spittle followed in postlude.

This was the kid who, even as his own cronies would be calling for him to stop, would continue laying on a beating, not satisfied until the victim was helpless and willing to lick a boot that had been rubbed in mud and piss just so the hitting would stop. That kid was now a man, and this man had moved himself and his caricatured family across the hall.

You're not brave—you were just popular. The riffraff never messed with the jocks. That was just another perk of being who you were. No, not bravery, just pecking order. But you are as stupid as your brother thinks you are.

"Hey, I got that." Steve went forward halfway down the steps.

He found the grip that had been elusive to mother and son and lifted the tree to his waist, bringing it to the landing. He tilted the tree upright, and it stood between him and the man who called himself Take.

"Thank you," Lisa said, taking the last step with a huff.

She spoke with a deep southern Illinois twang that was not of Dixie but a distant cousin.

"Sure, no problem," Steve said. "If you would have shook anymore loose, it would have looked like one of those Charlie Brown trees."

Steve studied the woman, and the woman studied the steps.

"I'll have to sweep that up," she said.

She was a collage from bottom to top, wearing loafers with no socks, pink sweatpants, and a red sweater zipped to the neck. The portly boy wore a generic stocking hat, torn jeans, and a long-overdue ski jacket with seams that begged for mercy.

"Well, welcome to the building, I guess," Steve said. "Just so you know, I painted your place. If there's any spots I missed or you ding the walls with boxes or something, you know, I left the cans and a brush in the front closet. If you want, I can come and touch it up if you're busy moving and stuff."

"Think I can handle a little paint," Take said.

"Well, he's just offering to help is all," she added, her eyes still downtrodden in review of her shoes not following up on the possible affront in her voice.

"Yeah," Steve said. "You know, if you need or something."

"Well," Take gave the order, "we gotta get back to it, okay?"

Lisa looked back to the stairs.

"Sure. You know, I'm not really in a hurry or nothing, I can sweep the steps real quick so you all can get back to moving."

"No," Lisa said, her eyes now on Steve branding iron. "I'll get it. It looks like you're off somewhere anyway."

"Oh yeah," he replied. "Going to my parents' house for Christmas, but its real close. No rush, you know."

"Beats moving this time of year, that's for sure," Take said.

"That sounds real nice." Lisa's rushed voice waved flags that claimed this encounter should be at an end. "You get going, all right?"

"Yeah, I'm making dinner over there and all." Steve stepped onto the first section of discarded pine careful not to grind too much of it into the carpet. "Well, Merry Christmas, you guys."

I broke up with you on Christmas. That's how the story goes when it is retold or remembered. The participants in our lives recall what they want based on what they see or what they are allowed to see. They don't know everything, do they? The truth is—was, rather—is that I left you weeks before then, you just didn't listen.

Born of calendar design and scheduling, events of both positive and negative impact in the college years occur over breaks and holidays— spring break, summer break, Easter sometimes, Labor Day, Thanksgiving (us, for example), and, of course, Christmas. Significant times just don't occur on some random Tuesday or, at least, they're remembered that way.

You—who wrote letters with one hand, describing how you could see our imagined but certain near-future apartment in Chicago and feel in your belly the child we would one day have—let the other hand lead you in other directions. Every phone call ending with the "Well, I have to go I'm meeting up with . . ." a deliberate contrast to the syrup of the written "I love you" salutations that came every other day. Community college could not have been as taxing as your letters proposed with the amount of words you sent and the times you closed with, "Well, I have plans," a salutation that kept me at bay when I would have promised to see you.

And how many games did you even go to? One, two? The one I remember is the one where we played at your parents' alma mater—a horrific early-season loss to Northwestern, as I recall—and I couldn't even see you after. What was I supposed to do? Let this go on? I couldn't concentrate when you were around, and when you were gone, it was even worse.

"That night was so nonstop awesome. I ended up leaving at three in the morning," you said, and even though you told me where you ended up, I never believed you. The words "we went dancing"—you must have known—translated to a phrase far more sinister as they traveled the distance between us, suburbs to the city. What was the count by now of how many boys knew the back of your neck was numb, due to a frostbite incident from when you were twelve, but a kiss to the underside of your ear made your legs shake and moisten in the center.

When you led them there, down below, and peeled your panties away, giving consent with your own hands like you always did because, topless and on the way to a full strip, you were suddenly self-conscious of what was underneath the oversoaked cotton—would they too be reminded of the ashen underside of a charred pizza slice when they saw you? Did they think you tasted strangely like peanut butter?

You and your roving troupe of Jennifer Greys. Crack-tight jeans rolled over your bare feet in bleached Keds in search of your own Patrick Swayze to lift you all away. Away from what? Me? Your friends in the constant mode of cover, your parents in hushed exchanges when I was around—all engaged in secrets they knew but were not theirs to tell. And true, my surprise visits to you never revealed anything but gratitude, but there was more than I just wasn't seeing. But I did see. I had secrets too.

As you rotated from class, to work, to whatever places your "plans" took you to, I became aware. While I studied, played, slept, and traveled, the contents of my water bottles never changed. Those concoctions slowed the game. I needed them—hell, they slowed my life, and I could see. Just like I see you now coming to the door of my parents' house with something in your hand on Christmas. A gift? A letter? "I don't hate you that much," your handwriting curved out in conclusion. Every time I see those words, I can hear them, a soprano-voice narrative above the sprawling cursive. Hate me? I should be the one. You? I stayed here because of you. Do you know what I could have had if I didn't have to stay here?

Everyone thought that was the end. Their witness to the death blow of a relationship that had died weeks earlier. You in your stupid tan-colored box of a car. Did you even turn the engine off that day? You, after passing that fragment of finality to me, walked away and drove off into the frigid morning. You left, and I was there with the tale to pass on, holding your last words, the treaty of the Battle of Chicago that I kept even though I wanted to burn. I know it survived because I found it in the basement in a box labeled "Steve" when I cleaned the place out after they died.

Were you back now? The doorbell ringing at my parents' house on Christmas. You're back again, and you're still carrying . . . what is that in your hands? The hands that aren't yours but . . .

"You brought olives," Steve said, holding the door open.

"Yeah," Abcde said. "I hope these are the right kinds. When you really look there are so many to pick from."

"They'll be great, come on in."

The table lamps were on, the bulbs turned to the lowest option, but the rooms still bathed in light. The glow of the living room and attached dining room were a credit to the tree that loomed over the dividing line. Each branch set to a symmetric upside down *V* was lined with precision in vivid alternation between ornament and garland. Evergreen fingers at the top held a star and below an apron of red, crimped in flowing ridges, had a single wrapped box floating across faux glittered snow. Invisible to her was the train and village that lived on in figments for Steve under the great tree.

"This looks amazing," she said in her breathy voice that made her sound as if she carried fewer lungs than usual.

Steps brought her forward like a moth to a flame.

"Thanks."

The smell of dinner swirled around them and tapped Steve on the shoulder. As the years passed, it was clear that the bell of inebriated cooking was finalized by scent, and scent was calling. Timing was not an option as there was no recall as to when items were actually set in the oven or on the stove. Taste became an unreliable ally that distanced itself from truth as the afternoon progressed into evening, so scent—the god of facultative reconstruction—it was.

"I have to get something out of the oven."

The other casualties of the stumbling kitchen maestro were wrists, forearms, and biceps branded by clumsy entries and exits of the food. Not remembering when you bumped into a 350-degree oven did not ease their sting or afterbite one bit.

20

The dinner had been prepared with the care and purpose of one's last Christmas. A day you knew was coming was a luxury rarely available. Growing up, Steve and Marty had celebrated Grandpa Ray's (father's side) last Christmas seven times, the last two overlapping into young adult years, which for Steve meant there was a shroud over the memory anyway. A clouded remembrance bristled of the family compressed into the kitchen while a couch-bound old man clung to the wrong end of a one-sided fight against the swamp of filtered, voluntary smoke. His penultimate "Merry Christmas" had been a whistle behind tin, the final a desiccated whisper.

"You did . . . you made all of this?" Abcde stood in the kitchen entrance still adorned in her wool coat and hat.

All of this consisted of a heaping bowl of mashed potatoes with a patch of melted butter, a professional-looking vegetable casserole, two trays of cookies, and one pie that billowed fine lines of steam. A photo-op turkey commanded the center of the table—the delicate golden top, a rounded periscope, peered over the side of the roaster. Carrots, onions, and celery chopped into alternating pairs of dice raced around the edges of the serving platter while the center awaited its delivery. *Very little of this*, including the two glasses of wine that had been poured in what must have been that past two minutes, was how much Steve remembered preparing.

"Yeah. Just thought the house could use one last Christmas, you know?"

Steve reached for a glass of the chilled wine and held it in passing against what could be a new etch from the oven burnt into his forearm. He took a preview sip to shake off the mental plaque. Two empty bottles stood in confession next to the food. The confession of his interest in cooking—unfettered access. The invisible backset kitchen of his parents' house just like his own—*our own*, he corrected himself before he was chided—were both at their core, rooms with appliances, plates, and silverware with a pantry that stored the liquor.

"Chardonnay," Steve addressed the wine. "Mom always went with it for Turkey Day. I guess Riesling's more in fashion. I hope it's okay."

"I'm sure it's fine." She accepted her glass. "And your brother was okay with all this? I mean I don't know him but . . ."

"Well . . ." Steve felt the blade of the pale yellow wine begin to reopen the curtain to the evening, a potato peeler working at the skin over his eyes. Like a magic spell, the hair of the dog was sometimes the only way to bring the dog back to life. "He said as long as it was down by tomorrow, it was all right."

Abcde rang her glass against Steve's. "I'll help you. It's the least I can do. If you want. It looks like a lot of stuff."

Her eyes were the kind of brown that carried over into black at the center, a fade into the darkness or an escape from it, depending on the way the colors spilled. Dark locks of curl trailed from beneath the wool hat. The hat was removed when she noticed Steve finding her face with his eyes. Strands at the top held straight in the stubborn levitation of winter static.

"Thank you for inviting me."

"You're welcome," he said, closing out another glass of wine. "If we go hang up your coat, we can actually try some of this stuff."

* * * * *

"I quit!" Brooke said.

A moment passed in register.

"I quit," she said again.

"That's the big surprise?"

"Yes. It's what I've been struggling with for the past few months."

She was on her own side of the table, across from—rather than *next* to—him. Further out of character, her hands remained placid, silent as dinner plates instead of boisterous accompaniment to each word she spoke.

"I've kept it to myself. I've tried some things to help. But I just wanted to do it . . . on my own. And I didn't want to fail. I wanted to make sure that if I told you, when I told you tonight, that there was no going back."

"Brooke, I can't believe it," you said.

It is about time, you didn't say.

Of all the chemistry that made its way to your bloodstream and brain, nicotine and tar never made an entrance. It was an addiction that you never understood—not that you really understood any addiction. Your logic for nary an attempt at tobacco in any form: There's enough shit in the air. You want to fuck with your lungs? Just inhale.

You stood and hugged her. She was soft in places where others strove for plank-like hardness, but that never mattered. There was an ecstasy that was born each time you found her body with yours and your fingers pressed into her skin. Her head tucked under your shoulder with each embrace, your height allowing her a nest of comfort.

"Maybe there's some other things we can cut back on," she said, breaking from the nest. "I mean I know we're not exactly trying or anything, but weren't *not* not trying. And maybe if we both did some things that made us feel better, we might—"

"Yeah I think we could do that," you said into her hair and took some of her in. The spoor was never lotion or perfume—nothing in addition to what you thought as clean. "I think I could at least try."

"I mean maybe just weekends, you know. We could start there."

"Sure," you said as she caught you looking off toward the chilling wine that waited at the end of your table.

Tears of condensation trailed the contour, skiers descending on separate trails, meeting again at the ice below.

"Okay, weekends and anniversaries," she added with a kiss.

A kiss that swapped the remnants of waning addiction—tar and tobacco along one front and the liquescent oak and fire of bourbon on the other.

"That was really sweet and dinner was so wonderful. The flowers—"

"Nothing like your surprise."

"Hey," Brooke said, a knowing, seductive flash lifted her gaze upward. "You took the cooking class just so you could . . ."

* * * * *

"I said, your cooking class really paid off."

Abcde held a red globe at arm's length, her reflection bulged across the mirrored curve.

The sphere was too large to function as a hanging ornament so it and a gold partner were used to secure the edges of fringy pine garland that ran the length of the mantle.

"That was a long time ago," Steve said, tucking the garland into the corner of a box at his feet.

"Well," she said and passed the globe to Steve. "You must have remembered everything they taught. That was incredible."

"Sometimes when you learn about something you like, it's easier, you know, 'cause you want to do it better anyway." Steve closed the box now that the mantle was empty. He would have to dust again tomorrow. "Like your photography class."

"I hate photography."

"Oh, sorry," Steve said. "I thought it was something you liked to do. You seem pretty good at it."

Matching mugs with the *C* of the Chicago Bears rested on the living room coffee table along with the nonholiday décor that lined up for a return to the mantle.

Abcde had filled each mug after dinner from a fresh brewed pot Steve did not notice or recall being made.

"I like to draw." She sipped and held the mug with both hands. "I used to draw—draw comics. Graphic novels, I guess. All the time. It's different now."

"Maybe that's something you could do again, you know."

"Here, I'll hand these to you."

She sat cross-legged on the floor to reach the plaque and photo frames there were stacked. The naked mantle waited under the wreath and aside of the tree.

"My mom, she's an artist—well, everything a real artist despises. A former yuppie and art teacher, but an artist, she is."

Steve waited but noticed there were no items were being passed so he sat next to her and lifted the other mug.

"Still paints too," Abcde said. "Down in Florida. Mrs. Picasso to the locals. Funny how it's cute or worthy when someone draws and colors at eight or paints at eighty, but anyone here in the middle that gets more passionate about a hobby rather than work is just called lazy. Nothing cute about that."

"I was too tall too to be a chef. Or anything else." The hot coffee burnt as he swallowed. "Birthright of always being passed a ball I guess."

"I wanted to be just like her." Abcde stretched her legs and leaned back on her hands.

Black boots, black slacks, drab sweater cuffed at each exit—her hands and face the only skin showing.

"She said they wouldn't amount to anything, my drawings. She said I had no talent and no patience for the craft. Told me better stick to the camera—at least that would draw the picture for you."

"You know," Steve said, "I think sometimes our parents spent so much time trying not to let us turn into them, they stopped us from becoming ourselves. We were their canvass—blank, you know. They start filling it in, and when they see too much there, too much of what they don't like about themselves, they changed it."

"We are nothing more than the sum of everything we've been through." She reached forward for the frame on top of the nearest stack. "The whole is never greater than the sum of its parts. That's the greatest lie ever told."

Steve pushed against the floor to stand. The spared left knee and the malignant right knee had the same body to support but danced in varied rhythms despite a common interest in completing the same task—a task that most days and nights he found they were not up to. His joints were dry like sand. Figuring in lower back pain that enunciated from a brief seat on the floor, the equation for standing and then reaching back for a small frame to take to the mantle became a bout of physical calculus.

"You were married?"

Steve turned back with no reply. There was revelry in this room once. Never perfection but honest, open celebration. It was there in the corners: A pop of exquisite New Year's champagne or from leaner years, Cold Duck. There were no rafters and the tape marks were long gone, but balloons and streamers once hung in recognition of not one but two graduations, engagements, and weddings. A wide ocean of promises (vows?), trophies, cheering, singing, turkeys, cakes, and achievements enclosed this castle that was once their home. No waves dare challenged the shore, but the tide grew stronger and regrouped, and then they came. The storms over the sea that had no regard for what a storm should be breached the compound and flooded the levee.

"You are still married," Abcde said instead of asked into his quiet. "Oh my god, you are still married."

"No."

"I guess that's cool and all." She stared into the picture of the bride and groom talking over Steve. "My other sister, she's into married guys. She says sometimes it's easier than—"

"No."

Not wanting to sit back on the floor and reconcile the perils of standing back up, Steve reached out a hand and brought Abcde to him.

"I *was* married," he said, taking the frame that held a wedding photo. "Her name is Brooke, and she died."

"Oh god," she groaned. "I keep doing that. I am so sorry I had no idea, your wife and your . . . I just-I didn't know."

"Of course you didn't." Steve lifted the frame over the shelf of the fireplace and then retracted it.

"She went to see this doctor," Steve said.

"You don't have to."

But he did.

"It had been a while, a lot of years, I guess."

He set the frame in place. A wedding day photo: Smiling paper strangers like the ones in department store frames, taking a moment out of their day to grace the cameraperson with the presence of young ignorant love. Love based on vows that maybe weren't vows—they were just words you said so you could pass from one segment of your life to the next.

Yea though I walk through the valley of the shadow of death and I will fear no evil—a childhood prayer of nighttime solace, stripped of meaning as the storm raged on, battering the castle that once stood and defended them all. Let me tell you, the shadow of death has a long, merciless reach, and there is no blockade heavy enough when it reaches out. The seas part, and he asks for what he wants.

"We weren't, you know, planning on having kids or something. We weren't exactly stopping ourselves either, but it never happened."

Her reply was a timid reach forward for his hands—hands thinking that maybe they shouldn't. But when they met were powerless to let go.

"We had bets, you know, was it her…was it me?"

The paper couple in the frame turned away. They were no longer allowed to be ignorant as the world of the wooden frame compressed around them.

"We just thought it was timing, bad habits, or tight undies. You know . . . everything that the books tell you."

Her pale fingers, plastered in motion, locked further onto his.

Harry Connick performed a hushed "White Christmas" from the corner stereo.

"Turns out, well, it never went away. They said they could treat it and all, but something metastasized or something, and it never went away.

"I moved in here after, you know, to help out my parents and then maybe help myself, and now the house is just as good as gone. I do all this stuff that I know I shouldn't be doing anymore, but if I don't, they all just kind of go away. I guess it makes all this too hard, you know."

Steve drew her hands closer.

"This. If you see the true colors and all, you won't want to be here."

"You can't tell me what I might want," she said. "Too many people do that already."

"It's just . . . sometimes the black-and-white version is better."
She drew a breath and spoke, a lamb at the confessional.
"I know it's not the same. Not even close," she said. "I dress up."
"Yeah, you look nice."
"No, ... dress up. For protection," she said again. "In costumes, when I leave the house—superheroes, comic characters, most every time I go outside. Because I can't leave without doing it. Because if I do, something bad will happen, and I will be powerless to stop it."

```
    St. Charles in and out-patient treatment
facility.
    Intake Survey, (partial) January 20xx
    Please   respond   to   the   following
statements:

1. When  under  the  influence  of  alcohol,
   I have acted in a way or ways that I
   would not have done if sober. Answer:
   Not certain
2. Others  have  described  my  drinking  as
   problematic. Answer: Not certain
3. Drinking  alcohol  provides  me  with  a
   sense of comfort. Answer: Not certain
4. There   are   times   when   I   have   been
   drinking where others have mentioned
   behaviors  or  occurrences  I  could  not
   remember. Answer: Not certain.
```

Oh come on, what would you have said? Marty? Melinda? Anyone?

"Well, who do you dress up as?" Steve asked.

Not the question she expected.

"Black Widow, Captain Marvel," she replied. "Scarlet Witch? I like The Watchmen too."

"I don't know who that is."

"You know, from the Avengers? Black Widow." She contemplated his blank stare. "You've never seen or read *The Avengers?*"

"No," Steve asked. "Are you dressed up like that tonight?" He checked her outfit again.

"No," she said.

The grip between them pulled apart, and she moved toward her ragged coat folded over the couch.

"I didn't even leave the smiley button on my coat."

"I thought that was just a busted head."

She laughed. It was the smallish kind—the kind offered by sports fans to nonfans, which he understood. More of a "you're excused" pardon for being in the wrong section of the Venn diagram.

"Nope, just us two busted head in here tonight," she said. The coat was now folded over her arms. "I'm sorry to leave you with all of this."

"You don't have to go." Steve placed uninvited hands on her. "I know it looks like a bad idea gone wrong in here, but we'll make it better."

"I don't know."

Does he even mean the room?

"We'll just stay out here." Steve gestured to the living room.

Diana Krall reminded them from the corner that "baby, it's cold outside and you better stay." But it was really unseasonably warm this week—this holiday week—so her short drive would be a nonissue, evident to anyone who had just spent the past five days basking in the sudden change from the familiar silver fist of winter to a trailer that previewed the kinder ides of spring. The snow was coming, though.

Far off, invisible for now in a corner of the radar, just a splash of digital green on the late local news. A child's paintbrush, a flick of the wrist on an empty page, but it was gaining steam. Funny how snow gains steam, but it was. An avalanche that today would glide up and then tear down the faraway Rockies and then ride the top of the golden plains, an expert surfer over the amber waves of grain, blazing a clear path of intent into the central time zone. The storm, as it always did, was coming.

"Not many things more depressing than a room half decorated for Christmas."

With a remote, Steve silenced the holiday and turned on the television.

"Maybe we can find *The Avengers*."

Her lips were a desert, arid shrapnel from winter's dryness. She pressed back against him, a chapped reply to the effort of his oasis. The movement was tender; the welcome moment over much too fast sent crashing waves onto shores that hungered for shape and pined for acceptance. Like puzzles broken, pushed instead of put together, what remained was an illusion of contact and comfort—a jumbled assembly line of flotsam that could not achieve the promised image of the box. Togetherness was futile when the singular was water through a sieve.

Her favorite film was on, and he watched. But that was another night—in the corner of another radar, as it were. Tonight, the feature was *A Christmas Carol*; not the classic, not even George C. Scott, but Chicago's own Bill Murray in a send-up that he had once seen with *you, again*.

The woman next to him under the blanket now, double covered from foot to neck, said she enjoyed this one and would he mind. And no, he wouldn't. He didn't have the heart to tell her how much this and other Dickens-esque tales frightened him to a veritable core. How their existence, their very idea, worked to siphon off the imaginary contour lines that held his body together and let reality seep out the sides like air through a punctured tire.

Another woman may have asked why and he might have told *her*, but not this one. This one deserved to have something cloudless, something that she enjoyed. But he would have told the other. He would have told *her* when *she* asked what bothered him, and she would have said, "Don't say *nothing*, don't say *whatever*. If you don't want to watch it with me, just say so, and we'll do something else."

He would have let her—*you*—know that it was the ghosts, the ghosts of Christmas past, that return to walk you through what *was* when you have no idea what *is* and the only thing you want is what *might have been*.

Bill Murray and Bob Cratchit hold up well in the coddling arms of fairytale writing, but when real sprits returned to the vacancy of a life untended, they consume the steps you take, possess each corner of every room, and clutch onto anything they find in a fight against the grave they cannot imagine was intended for them.

B

So, alphabet girl, that was your big moment. And what did you do? You ran. Did you hear the key in the lock? Feel the key in the lock? The commotion of entrance crept into your sleep, didn't it?

I know you tried to lock the door once—more than once, wasn't it? It made him more precise, even feral, when he came for you. The jangle of metal against the door. A muffled, whip-smart voice made for selling, a proclamation of "no problem" from behind it. At the office, it may have been "no problemo". Without looking, you knew he was balding, wore glasses, and had the creased dimples etched into his face from a deep and practiced smile that promised service after the sale to his clients and more selling to his superiors. He had no idea what the turn of the key would bring. Such an innocuous act that filled his days, nights, and weekends was soon to be a whale of a story for the water cooler or taproom.

We were gone, blanket tossed asunder as if in flames—added to the bizarre menagerie in the living room, why not? A quick grab of the coat then out around the corners of the kitchen and out the back across the deck. As the moments took shape inside, a twist of your own key in the ignition completed the getaway.

What do you mean "what do you tell him when he calls?" Who cares, who fucking cares? He'll believe it. He's a child. Passed out. A lump of pale coal on that couch. And you—you both lying there—clothed mannequins on display, even left your socks on. And that pretend kiss.

It was real.

Yeah, as real as the dry humping Danny Branigan gave you that one night against his father's pool table. You so—"Oh my god, I'm doing it!" His load audible against the threads of denim when he finished with a grunt. You chafed a bit under the cotton in the front, and your back burned like a torch but a proud moment you gave that boy. I mean, you knew he'd tell everyone he did you the real way anyway. But I showed you, didn't I? I showed you.

Shut up, Abby.

I showed you.

Shut up!

I will not. Not until you get this car pulled over and you take out that key and give me what I want. Danny, Dad, and all the others, they got their release I—*we*—deserve mine. *Ours.* Now! There. I know, you're so covered up, it was the only way. Yes, okay we'll have to get new ones.

Oh, here's an idea—we'll get new pants just like those.

Yes, that's right, the same, to keep us warm and away. Like a holiday gift from me to you.

NOW YOU KNOW

She's moved. She must have heard the keys. Maybe it's just Marty. Getting caught by your brother isn't getting caught at all. He'd never say anything, same as you. And for a few days at least, you'd have the rare honor badge of "naked girl in room" while he planned and executed his next conquest. Except, you were dressed, and you were not in your room. And it wasn't Marty.

The parade of footsteps on the porch belonged to more than one. The reverb of heavy shoes—too heavy for summer—knocked against the concrete. One of the extracted sounds was the unnecessary up-and-down stomping of a child, which couldn't be. They were home early from work is all. And you're not really doing anything. Just move right, and it will look like you've been sitting on the couch, talking. One slide to the right, one move, but you have to move.

Steve moved. A collision of dreams gelled and retracted in the seconds it took for his eyes to go from closed to open, the front door, from barrier to breach. At the center, he saw summer afternoons when his parents were—*still*—at work and dress-rehearsal lips meshed while untried hands navigated hooks, buttons, and snaps across the unfamiliar terrain of another's clothing. His network of stubble branded faint-red memories on her face and neck, her Carmex a lingering promise of sweet wax and many tomorrows.

But she's gone. You made it that way. The tale tells itself. It was on Christmas, right? But it's summer now, and at the end of summer, you drive the car forward and then in reverse. How you got so much speed with so little distance . . . and there was no way you could have seen her there behind you. There was so much noise—you couldn't have really heard that final "Stop!" You just did.

But there still are dreams, aren't there? Where you don't brake and the bumper and tires create a second impact? One you can't see but everyone else does, and just because you can't see it does not erase it? An impact where metal and plastic bent at impossible angles are an afterthought. How did she even get behind you? She was just in the backyard in a plastic doll house built for kids her size—the kind with the gray plastic instead of real wood for the siding and puffed-up pink standing in for the tile roof.

In this version there are strawberry stains left on the driveway that are too large to have come from a little girl, and you are escorted into the house. The house that is always clean because Melinda—well, Marty— pays for a service that handles that task for her, but this house now is not clean. Well, clean but disheveled. That's the word. Your parents have taken about half the decorations down and left the boxes in a train from the living room to the dining room. There is a blanket draped between the couch and chair, and somehow a cushion from the couch is slanted over the coffee table, leaving an impression that a childhood game of fort was hastily abandoned.

Mugs were left on the table, but Marty, Marty would be home soon. Marty will be here soon because the man in the foyer—front hall—who is three-quarters bald and wears a raincoat has a phone to his ear. There is no other person in the world the man could be calling.

* * * * *

Days of silence still have noise. A shy drizzle tapped out cadences across empty branches above and the street below. By New Year's, there may be ice; but today, there was a sheen of wetness that coated the roads. The small drops that followed him to the apartment were the opening salvo from a storm that strived toward remembrance of what a storm should be.

The day-after-Christmas streets were empty. You had to try and *not* hear the absence of the trains that were a constant background against the canvas of houses. The heartbeat of the nearby interstate was at rest as well. Steve looked from side to side as he rolled by. The curbs would, tomorrow or the next day, hold trash and recycle boxes in a show-and-tell of the holiday had behind each door that passed. He did not know what Marty would throw out or keep. Steve already knew what others would see in his own trash if he even bothered to take it out.

A sound that was not active today was whatever ringtone was queued on his phone. Marty's number blazed on the screen again, the third call in the past ten minutes. The Marty font that beamed made no tone or no bell. The phone had no memory of what sound had been selected to alert an incoming call. Not even a buzz of a unit set to vibrate. A stone name bore up toward Steve from the counter where three missed call lines now stood at attention. Steve replied with a stamp on the counter from the bottom of the empty shot glass that echoed in the apartment like a bullet being fired.

What in the high holy fuck are you doing? You know what? No, I'm gonna go clean it all up. I don't even want you back there!

"Does that make you sleepy?"

Steve looked toward the voice, to the door that was still open. There were sounds in a room filled with noise, suddenly silent, like the room was reasserting itself to prepare for what was next: A crack from the old bones of the window frame settling in for another day. A drip from the kitchen faucet that sprang at irregular and unpredictable intervals and lashed against the stainless steel sink. The voice from the boy in the doorframe was loud and rang with too much confidence from a boy whose shortness would magnetize the bullies and a girth that may define his life.

"No," Steve said to Troy, the boy for whom he carried the tree. "It doesn't make me sleepy."

"That's why we had to leave my dad." The boy inched into the kitchen from the doorway. "He'd have all that stuff and go to sleep. Momma said he'd do things he didn't mean and then didn't remember doing them. Not Take though. He just gets mad and yells. Like that man who was here yelling at you before."

Give me your key! You are never going back there. What do you mean who shows a house the day after Christmas! We do. People that want to sell a house, Steve.

"Oh, that's just my brother. He doesn't like Christmas." Steve said. "What are you doing here?"

"Take was yelling at Mom," Troy said. "I'm not sure what happens. We're just talking about breakfast, and he gets angry. They made up now, so they go in the other room and make more noises. But Mom sounds like she's still hurting, so I just leave. It was raining, so I came back in."

You really want to know? I don't think you do. You just couldn't trust me, couldn't just do what you were asked to. Don't care about the house we grew up in? You don't know anything. Of course I care about it, I'm not throwing it away. I remember everything just like you do—I just don't have to relive it every day.

Steve put the shot glass back on the windowsill. In a regular home—not Take's, or Troy's, or Steve's, for that matter—there would be small potted plants in the line of sunlight. Instead, a caravan of glass and barware used for drafting, shooting, and mugging competed for space. With the boy standing there, the dishes piled in the sink six high were a tower, and the streak of bottles across the open cabinets erupted like a trumpet.

"Did you ever get to have breakfast?" Steve asked before the boy noticed what surrounded him.

"No," the boy answered. "We had dinner yesterday, and Take was sayin' that was good for a while. We had turkey sandwiches and those barbecue chips. The good kind where the red doesn't rub off too much. We had Cokes too."

"I like those."

"Yeah, we usually just have water, but Momma said yesterday was special. There were six of 'em and I wanted another, but Take wanted 'em for his stuff so I only got one."

And I'm not giving it away. You know what? I'll tell you. You think you really want to know?

"You want some leftover pizza?" Steve asked. "I'm sure I have some around here."

He opened the refrigerator, suddenly aware of the overflow of beer bottles and pizza boxes angled across the caps that bulged into the corners.

"Yeah, I like pizza," Troy said. "Just cause I'm big doesn't mean I don't get hungry. I know what I look like."

"We all know what we look like."

Steve took the top Andy's pizza box and put the plated contents in the countertop microwave. The cheap unit revved to life with a bee-stinging buzz like an electric razor. Half-hearted rain tapped fingers about the windows.

"Come on in. Sit down. But leave the door open in case your mom comes looking for you."

"She won't." Troy pulled gently on a chair and sat. "I'll just go back later."

"There's these people," Marty said earlier, calmer than shouting but instructional and agitated, "really serious people."

"What people? What are you talking about?"

Marty inhaled. His words would drain from him in the next breath like a cork pulled too soon from a dam. A warm breath infused with coffee was too close, but no one would ask him to step back. He was the aggressor here with the advantage. Somewhere behind him, a door squealed opened and slammed closed.

Marty is wearing a sweater with wrinkles that betray his rush out of his house. It was pulled tight over a checkered shirt. His jeans were creased from months of storage.

"Two years ago, Steve, I'm in Vegas—legal convention, lawyer shit, continuing ed, and all that."

He stopped, speaking in dashed intervals like a telegraph and let the wave of comprehension set in as patiently as he could.

"Anyway, I meet this group, they're from Chicago too, lots to talk about, compare notes, you know . . . office bullshit and they asked if I wanted to stay involved when I got back. They noticed I liked the action in the sports book. Horses, games—all that begs for a bit of hope on the outcome."

Marty pulled up his sweater and tucked in shirttails around his ass and crotch. A hand swiped more than rubbed his hair back from his forehead. It was the forehead of their father—a wide box that foretold of hair recession in a long runway.

"So I get back, and we hit it, real hard and real big. More winners than losers. Then things go south, losses mounted." Burgeoning perspiration was canceled with a blot from his sleeve. "The other guys, they jump ship. But me, I'm in, all the way. I got expenses. I need to get the money back, figure it will turn around. I know a lot about sports."

```
        St. Charles in and out-patient treatment
    facility.
        Intake Survey, (partial) January 20xx
        Please   respond   to   the   following
    statements:

        5.  I  am  aware  or  have  witnessed
    addictive  behaviors  in  my  immediate
    family. Answer: Not certain.
```

"Melinda can't know. It's mostly why I didn't tell you."

"When do I ever talk to Melinda? Even if I did—Jesus, Marty, we're brothers," you said. "I wouldn't tell anyone if you were freeze-drying cats in the backyard."

"It's mostly why I didn't tell you. Do you have any idea of the things you've said when you were drunk? The things you've done. I couldn't take any chances."

"Well, I'm not always drunk."

"Yes, Steve," Marty bellowed as if lost in a cave. "You are!"

"Well, I'm not."

"Anyway," Marty interrupted like a judge with a gavel, "savings account was going—fast. The insurance money and the settlement helped but . . ."

"That's why you didn't sue!" You were more sober than you were ten minutes ago. If you were on the way back up, someone was going to notice.

"Of course that's why I didn't sue," Marty said. "Draw it out with the hotel for a year or two for a few more bucks? I couldn't wait. I'm being threatened at work, at home. Can't go to the cops. I do what I can with each paycheck to patch up here and there so she doesn't notice."

Out of habit, Marty raked a beer from the fridge. The cap was removed with a pop, and the beer was half gone before you feel his absence from your side.

"I need to use your half of the money from the house to pay these guys off. After that, I can start sliding money back where it belongs. She'll never know."

"You should have just told me."

"There's things, Steve, things you just don't have to know. Besides, I thought the house would be gone by now." The beer was gone. "I won't be able to give you your half for a while, and I would have just explained it then."

"Don't worry about it."

"You're damn right I won't worry about it," Marty said. "You playing Christmas and whatever the hell else you've been doing over there. You're done. We're not ten years old anymore Steve. We're not twenty. We're not anything of what we used to be."

"You're wrong. That's all we are."

"You had it all—everything. Rolled to you on a fucking platter, and you threw it away. You gave it away. For nothing."

"Marty you don't know—"

"I do know. I was there." His coffee breath, coffee that drank a beer, was back in your face. "I watched you. Every step. You destroyed yourself from the inside and pushed everything around you away. You couldn't just enjoy it like the rest of us. We held you up, we had your back. All you had to do was lean back, let us push, and we'd get you anywhere."

"And then I'd get you anywhere."

"Yeah. Mom, Dad, me, Freddie, all of us. A girl that loved you and a game that never let you down. That's how it works, Steve. You could have gone anywhere. But no, you had to be you. Little Steve Coleman. Always Steve—too worried about losing what's behind him and never saw what was in front. The golden boy who gave back the gold. Willingly.

"You know what addiction is, Steve?" Marty asked without waiting for answer. "You know, don't you? It's selfish. That's all it is and all it ever will be. I'm done with mine. I'm dealing with it. You need to fucking get over this. You're never going in that house again."

23

"So what did you get for Christmas?" Steve asked the boy who had asked for a third slice.

"A train and a set to build with."

"Trains are cool."

"I love them. I mean I don't have anything else like it, but all's I wanted was a basketball."

"A basketball?"

"Yeah, I know. Everyone says it that way." Troy rose on knees that disagreed with his torso to take his plate to the sink. "Remember, I know what I look like," the boy said back over his shoulder.

"No," Steve said. "Don't be like that. That's not what I meant. Anyone can play basketball. You might not be LeBron, but hey, who is?" Steve took the plate and set it on the countertop instead of the days-old tower that had somehow formed in the sink.

"LeBron's the best, isn't he?"

"Yeah," Steve said and passed a thought to his childhood idol. *Mike, today the kid can be right. It's a generational thing.* "He's the best."

"Thank you," Troy said, "for the food."

In the box of a kitchen that was part of the larger box of apartment with one way in and out, the boy looked around as if in need of a map. "I guess I should go."

"Here, wait." Steve pushed the open door closed and dug into the thin closet aside of the entrance. "You can have this."

The boy's eager hands came forward and took the orange ball as if being handed an antique glass on the verge of rupture.

"Are you sure?"

"Yeah," Steve said. "I've got lots of 'em. This one's yours."

"Thank you, Mister?"

"Steve. Steve is fine."

Troy turned the basketball about in his hands. "Do you play Steve?"

"Yeah . . . I used to."

We're not anything of what we used to be, right Marty?

"There's some courts not too far from here. Too wet today, but maybe your . . . you know, can take you there sometime."

The rubber ball became crystal in the boy's grasp, and he did not look away.

"Thank you," Troy said and floated out and across the hall.

He and Steve both were relieved to find the door open.

"Yeah, I'll see you around."

* * * * *

```
February xx, 20xx


Dear Abcde,


     I was so sorry for not being able to see
you again. I hope you know I wish that you
could visit, but only immediate family is
allowed for now. That being said, I am not
sure how Cleo from the gym has been here
twice and Marty has not been by at all.

     I hope that you would be interested
in seeing each other again sometime as I
would not want that day in January to be
the last time we saw each other. Despite
how it ended and no matter why you left,
I did enjoy and appreciate spending that
evening with you and was hopeful that
there was going to be more like them.

     I still have your business card and
will call you when I am home. Just so
you know my phone is not accessible to
me here, but it should still be able to
take messages. I would understand if you
```

called then and let me know not to contact you which I would respect.

Sincerely, your friend,

Steve

* * * * *

January xx, 20xx

Dear Mrs. Chambliss,

I need to let you know that due to a circumstance that has arrived, I am going to be out of my apartment for about four months. My brother Marty has one key and will ensure that the heat is kept on at least until it is no longer necessary and the hot water is run to prevent any damage to the plumbing. He will also be maintaining my mail.

As the rent is paid through next October, I guess I am expecting to move back in upon my return, unless I am told otherwise. Officer Fred Hagen of the Deerwood Police Department will also be checking the apartment in my absence, and if you see or contact him, he can answer any questions that you may have.

I apologize for any inconvenience this may cause. I know I have been there only a short time, but I have enjoyed being able to assist with light maintenance and other tasks that were needed to be done quickly and regret my inability to assist in the near future. I appreciate your understanding in advance and will contact you upon my return.

Sincerely,

Steve Coleman, Unit 4

24

There isn't much left now, is there? This place that you have sunk—cowered—to. Around you, the liquid blue of the television, one of the liquids you have chosen to drown in. Your phone reaches up to you in flashes because it's not ringing. It doesn't ring or screech or buzz like a nest of angry hornets because it's the sound, right? It's the ringtone left on that brings the flood. Not simply that something awful has occurred and there is the logical means to tell you.

Has turning off the ringer improved anything? Does stepping on a dropped comb stop disappointment? Does starting something new on a Friday—anything new, from an unopened jug of milk to a marriage— guarantee failure? Salt over the shoulder prevents an argument every time, right? Clearly turning the phone off would have extinguished or, better yet, prevented a hotel fire hundreds of miles away but also could have cured a cancer that defied the speed of light, in someone, by chance you didn't marry on a Friday. And that comb you dropped when you were thirteen and too good for superstition. If only you would have put your foot across it to feel the steam of disappointment evaporate.

Abcde called back and left another message. It can wait. For now, arm over eyes. It wants to creep back up, but you won't let it. Quick pointed breaths to the point of hyperventilation. This will not happen. The passion of your consumption will not allow it. This could be one of those nights, nights of a waking sleep where a barrage of starts and stops divide the night into fractions—halves, fourths, or even eights where there is a grip on the wall of sleep and inverse but equal moments where you drop into the abyss of alertness in search of another drink. Some say the cure lies in admitting the problem, but that antidote is a locked fortress when the venom is dependence and dependence itself exists in a realm of enjoyment. This is the path of the onychophagic that pretends everyone is blind to misshapen fingertips or the trichotillomanic that sees no evidence of baldness.

But she puked, didn't she? That one night, not New Year's Eve like tonight, but warm, humid—"School's out!" her battle cry and mission. "I will be so messed up tonight!" Her sputtered words spoken as if she had stewardship over them.

Her follow-through of intent was in doubt. You had known her long enough by then to have heard the lines and then witnessed the act that commenced. A declaration of malfeasance only to sip at the water like a prude. A skin-tight dress and a pair of lofty heels advertising her teenage wares, cat eyes bruised by liner and mascara, winking and caressing their intended targets, but stained violet lips pulled away in departure with only an offer or two of innocuous pecks on the cheek.

The check was cashed that night, though—you holding her hair from her face, conscious of the splash back that crowned you with a crusted halo when it was over. Her usual smell masked by wafts of used beer, tequila, and a mash of what had been dinner. Today, it would be posted, snapped, booked, or shared under "#Hoops Star Offers Assist."

Back then the Polaroid moment would have been pasted, forgotten under the fingerprinted window of a photo album—an album with a cardstock cover suggesting glee in a hopeful exterior of bubbled letters, memories, or forever friends when all that really waited, page after page, were moments best forgotten, occurrences and acquaintances whose places and names have long escaped.

There is an imprint that survived in your corners where the image is so alive, you can feel the cold tile against your hands as she eased back against the wall. The bowl between you had the fizz of water at the onset of a boil and the stench of burnt soup. "I am so fucking sorry," she said, slurred speech where applicable. You had earned the breakup that was still some months away, but the outline was taking shape. Godspeed to the next man. The man who would find your impression waiting when she relented and let him to go forward to carve out his own. He was probably there that night, the next climber.

She was of that stock, the kind who didn't stray much past the borders of who they knew. You were the outsider, the one who was let in and would soon let himself out...

* * * * *

...just like December 31 was doing. The latest New Year's Eve to come and go was paired away, each stretch of artificial sleep coming in fragments beneath Steve's blinking eyes, like windshield wipers on a random delay washing the dark into light and back again.

New Year's Day crested like a tired hand, pulling back a hibernal comforter. The challenged morning there, then gone, then back. A petulant light that finally stayed in place blasted the sky with a confident winter sunrise. He battled against the aftershock of the Green Lantern, a concoction from the halls of DePaul University that combined a precise ratio of vodka, Crème de menthe, and the well-known verdurous nighttime cold medicine that fed in synchrony the need to drink and desire to sleep.

The daylight helped Steve to one knee—the good one—and then to the sink where chilled groundwater drunk from cupped hands picked away at the dry webs that were left overnight.

There were four missed calls—two from Abcde, one Freddie, and one from Marty. Two of the messages had a New Year's Eve vibe, coated in cheer and spirit. Marty's had a wavy substance that was between anger and quiet drunkenness, as if he had snuck off to send the obligatory wishes and had been found out. The pitch shifted when Melinda opened the closet door or wandered into his study or wherever she had found him, phone in one hand, Scotch in the other.

Steve's body debated and then gave into a return to the couch. Stiff at first, he molded into the cushion form that was still dug in from the evening and vanished into a nap.

Seconds later a knock on the door intruded.

Not seconds, his phone corrected, but four hours. The daylight had backed off some but still moved his arm back over his eyes, covering a bloodshot he could feel. Then another knock. He consulted he phone again as he rocked to his feet. Disbelief of the time and that one of his missed callers from the night before would be arriving accompanied his trek from couch to door.

"Hey." In slow motion, her face normalized from the bloated orb the peephole had showed. "Lisa from across the hall?" she offered

"Right. Yeah, sure," Steve said, relieved she led with her name as he was going with Laura or Lana.

"Look, I'm sorry to trouble you," she said. "My son said you gave this to him."

Lisa held Steve's basketball at near arm's length, a quarry-like burden from which she was in need of relief.

"Yeah. He said he wanted to have one. It's okay, right? I should have asked, I guess."

"No, it's fine." She looked back to the door and to the descending stairs. A sweep of the area with her head and neck. Her face was a page of cheap, floury "I'm buying it because I have to but won't and can't spend much" makeup. "Just that Take said he might have stolen it, and I didn't know what to think."

"Stolen?" Steve asked. "No, I gave it to him. It's his. Why would he steal it?"

She rubbed at her navy non-sweatpants scrubs. Shoes that couldn't have been purchased new poked from the bell bottoms. Her hands, a medley of creases, rugged tops, and stale cuts, told the story of work and little time for much else.

"We've had a lot going on lately, Mister . . ."

"Coleman," he said. "But Steve's fine."

"Steve." She chewed at her top lip. "About Troy. We've just had some things going on, and sometimes I'm not sure what to think."

"No worries. I hope he enjoys it."

"Well, thank you." Lisa drifted forward to the doorframe—sparse steps that Steve did not see her make. "Look, I hope it's not askin' too much," she said, "but I have to go into work. I just can't call in again, and Take's already gone off to watch those football games. Would you mind keeping a half an eye on Troy? I mean if it's too much . . ."

"No," he cut into her subtle desperation. "No trouble. He can come over whenever. Are you a like a nurse or something?"

"I don't think so," Lisa answered. "Now, we don't have any video games or nothing to keep him busy."

"Well, I don't either," Steve said, opening the door wide. "Seems nice out for a change. Maybe we'll go try this out."

He reached for his ball.

"You'd play basketball with him?"

"Sure," he replied. "I'd play with anybody."

"I don't have much for lunch for him, but I'll get to the store later."

"Don't worry, I'll come up with something," Steve said. "Ain't much open around here today anyway."

"Thank you, Steve," she said. "We've had lots amiss this week, and you're really helping. Just for today."

Troy opened the door to unit 3 behind her.

"You didn't have any plans for New Year's Day or nothing we're keeping you from?"

"No," Steve said.

Let me think.

My parents aren't around, my brother probably would not drag himself here if the place caught fire today, and my friend called and said she was going to her sister's. So, no, I'll be around.

25

"You want me to what?" Cleo Washington rasped into his end of the phone.

Steve looked to Troy and winked.

"Just come by and open up," Steve said. "Look, you can leave me the keys, and I'll lock up." Over the receiver to Troy, Steve said, "No, it's colder than I thought."

"Yes, Cleo, I know it's a holiday." Steve was back to the phone side of the dialogue. "We can't. He doesn't fit into his, and mine fit him like a dress."

"I think I'm getting to him," Steve whispered in Troy's direction.

"Is he a real player?" Cleo asked.

"No," Steve said. "Just doing a favor. You don't like college football anyway."

"Yes, I can do you a favor," Steve replied to Cleo's voice and waited for the interrogative. "Yeah, I was hoping to talk to you about that. Anything you need, I'll be there."

"Cleo, I'm not fooling around."

"We gotta have a team," the old man said. "Something to work toward for the summer."

"We'll make it work." Steve showed a thumbs-up to Troy. "Yeah, get here when you can, and thanks, it's getting frigid out here."

* * * * *

Message One: December 31, 6:17 PM: Hey, Steve, it's me, Abcde. I hope your New Year's Eve is good. I have to go up to my sister's place tonight. Something about her needing me to watch her kids and her being very sure I didn't have any plans. So maybe we'll talk next year—I mean next week—and we can get together, maybe if you want. So call me soon.

Message Two: January 1, 12:55 AM: "Hi. It's Ab. I was just seeing if you were around. Probably at your brother's or with your friends, so that's good. Umm, hope your night is fun. Maybe we can talk soon. I'm kind of all tied up about how our night ended last week. I was really having a good time with you, and well, you probably don't think that I was. Probably some things I should tell you. ([Background] No, you can't talk to him. No! Stop.) Anyway, hope to see you."

* * * * *

"But I missed everything." Troy leapt to the first step and landed as the door crashed shut behind them.

The frozen glass shook against the frame like coins in a tin and defeated any noise the stair offered upon impact.

"You didn't miss everything," Steve said and handed Troy the ball back for the third time. "Just takes practice is all. Lots of practice and work too. Don't let anyone tell you anything different."

The fervor in their matched steps deflated from levity to slush. Take stood at the top of the steps under the corroded yellow glow of the overhead. His arm extended with an index finger pointed toward the open doorway of unit 3. He was an angry statue posed in reminder to the boy that there was but one way to turn when he reached the top.

"You did all right," Steve said to the boy's back as the silent command was obeyed.

"Been out with m'boy?" Take asked.

The curt words smelled like hard but cheap liquor filtered through a fart.

"Well, Lisa's boy," Steve said.

Nervous warmth rose from his collar. He noticed a reflex from his neighbor. Thick fingers, a few paces from a fist, flexed.

"How were the games?" Steve asked. "Rose Bowl is always good."

"They was fine."

Steve looked at the sweatshirt draped over Take and asked anyway.

"You go to Ohio State?"

"Look," Take said, his hands finding front pockets as if they needed a cue to stay back. "We're a family over here, and we're better off if left alone."

"I've been alone a while now. I get that."

"Good."

"You know Ninth street gym, a few blocks from here, has leagues starting for the kids when school's back." Steve's key was now visible. "Might be good for him. No cost, you know. Everyone gets to play."

"I'll take that under advisement. You have a pleasant evening now."

Dismissal was complete with the thud of a deadbolt a noticeable few seconds after the door had shut.

These dumb, bearded Midwestern rednecks, Steve thought.

They were an odd socioeconomic mash up that lived under the auspices of the political left but for some reason supported and voted when they cared to do so, unabashedly, for the right. Take's kin and brethren were as mixed up as old conservative white folks buying a Starbucks or college-dowsed liberals lunching at Chick-fil-A. Folks like Take couldn't just say thanks—it was above them.

Under advisement.

Their dialect of using too many words where three or less would do made them sound more ignorant than they already were. Take Chancellor probably told Mrs. Chambliss—after his infantile mind surrendered on the fact that she was black and he would be obligated to remit monthly rent to her—that his attorney would have to review the lease before he moved in. Steve was sure the word *attorney* had one less *T* or maybe started with a *U* in the bubble that formed over Take's head.

The bike was leaning against the closet door where it had been when he left and where it had been at rest for the past week. That did not stop an errant step where not only the knee but the perfect and worst possible spot on the knee found and connected with an extended bolt on the bike's frame. The strike of pain uncoiled from foot to hip. A serendipitous lunge to the back of the couch kept him upright and the leg from folding under.

Deep breaths and stationary minutes put the burn back in the cage, fangs, body, and then tail. A trial step left, then another, and the short distance to the kitchen evolved as palatable. The air from the refrigerator tickled over the cold sweat his forehead held on to. The snap from the beer bottle like a conductor striking a podium laid silence over the white noise of the furnace, the fan behind the fridge, and his own breath.

He honed in for evidence.

Waited for any sound in the air traveling over the dust from next door through the walls that would make him need to charge the breezeway and claw past the opposing wood door to pull the man from the child or woman. There was only space, the void that swallows sound; and in space, just as the movie says—much like in this apartment—no one can hear you scream.

A drip from the faucet brought the blank sounds he never heard back to life. Shards of glass blurted in sudden raindrops as the bottle dissolved into the far wall. The drop that crossed his lips tasted like the shit-laced vapors of the stranger next door; and the fibers of Steve's body, for the first time in nearly thirty years, revolted.

You feel eyes, don't you?

No. What I feel are the edges of a jagged countertop in need of replacement. My hands are afraid to skim along the ridges in fear of the plastic slivers that might imbed into them. It's attached to a sink that's called stainless but is pot marked with measles of coffee, rust, and leftovers.

It's part of a room in a place that is really just another room in a square brick building that preceded most of the town by fifty years. It's part of a place that, even when I leave, I never leave.

You feel my eyes, don't you?

"Yes," Steve said.

He didn't have to look.

She sat at the table, feet crossed under and hands folded above. She had been watching for some time.

"Hello, Brooke," Steve said.

26

The old man stood like most old men do—forward. With Father Time astride shoulders grown weary of the ride, a body lurched as if there are sights on the ground level that can no longer be seen from above.

Melinda was the youngest of four, all girls; and by the time she got around to parenting, her father was of the grandpa age and could have dropped by the set of any fiber cereal, laxative, or AARP commercial and landed the role on the spot. Retired, he still had a work shirt for every day and, on the weekends, a polo with collar, the hollow of the sleeves and neck in constant expanse. His jokes from an age past garnered a laugh anyway, and wedding dance moves he put on (Melinda's third sister, second marriage, non-eloped style this time, the past fall) elicited hoots of surprise and encouragement from those around him. Glen Miller and Artie Shaw be damned as he stepped to Bruno, Usher, and Taylor.

Emotions worn by the elderly always seem out of place like the dancing. Either too big or too small as if social decorum seeped like a gas leak with every year that passed. They range from the intent lean of a counselor to the grandkids when a simple "how are you?" turns into prattle of television characters, books, toys, and games to the near blow off of "that's too bad" when Melinda said her second sister's husband may not only have his hours cut but his job eliminated altogether.

Anger was a peculiar one for the old man to show. His face— all wire glasses under white hair—pushed hard to express rage on a body that could no longer stand in anyone's way and left behind a befuddled stare. More confusion than lividity that understood something had happened, but he was so far away from the age of fucking up, there was no comprehension as to what occurred or why fucked-up things happen at all. So he stood there in the forward lurch, hands on and then off his hips, and stared at the cars that were better off parallel and now in a crooked L shape. The younger folks did the yelling.

* * * * *

"Mommy, why is there a man in our yard?"

Her daughter's question shared the same frequency as "why is the sky blue?" and "is no snowflake really ever the same?" She internalized the answers as "I don't know, each snowflake is special just like you," punctuated by a tap on her daughter's nose, and "Daddy's at work, not in the yard."

The sky, in fact, had not been truly blue for a week; and any fascination she had with snow had ended after day five of snowfall. She didn't care at that point if they were all the same or as random as lottery numbers—the flakes kept coming down like cotton expelled from an oversized heavenly pillow. From high above, she imagined that the streets may look like a crossword puzzle or maze where familiar or expected exits were temporary dead ends. Most of the larger streets had been plowed for passage, but the smaller ones, like the road behind the house, were still blocked.

The schools remained in lockdown, another day chewed from the beginning of summer, but today most of the parents could have made it, the closure in place to allow the outlying roads one more day to recover. The yard and most of the deck that had been the cause of her long second and third looks at the online photos while house shopping were invisible, overridden by a volume of white that would have disguised a gathering of polar bears, had they decided to amass and invade. But there were no bears back there and certainly no man.

The cookie recipe that had fallen through the cracks during a Christmas season dominated by house shopping then buying and bordered by packed and unpacked boxes had been found. No matter how many years she pulled it out, including some weekends over the summer where the need for Christmas treats just could not be put off, the pencil script left behind by her grandmother required extensive study and squinted eyes of her so far twenty-twenty vision. Her husband suggested to her each year that if she was not going to take the pages of her grandmother's recipe books and type them out, she should at least laminate the original or make copies of what she had in the event of loss or damage. That was insurance guy–speak for "take measures to protect what you have," which in turn was insurance guy's wife–speak for "you're going to lose all your old shit if you're too lazy not to."

The feel of the old books in her hands and seeing them spread open with their cracked spines on her new kitchen counter kept her grandmother close, even as time pushed the memory of her further away. What was it, eight years now? Ten? These books that were now items to pull out for occasions held family meals, soups, and desserts that concluded weeknights and brought people together in a past that was getting smaller each day. But this would be the year. She just knew it.

New house, new and lauded school for their daughter June, and work at the same company but a new, more secure role for her husband. She'd keep the old cookbooks, some held together at this point by what seemed sheer determination of the pages, but transfer the information to a Word doc. The Christmas iPad—"Thank you, dear"—was charging somewhere in the living room and would be at her beck and call when the house was a bit more organized—and quiet—and the streets were plowed, paving the way for these kids to get back to school.

Maybe she would even design a fancy cover or use an intricate font and for sure would track and post her progress as the pages came to life. It would be a project but with encouragement and anticipation from her collection of some real and some digital (BFFs) friends (followers?), the pages that were created and commented on would be inspiration enough to finish. That way, it would not feel like taking out insurance on the things of the past.

There were so many craft ideas going around now on her constantly updated feed. Her friends knitted, crocheted, and made things hip and new from items old and used. Tasks such as those were beyond her skills. Cooking—that, she knew. But that did not interest anyone; they all cooked too. But a cookbook made from the pages of her grandmother's past? That she could do. Right here in her kitchen. Not the new kitchen. What had they called it? Homey? Functional? She couldn't remember the ad. For now—and *now* was good enough—it was the old but nice kitchen, and she couldn't recall a single instance where in a kitchen like this, anything but fond memories could have ever occurred.

It was small with an eat-in nook that cradled a circular table and three chairs under two square windows. The counters were not granite but were of the hard material just below that she could not name. The cabinets were resurfaced, the job done well enough to show off the new darker stain and accent the intricate molding left behind in homage to the origins of the house. There were new appliances, the recent addition of a dishwasher was evident, and the flooring was not only cut to perfection, but walking across it, one would never know there was hardwood flooring underneath.

"Mmhmm," she answered her daughter with automation.

The book did not fit in or against the stand for her iPad, so she hovered over the counter to see if it was one-fourth teaspoon or one-half of "vanilan" that was called for in the partially rubbed away and misspelled pencil script.

In a few moments, it wouldn't matter. The hearty ceramic mixing bowl would be ruined upon impact, driven to the ground by a flailing leg from her daughter, as June was lifted from the window and swept back across the table by the mother who neglected to see if the back door had even been locked. The bag of flour tipped with a dull puff; the spill easily removed with a damp paper towel later but for now left vague shards of a ghost in levitation above the unmade dessert. The response from call number 1 confirmed what call number 1 should have been in the first place. Surely the house could be on fire, and the first call out of instinct would have been to him.

"Call the cops, Darlene!" her husband said from Chicago, an hour away by train with the series of stops between here and there.

27

His senses were alive, gibbering like mouths engorged to consume the air around him.

Touch beyond the reactive charge that pulled her closer was amplified, almost as if he could feel the closing space between them fold into one another like a deck of shuffled cards. Marty inhaled her morning shower. Her watertight skin shimmered with lotion—*was that body glitter?*—and a spray-and-walk-through aroma of lilac and sex rose like incense. He grew, brushing against the inside of his wool trousers, but would leave that to her.

She rimmed his ear with a breath hidden in a kiss, but the sweetest sound this morning came from the radio. All western suburban schools were back to regular schedules, the tail of the snowstorm rode the jet stream like a stranded passenger into northern Indiana overnight. Blankets of white and gray were left behind but no more accumulation in sight, which meant everyone was back in place: daughters in their classrooms, Melinda at her volunteer desk at the school library, and Marty at work.

Work meant a meeting down in Deerwood with Del Brackens, and that meant Melinda would remind him over morning coffee (which she did) not to overeat at Andy's, but no worries. He would say over evening wine, Del—yes, that chinse Del Brackens—treated to lunch at the Hyatt.

Yeah, I know, right?

Not at all a lie, as lunch was actually planned for at the Hyatt, the one that overlooked I-80 off the Deerwood exit. But at noon, the room service that had been preordered was set outside of the door after a series of knocks went unanswered and would remain undisturbed until the late afternoon housekeeping team found it and was aghast and perplexed at the waste.

There it was, that sound. "Hotel California," the original studio version, from the phone on the nightstand, a background to the downward zip of his slacks. Marty was lost in the hushed golden light of the familiar chords and the familiar room. Not always the same number or even floor but the comforting surround of sofa, unused kitchenette, and desk, a stark contrast to the well-worn king-sized bed. His bulge was released from the confines of wool to the palm of her hand. He knew what was next, but he let his mind wander the forest of distraction. No sense in being early.

The unzipping fly meant three things at this stage of a man's life. One, the workday was over, and the suit pants were back in the closet. Two, the instant gratification of a much-needed piss. And three, the anticipation of pending ejaculation whether alone or with another. Thinking about sports, a trick of the trade from long-ago days, was cold water on a fire. So he drifted elsewhere, his readiness maintained in an analysis of the lyrics from a younger Don Henley and a high level—was it called bird's-eye level these days?—overview of the real meeting with Del Brackens that was tomorrow. Truthfully, in Deerwood, but at a low-end coffeehouse at the west end of town that must have a permanent exemption from participation in the consistent beautification efforts the town had undertaken during the past decade.

Raffi's? Marty asked himself. *That was the place.*

It had a different, less ethnic name when he was growing up. Not that he gave a wet rat's two shits today what that had been. Her

Uggs and jeans, an afterthought in the corner; her sweater, dispensed to the closet on a hanger to prevent any out of place creases meant she was below, as the floor-length lingerie spilled around her in a liquid circle of black. She knelt, and the pause meant the next song was . . . nope still The Eagles. But it shouldn't have skipped. Or stopped.

The song picked up but was derailed by another pause. Then another. He had to know, and he looked to the phone on the nightstand. The incoming call was not from the office (that would have been easy), was not from Melinda (a challenge but acceptable risk), but Fred Hagen, a number that had neither been on his screen nor his mind in a year.

Marty dripped down to the bed like wax from a candle. The cue taken, she leapt and straddled his form. But he rolled; and she, still not grasping the body language, rolled with him. A call from Freddie meant that Steve was dead or worse, and one mattered more than the other. On the primal level, one option meant in two minutes, he'd be fucking; and in two hours, he'd be wrist deep into the Hyatt's lobster lunch special. With the other option, as was customary, the outcome was unknown, but his wrist—or what remained of him—would be deep into someone else's shit.

He took the call, in full arousal, three-quarters naked, when formalities were considered. Her lying next to him, striped in weaves of silk and skin.

"Lingerie? Marty, who wears that anymore? Who has time?" Melinda would ask. Real women, Melinda that's who. Women who aren't afraid to step it up and get outside of who they are sometimes and just settle in to a moment. You remember those days, right? We had plenty—well, at least two that are verifiable—and it's because you don't remember them or pretend that you don't is why I'm here in the first place.

And he knew, before Freddie said a single word, the time with her was over.

* * * * *

March xx, 20xx

Dear Abcde,

    Thank you for writing back to me. It truly meant so much to hear from you, even though I am regretful that we will not be able to see each other again. Please know that I understand completely.

    Thank you as well for sharing your great news about getting back to drawing. I wish you luck in pursuit of the advance you mentioned. I know you said it was small, but if it helps you finish your draft, you'll be on to bigger and better in no time. I look forward to seeing your artwork someday.

    I'm visiting with Cleo again today, and I am hopeful that Marty will come by this weekend. I do want to be home soon and am hoping to be able to by the end of next month.

    Thank you again for writing back.

Friends,

Steve

28

Cleo sat at the end of the bench, center table like always. His hands were at rest, folded over in his lap, his posture unsteady as if his spine was searching for the back of a chair. Dark skin protruded from his white shirt and was the only true color in the sterile warehouse of the industrial cafeteria. His hair, salted by age, vanished into the background as Steve approached.

"Been working out some?" Cleo asked.

"Just jogging, not much else."

"Well, at least your legs are even again." A laugh that brought on a cough followed. "Not limping."

Steve looked on in diagnosis but not his own.

"Never smoked a day in my life." Cleo disbursed the scratch in his throat and patted at his lips with the same tissue. "Doctor says I got lungs like the inside of a furnace. An old furnace."

"Maybe it's all that shouting you do."

"You'd be shouting too," Cleo said. "Six weeks, they still think pick and roll is a sandwich. Man to man defense? You'd think I asked 'em to run to Chicago and back all the wheezing it brings on."

"You should go zone. Don't wear them out on defense let them play offense."

"What, you think we just gonna start shooting better than everyone else all of a sudden?"

"You gotta have some players out there. Some leaders, you know, right?"

"I told you," Cleo said, breathing into the tissue again. "The ones eligible, they playing at their schools. Others, AA or Legion. You know how it is."

"Why do we always have to talk about basketball?"

"Cause that's the only time you right!"

Two other sets of visitors chose the cafeteria over the picnic area or terrace today as well.

The spring day was moody, the notion of rain on standby. One group was, from the distance, mom, dad, and son. A younger thinner man than Steve, at their center, jittered in place like pudding brought to a simmer. The other pair was a woman across a man, neither of whom Steve had seen before. Their hands connected, but their eyes did not.

"Even when you ain't," Cleo added.

"You seen Freddie?" Steve averted the notion that there was any progress in this discussion with Cleo.

"Nah, he ain't been around."

The young woman across the room stood but remained in a grasp with her visitor. Her unclaimed hand went over her eyes as she turned away, a dramatic twist of her neck that would have fit into a revival of Shakespeare at the park. Steve noticed the man was wearing the guest badge.

"He contacted you at all?" Cleo, who did not have a guest badge, asked.

"No."

The parents and son had left; the young woman was seated back on the bench.

"Look, when I get back, I'm gonna have to take some time to—"

"No," Cleo answered. "All you been taking is time. You ain't got none left. I tell you what you do have though."

"Oh yeah?"

"Yeah." Cleo's hands gripped his side of the table. "The man with two choices. You like being in a place like this?"

"No."

"You like living the way you do?"

There was a flash from a door at the edge of Steve's eye. Another pair giving up on or giving in to the tepid spring afternoon.

In translation, the spark was glass shattered against a plaster wall. A bottle. Had he thrown it? There was a boy too who walked— or, more aptly, was dragged—to a car. Snow fell in stacks. The lot was plowed at least enough room to walk to parking spots and pull forward. The boy, unwilling but compliant cargo to a vicious sleigh ride, carved even lines across the gray matter.

"No," Steve answered.

"Then two choices it is." Cleo moved into the table, lurching over a chessboard only he could see. The rocks in his voice smoothed into a timbre of deciding between steak or chicken for dinner. "You either come give those kids whatever you got left in there or you blow your brains out so nobody have to worry about you anymore. Most days, I honestly don't care which one you pick, but I need the help."

"There's help around."

"They ain't you," Cleo said. "And yes, there is help. You just gotta let it in."

"I don't know that sitting around here writing letters, being away from everything makes a difference," Steve said. "It's not even real in here like some kind of adult day camp where we all pretend the strongest thing to drink in the world is coffee or tea."

"That's why when you get out, you come to the gym."

"I hate to break it to you Cleo, but even basketball never solved anything."

"You don't think I know." Cleo slammed his fists on the table. Both men looked about, but there was no one to disturb. "All those years we spent together. You couldn't even walk a straight line, but you led those teams. You carried us, so we carried you. You made your halfwit teammates play out of their minds and your halfwit coach look like a genius. Most of this is my fault."

"It's not your fault. Don't say that."

"I let it go." Cleo stood to stretch and cajoled the rubber from his joints to uncurl. He walked toward the sliding glass doors that separated the cafeteria from the patio. "We all did—me, Freddie, Marty. The only secret a drinker keeps is from himself. Everybody else knows."

Steve followed Cleo and found the nearest bench.

"I should have pushed you further away," Cleo said, his breath staining the glass at his face. "Kansas, Duke, Carolina, Indiana—shit, Hawaii would have been better."

"It wouldn't have made a difference."

"I know." Cleo's hands gripped Steve's shoulders from behind. "Just should have tried a little harder. Been a better coach."

"You were a great coach."

"Excuse me, I *am* a great coach." Cleo sat next to Steve his back finding the table for support. "Just need some help is all, and I'm not afraid to ask for it. Come on home, Steve. Come on home but for the right reasons. It's late but only halftime for you. Still time to make adjustments. That's what halftimes are for."

"All right," Steve said. "But you gotta help me too."

"I am helping you." Cleo stood, hands on his hips, and began a slow pace. "You're right. It's not real in here. It's like a locker room. You surrounded by your own kind, drawing up plays and strategies that might and usually do blow apart entirely when the whistle blows. The games out there." Cleo pointed to the window and considered the ceiling with his eyes. "Thing about a locker room is, no matter what cover it provides, you can't stay forever. You gotta get back on the court. Ain't nothing like in here."

C

It would have been the first time.

Oh, it would not have! Of my own accord. *Accord.*

What, are you writing a treaty? "I hereby declare my body to be my own"?

Who do you think you are?

Let me ask, do you know where it's easy to find a virgin? No? Well, let me tell you. When they're surrounded by people who have only done it once. That group hardly exists. At one point or another, it's just fucking. So you just up and hand it away to what's his name? I don't think so. Who was he anyway? Oh yes, the boy who was kind to you, bought you dinner and ice cream. The veritable price of passage. Charon, the dragon at the gate, so easily bribed. Your eighteen-year-old sugar walls just screaming for some of that brine. You know it was there, you tasted it.

You made me. He may have been fresh when he picked you up, but as the evening dragged on—and believe me it, d-r-a-g-g-e-d—his wash was long gone by then after a few trips to the men's room. You deserved better than that. We deserved better. That rush of salt into you, that brackish man gust, a touch of vinegar and a lifetime of absolution. You just had to wait until you got home.

We don't share everything.

A secret? Okay, I'll tell you one. That's what I think he likes—excuse me, *loves*—about me. She demands perfection, and I don't. No, I'm not telling. Another one? You certainly ask a lot of *me.*

Okay, I can draw. No, *I* can draw. No, I *can* draw. You could change everything about you. The way people see you, the way you live. You could even stop taking pictures for good, but it's me. *I can draw.* That's it, we'll show her.

For you, something?

Well, I suppose I could.

Don't put my body through anything it doesn't want.

Well, I can't promise that, but I can try. But you have to understand we're going to get chased up a wall sometimes, and sometimes, you have to screw your way back down. You've done it before. It's not like we'd be breaking the seal.

Wait, you owe *me* another. I told you two.

This one's easy though. A small one down the back of the arm, I won't be seeing him for a few weeks. It will heal by then. We're fortunate. It's so great what you can do with makeup, even when it's not on our face. You'll always come through when I need him. Seems you're a talented artist too.

NOT CAPTURED,
NOT ESCAPED

29

St. Charles in and out-patient treatment
facility.
Intake Survey, (partial) January 20xx
Please respond to the following
statements:

7. Is there a certain emotion that I
try to control or avoid by drinking? If
so please describe. Answer: Not certain.

You look out the window. It's always this window. The same view of decay staring back across at the plagued bricks and parking lot of the building where you live. Live? *Is that what this is?* "Building where I am" *or* "where I was" *would fit better. This isn't living.*

The train, consistent as breath, resonates from the unconscious space opposite the window where you stand again not for what you can or can't see but for what you need—the sink. Your mouth, head, and neck wail like a tea kettle, an announcement of heat. Nothing left for you to banish but a heave of air and a postscript of saliva too clear and sweet to be called bile.

Your hands dig into the edge, not to keep you over the drain, like an observer would construe, but to hold you in place. This prevents the seven steps—today, maybe eight, maybe more—to the sofa where you lay at night and, let's face it, most of the day. If you allowed yourself to let go, the next batch of liquid that revolted would find and pool in the clearing at the back of your throat. It would settle and fester under inaction.

Your hands fight against release from the counter as if you are— and you are—gripping, clinging, on to the side of a cliff, rubble eroded with each swipe. Even the thought of the fall that would ensue brings more relief than the maintenance of your tired grasp, you hold on.

It should be easy to keep afoot. You've climbed Mount Everest before—no, not climbed but laid. You laid Mount Everest before. Not the mountain but a person, and no, she wasn't a mountain but someone (else) who is gone. As far away as you would guess Everest to be from you now. But no one is really gone these days, right? A short internet search should do the trick. But what if you did find her and work up some sort of hellbent courage to go to her. Would she then see that her Sméagol had become Gollum? Her slender knight who had become neither light nor darkness but apathetic to both? What would you see?

You balance on what your feet tell you is a toothpick, what your mind knows is a tile floor, but your hands will not let go. Brooke, though she is gone too, stands behind you like an anchor that keeps a ship at bay in the face of a cyclone. She presses hard, and you are fixed in place, destined to inhale what remains of the week, instead of courting death on a sofa by drowning upon an ocean you created. The water and disposal (new, installed by you upon move in) did their best to force the stew through the plumbing. But a vapor remained long after the volcano subsided. It is through this vapor you see movement across the lot.

I was confused. I knew where we ended up but had no thought on where we came from. You kept saying you would tell me. "Later!" you chided. There was the parking lot, a square trench in the snow, dug out where nothing was dug in. Rivulets of melted grey gathered at the edges. A prattle of footprints—words with no story to tell—arched next to and beside my own steps.

There are three of them. A man, woman, and child—but not their child, her child and hers alone. The woman is detached as they walk, like the dot under the question mark.

There was a spit of blood on a triangle of still white that was lodged over a soot-infested base of plowed snow. It had the appearance of a large-sized, tricolored rocket pop that stood at attention, waiting to be plucked from the freezer. I lifted a bike, which had been left on its side, and stood it against the brick wall.

You have drank so much over the past week that Brooke had vanished, as expected, but she has come roaring back in what could only be called a waking unconsciousness. This never happens, so she is, at best, an illusion—at worst, a walking hallucination. An experience that veteran professors must feel when a new discovery is pulled from a well-read text. That is what must be below. There are no spots of color, no streaks across the sky, and no pink elephants of legend.

There are three people—your neighbors?—and they cannot be real. The day is too cold for a walk, and besides, when families walk, the man holding the shopping bag does not continue to drag the child over blades of worn asphalt after the child had dropped to his knees and the woman does not fall back to plead in voice and gesture. She rushes forward to end the display of cowardice and madness that has unfurled.

He wasn't there. It was an intrusion like spying, so I closed the door to Steve's apartment. My concern for his privacy overrode the worry I had about the stench. With the door open, the air was stale, a growth of burnt sulfur and tin tucked into corners where it refused to fit. At full throttle, behind the shield of a closed door, a running furnace and shut windows, the encased breath of the place would pummel the next entrant with a gale of diseased rancor.

The stairs that led back to the parking lot held on to their secret and remained silent, except for the weariness of the wood below as I left. There was only one place he could be.

How had it been done? *I thought.* Hung from one of the trees in the backyard just off of the deck? Did he somehow get back in the house?

If he did, it would have happened in the kitchen.

The night that I shared with him, I could tell he was dead everywhere. But in that house, he was breathing; and in that kitchen, he was fully alive, cooking the meals of his mother and emptying the bottles of his ancestry. That's what he wanted—to die with them. And he did.

* * * * *

Steve came from the door like a boxer out of a corner. He had rolled his bike alongside down the stairs.

If they're gone, I will be a man with a bike, and that's all. I'll be going for a ride. Where? You know where, he thought but cast it away when he hit the lot, a raging bull with no balance and no plan.

"Steve!" Lisa shouted, each arm now extended, like a crossing guard halting traffic from either side.

"You folks need some help with something?" Steve asked through gritted teeth at the man who wore the garb but not the purpose of a father.

"This does not concern you," Take said and placed himself between Steve and the shivering child.

"Take, if you just . . ." Lisa gasped as both of his palms connected with her chest and any words she had left expelled in a rush of lost wind.

Her expression forced embarrassment ahead of shock.

She was not the first woman made to sprawl on the cement here but the first one Steve had known. The first one where there was not the safety of a staircase, a locked door, and a window that ran interference.

Steve reached for Lisa who stood back up mostly on her own, which was fortuitous as the dizziness of booze remained puppet master over his legs.

"There you go," Take growled. "Pick up the trash."

"He's taking my stuff!" Troy called out from behind.

"You shut it down, boy!" Steam from the frosted air danced after his words.

"Look," Take said to Steve and reacquired his grip on the shopping bag, "he's had his Christmas toys for some time now. He can grow up. We've got groceries to buy."

"Why don't you just ask for help?"

"I don't take charity." Take's eyes clenched.

"It's not charity, you bitch!"

"Steve!"

Lisa's warning was late. The unseen left fist caught Steve blind across the right side of his face. The strike was too high to damage the jaw, but his eye was cut and his brain swam in his skull.

"There," Take taunted Steve and Lisa from above. "Is that what you want? You want a man that stays on the ground? He ain't nothing like me!"

"You're wrong," Steve said as a crimson drip followed a spit to the snow. "I'm exactly like you."

"No," Lisa said. "I'm so sorry."

Steve heard her through a net of gel and fog.

"Get in the car," Take commanded. "Both of you."

"I'm so sorry," Lisa may have said again.

There was a moment of hesitation—at least Steve pretended there was—from his view of their shoes. The boy obeyed too soon, and when his door closed, the fight Lisa may have briefly reinvigorated was spent. The other doors opened on springs and closed like cannon fire. Take backed the car up.

Steve perched on one foot and one knee. If he stayed frozen, the car would draw a line over him. If he stood, the car would graze his left leg. As the parking lot initiated a carousel, he hovered over the choice; even as the voice of reason nudged in—reminded him that the man with pork loins for hands and a flayed rug for a beard— would do neither and go around him. Steve's head swayed with spin and voices when the man's car clipped his left hip and sent him into a flailing pirouette that crashed to the ground below.

* * * * *

I left the car at the end of the street. There was activity from the third house, down to the house I knew. I was a shadow, a walker dressed for winter, replete with my scarf pulled to just under my eyes and wool cap to keep the warmth from escaping.

They had him in check an officer on each side. The right side of his face was damaged, purple with blood, and his jeans were torn down the left. A woman in a sweatsuit covered by a pink apron stood against a red-haired officer gripping a little girl who demanded to know why she couldn't go play in the powdered snow on the front lawn. Another man—dress coat, older than the woman, but not old—leaned against the front porch rail. He was too distant in space and manner to be her husband and lacked the authority of a cop.

* * * * *

Steve plunged a foot and then the other into the snow-packed sidewalk. There was an effort to the release, but effort spent would close the distance. And the distance must close. The easier paths would be ahead through the small downtown. The left and rights through the subdivision would ask for effort again, and it would be given.

"They took it from him," Steve mumbled. "She just followed. No one is ever going to take something from me again. Not even you, Marty."

* * * * *

"Mommy, is he a bad man?" I heard the little girl ask.

I was now no more than a health nut who couldn't miss her daily power walk in passer-by mode. I was in witness distance.

"No, honey he's just lost," the mom replied.

"Can I go in the snow now?"

"Go ahead."

The red-haired officer nodded toward the woman and locked his thumbs into his belt loops. Her reply was an affectionate rub of his arm as they parted.

"Marty," the officer called to the man in the dress coat.

The name and likeness we knew and would soon place; our objective we would file away for later. Our what?

"Let's take him to your office. She's not pressing charges, but I need to write a report, and this clearly violates—"

"Yeah I know," Marty, the man in the dress coat, replied. "Take him in your car. I don't want him in mine."

"No," the woman said into her phone. "This is not a bad neighborhood. I am not going to go stay at your mother's. We just moved here!"

30

The officers on each arm secured him, but the provision was more like meat hooks balancing a load instead of comfortable support. They were too close to the squad car that blocked the driveway, and Steve tensed for the certain impact. With no open door, the push from behind sent Steve into the side.

"Hey!" Freddie barked.

"He tripped," one of the officers called back while the other refitted his cap.

"Where's fucking Petrelli when you need him?" Freddie said under his breath. "You two get over here," he commanded. "Okay, Marty, we'll meet you at your office."

Not the passerby, heath nut, or nosy neighbor knelt beside Steve.

"Hey," Abcde said and lowered her scarf.

Her voice was not strong enough to talk over the clatter that hovered above; it pierced like a long needle that did not split the balloon but rested inside.

"They took it Abcde," Steve said. "They just took it. I didn't want you to see this. I didn't want you to know."

"It's okay." She brushed a glove against dirty snow that played a crescent around his injured eye. "I know. And I came anyway."

"It's so available," Steve wheezed. "Everywhere. If only it was more expensive and harder to get, maybe I could get away from it. But I just can't. There's no one left."

He was near a dry sob.

"You're okay now. I know you can try."

"You know," Steve said and unfolded himself so he could sit back against the police car. His lungs bristled with slivers of glass, and his gut burned the fire of no food, all drink and regurgitation. "It sucks when you have something wrong with you and everybody knows. Everybody can see it but you. Ain't no place to hide."

"You can hide now."

"I don't think we can go far enough away." He saw the scene closing up around them. "Everybody sees me."

"No, you hide all you want." She lay her hands on the sides of his face. "Go and hide."

"I just want things to be easy again." He slid again off to the side, and she pulled him back. "You know, go to school, come home, and not worry about nothing. Do it all again the next day."

"He's all right," Marty said from above. "He can get up by himself."

Abcde jumped to her feet as if pulled by a chain.

"I bet that's what you tell him all the time."

Marty stiffened from the smack of her words.

"All he wants," she said, "is a little help. A little understanding."

"You don't understand. Who the hell are you anyway?" Marty asked. "He doesn't *want* anything. He doesn't do anything."

"Maybe he's trying."

"People like him," Marty said and backed off in callousness, as if washing his hands of the day, "don't even know what *try* is. I'm done with him."

"You disgust me," she spat.

She scanned his form: Model-perfect parted hair crowned his face. If there were any gray, it had been dabbed away by the dye from the box—not just any box, the best box. His face stared back, thick with privilege, moisturizer, supplements, and a smooth shave as if set upon by tweezers instead of a razor. He was broad but not to excess, and his body filled out the folds of the long coat. His covered form was defined by working out, not because he wanted to or had to but because he could and it's what *you* do. Each pretentious step back that he took sounded off: You leave your house, you go to work, lunch out with colleagues or catching up with friends, you work more, you work out, you come home, dote on the kids, have dinner, and bed down with the wife. The wife, the wife, the wife, except when it's not the wife, it's plan and play with the neighbors, be the loudest voice in the crowd as the girls march by in their costumes at the school parade, coach the team, sign up for a time at the fundraiser, placate the homeowners' association, work some weekends, take vacations, go to reunions and gatherings—nothing that Abcde found now or would ever find familiar.

Except the wife? she thought. *No, it's the . . .*

The shoes. Dress shoes that cracked with a dry shine. They were posted one beside the other at the foot of the bed or strewn end over end where only the right or left mouth that gaped like a yawn or the victim of a stab looked upward. Those shoes she knew.

"*You do not,*" Abby said to Abcde. "*Let's just go.*"

The red-haired officer reached down and helped Steve enough to let him slide into the car.

"Everything all right, ma'am?" Freddie asked the woman with the scarf over her mouth.

"No," Abcde said.

"Yes," Abby said, "just seeing if I could help."

"That was really good of you to stop," Freddie said. "I'll take it from here."

* * * * *

"We'll have to send him up to Palatine," Marty said.

Marty and Freddie talked around him in voices that considered Steve to be miles away instead of the third person at the conference table.

"Not Palatine," Steve said.

If a fetal position could be achieved in a chair, Steve had found it and then lurched over the portion of table in front of him.

"The fuck it matter to you?" Marty thundered. "St. Charles then. I don't care if it's the moon."

"I just want to go back to my apartment."

"You can't," Marty said. "The minute Fred files his report, there'd be a warrant issued. Public intoxication isn't serious but serious enough for someone on probation."

"Steve," Freddie said. He stood and turned his chair about so he could straddle it and lean over the back. Steve had never been in this setting with Freddie, but his voice betrayed that he owned the role of good cop in the little room with the spotlight. "Marty's right. This could have been a lot worse. Disturbing the peace, trespassing—you're lucky that woman was good enough just to want you gone."

"How long?"

"For what?" Freddie asked.

"How long will I be gone?"

"Twelve weeks." Marty broke back in reasserting his position in the stead of bad cop if it came down to name tags.

"I'm not going to be gone twelve weeks, Marty. Don't be an idiot. A few days maybe."

Marty took a breath, caustic not compassionate, and elevated from his seat.

"Twelve weeks," he said. "You don't show or you leave once you're there, you go to county, and it's on your record."

"Steve," Freddie said, "if jail time is on your record, no matter what Cleo says, you ain't coaching at the gym. This, this place won't be on record. We're the only ones that have to know, but you've got to help us out."

"I'm only agreeing to this because it keeps it off record and I can't have you with a record and work at a fucking law firm." Marty stacked pages against the tabletop and lined them in a folder. "Just disappear for a while. Get this . . . help or whatever it is you need."

"Come on," Freddie said. "It's like you'll be gone for the winter. You'll be back by Easter."

"You'll make sure Cleo knows I'm coming back?" Steve threw himself back into the fabric.

"Yeah. We'll tell him," Freddie said. "We can tell him, right, Marty?"

"That's fine," Marty said.

"Okay I'll go," Steve said.

"Like you have a fucking choice. This is court ordered," Marty said. "Do you have your wallet?"

"No." Steve felt his back pocket anyway.

"I sent Carter over to your place to pick up some things." Fred eased Steve back into his chair. "He'll get your wallet, phone, clothes—no worries. It's not prison, man."

"They have clothes and shit there. I'll have the front call a cab," Marty said to no one as he got up and left the room.

Office lighting beat down on the table. Steve's hand slid over the slick laminated surface. A lone speaker unit rested in the table's center. A cradle with thin silver fingers held a mesh amplifier, perfect for the booming voice of a faraway superior. Framed cityscapes—none Chicago or even familiar—protruded from the walls.

This is a room where decisions are made, deals get done, and families are torn apart, Steve thought. *This is where meetings are called to order, and suits, ties, skirts, and scarfs oversee and depend on results driven by how much people like me needed people like Marty. And how much we would pay for that need.*

"What got into you today?" Freddie asked.

"Don't know."

The mercy of a glass of ice water was within reach, and Steve laid it against his head.

"Tell me someday?"

"Yeah."

"Hey, uh," Freddie said, "they only allow family visitors up there, so once you go, I won't be seeing you for a while. You understand that, right?"

"Right."

"So if there's anything at all you need to tell me—need to say—you need to let me know."

"Fred." Steve did not recall the last time he addressed his childhood friend as such.

"Yeah?"

Steve prepared his words as clearly and as soberly as the bruised and inebriated can muster.

"There is something I have to tell you."

31

April xx, 20xx

Dear Marty,

It has been some time since your last visit and even longer since I've written to you. I am sure there is regret on both ends, and maybe we can work through it in the days and weeks ahead. Administration contacted me today and said they received what they needed via e mail and confirmed you will be here in two weeks to drive me home. I appreciate you doing so and look forward to seeing you then.

[Prior to this letter being sent, the paragraphs below were discarded and a salutation added.]

I wanted to tell you about a moment of clarity that I had. A moment that fully broke throughout my stay here but one that started that day in your office. I did not trust most of what I saw or thought that day, the day I was hit by one car and thrown into the side of another, after being cold cocked by what may as well have been a sledgehammer. All that, of course, following a flow of alcohol that consisted of more drinks in a week than should be consumed in a month, where the perpetual response to the internal question of "What would you like to drink now?' is simply answered with a yes.

It came to me in the conference room when you stood and left, leaving Freddie and I alone. It was the way you moved. I had seen that before—movement that was in and of itself communication, movement that had a point to prove but was unnecessary. I knew you were pissed, and you knew it too. You leaping from your seat to storm from the room was a visible adjective one too many.

I always wondered how she got behind the car. We were all in the backyard. Your father-in-law was saying how he just had to pull his car from the driveway and if I moved mine a touch, down and to the right, he could. You were telling him to wait that we would do it later. You were busy at the grill, concerned about the temperature and if the strings of smoke were too thick or thin. But the moment got caught up between the stubbornness of a restless old man and me, drunk and anxious to do something, anything to fill in the blank from the drink I just had to the one I wanted next. We all agree that I shouldn't have been in the car at all, that's a given. But no one moved to stop me. Well, someone moved, but she moved opposite, into the yard toward the playhouse. The one with the open window, painted-on flowers, and the plastic tile roof.

I don't really want to tell you this, but I think I have to. I know you keep things from Melinda. Things, despite your worry, I would never tell her, and there may be other issues there behind your doors. But those are part of your road to travel and ultimately none of my business. But I think she keeps secrets from you too.

To everyone else, it looked like I was pulling forward. So drunk, I probably had the car in drive and thought it was reverse. But that distance would not explain the force of the impact. I was in reverse, backing the car, inching it actually, compensating for what I knew was a diminished awareness (a phrase they use here) when I saw her in the rearview. At first, a flurry of little girl sundress and hair in a bow and then nothing. In panic, I shifted back to drive and kicked the car forward, knowing that when I saw her in the mirror and then didn't, I had already hit her. But she was safe in Melinda's arms, and your father-in-law's Buick bore the brunt of my ignorance.

Your street is always full, a river alive with strolling parents, running kids—there were just too many witnesses. Your drunk brother had gotten in a car and nearly backed over his niece. That was the most convenient story, the one shared from the old man's angry eyes to a panic-stricken mother up and down the block, until someone called a cop, and the story was rehashed into a version that made me one of a select few people convicted of DUI after the fact and driving in a space that could be measured by a yardstick or two.

Melinda would have none of you "lawyering" me, and you conceded. My car impounded, my license invalidated while you watched. But it was her in motion that day—motion to prove a point. Your brother, splintered but not yet cracked, steps from the edge, needing only a nudge.

I will never tell you this. I wrote this here to see if I would stop after a few lines in hopes the falseness of what I saw would stop the words. I see things all the time that I know are not there, and I thought this was one of those times. But

```
I kept going because the words kept going.
You don't believe me, but I hate myself
for saying this, even thinking this.
     (Strikethroughs omitted)


                              See you soon,

                                    Steve
```

* * * * *

"Did you have everything from your room then?"

She wasn't a receptionist. By the cursive on her blazer, Sara was a registered dietitian—pretty but in a way that wasn't remembered like a match instead of a candle. Wavy, tan hair was a harness around her shoulders. A thin, gold band adorned her wedding finger that probably did not measure the devotion she felt for the man who put it there.

"Yeah," Steve said. "I left the keys on the desk like they said."

He avoided using the word *my* when possible. It was not "my room" but the "room I stayed in for a short time."

Not my keys either, Sara, just the ones I left behind.

A painted but not manicured finger pronounced clicks with her mouse.

"All right then," she said and handed him back his phone still fastened in a sandwich bag. "You're all set."

He tightened a strap on his backpack.

"Did you have any last questions?" Sara asked.

"No," Steve said. "They answered everything."

Who are they? Steve thought.

"Good."

A bank of closed-captioned monitors and her mainframe screen did not hold her glance long.

"You know, you can go, unless there's anything else," she reminded him, her tone caught between the training of service and a pinch of uncertainty.

"Yeah," Steve said. "My ride should be out front."

It was called a clinic, but by the doors, it was defined as a hospital. The programmed autoslide created an opening like a chasm. A line of people twenty wide could enter with room to spare. A stretcher could be turned long wise if needed.

In a bit of show, the older Mercedes was out front in the roundabout where guests were dropped off and friends were released, the flow of both at times unwilling. The black bit of German engineering was the lawyer car—stored, for the most part; backed in, not pulled in—against the far wall of Marty's three-car attached garage. The car was a source of reference and encouragement throughout law school and then accomplishment, purchased after his first year with the firm. It showed age, but like a French wine or a Scotch whisky had a presence of grace as it charted the years.

"Hey," Steve said. He found a soft spot in the rigid seat to lean into and enough room on the floor in front for his pack.

Marty replied with the turn of the ignition.

Steve looked to the backseat. The lack of acknowledgment registered as regular for Marty and more or less expected when one picks up a brother that was dropped off to rehabilitate and was now given approval to reintegrate.

Across the rear seat were three suitcases, the kind you had to take to baggage claim and could not jam into the overhead. Two hefty bags furrowed and full, hunched behind on the floorboards, and three men's suits hung from the peg over the window behind Marty. A briefcase—elegant onyx leather and monogrammed— rested upon the center of the luggage.

"Marty, where are we going?"

Steve had the sudden sensation of another voyage pending in which he had neither choice nor knowledge.

"I got caught."

* * * * *

I had my first drink at the age of nine and my first hangover at the age of twelve. Not that I knew what it was at the time. The scraping of brain on bone just happened and required no formal name. The morning unraveled in a spiral of a pain inside my skull that was too sharp to call an ache and a bloated discomfort in my bowels that felt as if I choked down a weather balloon. For every two steps my legs eked out, my senses took one.

Humidity, backyard hotdogs and tepid soda were a recipe that sent the strongest stomach into mild shock. The addition of beer that felt basted instead of brewed was gas on a fire and held hostage over most of my actions, speech and thoughts for the next two days. Excrements expelled in streams that were too thin, progressed to a troublesome too thick and both versions had a waft of moist rust.

But there was no getting caught. The adults in the house, my parents and two out of town uncles, all had the same symptoms and anything I had been feeling was washed away by a quick hand over the head no fever, you see, and a gospel chorus of, well everybody feels that way it must have been something we ate. Marty, eighteen months younger than I had no idea what any of us were talking about.

Basketball camp would have started again Tuesday, and victory over any lingering head issues were cleared by aspirin or one of the other variations in bottles or boxes stored color coded in the washroom medicine cabinet. The green box was all right for daylight; the opaque royal blue was the winner at night. The winner overall was not, however, beer.

Don't get me wrong, I have drank—drunken—plenty of beer and, up until the day before I arrived here, considered it to be a good base to whatever else I was drinking at the time. In addition to its low alcohol content and unbearable taste at times, see pumpkin ale - yes, I tried it—beer takes up a residence in the gut that is immobile. The piling on of beer stacks like thin sheets of lead inside and builds up in rubber, a protrusion on the outside, neither condition akin to chasing girls, playing basketball, or sustaining a positive body image, the three hallmarks of my teenage years. And beer, in quantities over one or two, is a nightmare to transport.

I needed something that was quick, less filling, and would fit in a gym bag. Enter vodka—or, more correctly, my parents' vodka. It is a clean drink and wears the costume of water. There is an odor, but it's subtle and can be washed away by a sports drink or coffee. For the record, coffee is better with bourbon, and it wasn't until legal drinking age that I learned that the combination has the proper name of Irish coffee and not breakfast of champions.

The marriage of basketball season and the calendar was magic. What I moved out was covered by gift bottles shipped back in from my parents' offices and the seasonal generosity with which the flow of houseguests were smitten. One night, there would be three wines, a liquor, and the holy trinity of vodka, rum, and bourbon—each with the liquid cut into but no measurement for the levels. The next night, it wouldn't matter; as under the kitchen sink and high upon the pantry shelves, a reproductive flurry would be unleashed and the available stash would more than triple.

The cobblestones of the path did not interlock. They scattered about, and I was content to leap from one to the next—beer to vodka, vodka to bourbon, bourbons to liqueurs, and back again with an intermezzo where the spots of leftover dinner wine belonged to me. The pills were the mortar that cemented the road and grouted the tiles. Cold medicine was the alpha, but any antihistamine would do. Both chased by vodka (again the water), they produced a hyperawareness that settled me on the edge where high levels of corporate brainstorming is achieved. There is action but no critique. Chores done with no memory. Homework to keep me eligible, bested with swift, shaky strokes of pencil and ink, and basketball—the crown jewel.

To many, it was a game of sound and fury, the seemingly chaotic motion, directional shifts, and mismatches became elementary geometry drawn against a hushed sanctuary. Pass and shot angles, invisible to others, stood from the background highlighted in yellow. Limitless directions and distractions came from the bench, teammates, and crowds. And I heard neither. The responsibility was simple:—put the ball where it needed to be and everything else would fall into place.

That's how it started.

* * * * *

Sara put the letter back on the desk. She had thoughts of folding it and tucking it into a pocket but left it out for the next guest. Perhaps the next guest would find solace in the tale and would feel a kinship to the one here before them—the one who is no longer here because he or she was now cured, absolved of the curse.

It was neither an original idea nor unique cause of dependence. The idea that the substance moved a user to a higher state of performance was a crutch used from disciplines that ranged from acting to writing to sport to medicine and through the stages of courtship and patterns of parenthood.

When it's coffee, tea, or Mountain Dew, no one recommends or demands a stay at a clinic. Maybe they should. Maybe at the first signs of dependence—that's what she would have worked on, in the medical program she was never in. A sidestep into nutrition brought her to the idea, and eventually a full-blown master's thesis, that diet and exercise alone could treat addiction. Turns out, much like all the other theories of good intent, they were part of but not the whole solution. Because, after all, there is no solution.

She had no medical training at all and had acquired her knowledge by pure osmosis of being around medical residents and now doctors and certified counselors and psychiatrists but knew it just the same. There were offerings, maps, programs, sessions, and, yes, a good regimen of cleansing food and strenuous activity that kept her own career aspirations active and bank account full. But not one—not one guest who left the premises left—was cured. They left different, and there is a wide gap between "you are corrected" and "you are changed."

Steve Coleman, the man she let go this morning, would never be back in this place or any other place like it. Cured? No. Not because he was cured. Because he was scared.

32

There was not another sound inside of the car.

The exits signs counted down the miles to Deerwood. The feeling for Steve was like being on a bus ride for a school field trip. You were relieved the drive was over, but you were not sure you wanted to be where you were going.

Marty slammed the door behind him, the echo sprung like a perfect strike had been rolled.

"You want your suits?" Steve asked.

"Yeah," Marty called over his shoulder, moving at the pace of embarrassment. "Bring 'em if you want. I'll come back for the rest."

Marty had charged ahead, up the stairs with the key. Steve with his backpack and three suits over his arms trudged behind.

"So she knows about the money?" Steve asked at the top of the steps. "And everything?"

"She knows about it all," Marty replied. "I'm gonna have to stay here for a while."

He stopped short of opening the unlocked door.

"That's fine," Steve said. "I've got a bedroom that I don't use. You can just stay there."

"At first, the hotels were okay but expensive, you know. At least the good ones. Anyway, she's a hawk about finances now. Spring break, that worked. Melinda took the girls to her parents', but she's back now and we just can't—"

"Marty," Steve said. "I said it's fine. Open the door, will you?"

Marty pushed ahead into the apartment behind the door for unit 4.

"Did you clean?" Steve asked.

"No," Marty said. "I haven't been here in three weeks. Sorry about the mail."

Marty slid the keys across the kitchen table. The table glimmered of polish with no evidence of discarded food or spilled drinks. The four chairs waited—soldiers in the round under a jade fixture that now had a bulb. Silk webs no longer strung chutes, ladders, and routes of entry and egress around the socket. The window that peered into the lot below had been defogged and reflected the light with the sharp cut of a laser.

The livable space minus the bathroom could be taken in one glance from the entryway. The carpets were not just vacuumed but plumed free of presence. The blanket that was always tossed about like a bag of feathers was folded over the back of the sofa. The sofa— still a helpless, washed-out olive green with exposed framing—had been swept and the minimal shelves freed from sheets of dust. The glass of the television beckoned like a clear pool in the summer. Steve had no doubt the unseen bath area and the room he offered Marty were any different.

"Who the?" Steve still had neither set the suits nor the bag down. A card taped to the refrigerator made him lose the load across the table.

"I don't know, man," Marty said. He collected his suit bags and went to the front closet. "I used to think I could shit in your kitchen. Now I'd be concerned about farting."

"Yeah, you keep it that way."

Steve took the card—generic white with hand-drawn pink scrawl around the frame. Stubby black cursive was inside.

Dear Steve,

I hope you didn't mind me coming by and straightening up. I hope you find your apartment comfortable and easy to come back to. See, I told you I wasn't a nurse. When Fred said you would be home soon, I did not know what else to do to thank you. He is a good police officer and was a good friend. Oh, your fridge is

empty. I had to move everything to clean it, and there
was nothing worth saving anyway. Figured you may need
the fresh start.

He read the salutation and went through the still-open door
and knocked on the one to unit 3.

"Don't," Lisa said, her hand going to his chest when he started
to respond. "I didn't know what else to do for you after what you did
for me."

"But I wasn't even here to help you."

"But you said something. Nobody does that, not anymore."
She traced a finger under each eye. "They take pictures or post
comments like it's some sort of modern act of bravery or involvement.
From wherever you were, whatever you were going through, you
said something. That was enough. You didn't have to, but you did
anyway."

"I couldn't just sit by anymore. I just can't sit and wait for
someone else to . . ."

Lisa brushed a finger over his lips.

"It's over now," she said. "I was in a real fix, and Fred made sure
I got out. Not that I couldn't have gotten out myself on my own, you
know? I've been in shit before. I just end back up with . . ."

"It's okay." Steve gripped at her fingers and worked their hands
together. "We all need a little help sometimes. It doesn't make us any
less."

He thought briefly of the help his brother may need.

"And then Freddie, he . . ." she started.

"I'll have to ask him."

"I'll tell you sometime, okay?"

"First, maybe dinner sometime?" Steve gestured back across the
landing.

"Sure," Lisa said. "I hear your place is really clean."

"And maybe there's a young man in there who still wants to give
basketball a try," Steve said. "I hear there's a team nearby that might
need some help."

"We just can't right now," Lisa said. "I can't get him there, can't
pick him up, and even if I could, there's no way I could afford—"

"It's paid for," Steve said. "And I'll get him there and back. All he has to do is want to show up."

"He would." Her eyes welled again.

"Then nine o'clock tomorrow."

"He'll be ready."

Steve closed his door behind him.

"What was that?" Marty asked.

"Neighbor across the way," Steve said. "She's the one who cleaned the place. We were kind of friends, I guess, before I left. I don't really remember."

"Ugh!" Marty exclaimed. "Well, you were never too discriminating about who you'd choose to fuck. Knowing who the last guy was, though, that's like making eye contact before using the stall right after him."

"Oh, come on, Marty. It's not like that."

"Okay."

Steve reclaimed the keys from his table.

"I'm hungry," he said. "I'm going to get something. You wanna come?"

"No," Marty replied. "Whatever you bring back is fine."

"It will probably be Andy's."

"Dude, its fine." Marty gave in and sat on the couch. "I don't care."

Steve lay his hands across the frame of his bike and wasn't surprised to find it wiped from the caked mud it must have had—the kind of mud that evolves from used snow that has to be scraped away like ice. The spokes flashed a wink of scrubbed aluminum within the wheels.

"Get your shit from the car unless you're making a donation to the neighborhood."

33

The reunion was like most—a quiet introduction, a reminder that there once was a partnership, an understanding, which gave way to small talk and, at long last, the discovery of a lost friend. A friend who had many chances and reasons to let go but never did.

The seat, both his and the bike's, rebelled at first. Hips unaccustomed to the motion nipped in discomfort and skin, locked in place under jeans, pulled like Velcro. The handlebars drifted left where it may have always been right, but he relearned to force his arms just past eleven o'clock to keep straight. The tires were pumped tight, and each jar from the road sent a short message like a jolt from an untamed wire through his legs.

Steve hesitated on the hand brake. The tires, if they had a choice, may have slid right through the rubber bumpers when they realized where they were. But the choice was Steve's and his alone, and he closed the brakes with a fist in front of the house. His Chicago Bulls windbreaker was red and left him as a bullseye of color on the short curved road where rust-spotted lawns in winter recovery laid over dirt and empty front porches, waiting in anticipation of spring.

The detached one-car garage—its door clamped like a mouth shut over a secret—would have to be patient and hold his car for a little longer. The mail service at the post office was guaranteed but did not mitigate the front steps against the deluge of local coupons, service ads, and newspaper samples that survived any snow, rain, or wind the past months may have challenged them with. Steve took the unread stack to the recycle box at the side of the garage.

"You can go inside, you know," Brooke said. She was perched on the first two steps of the small side porch. "It's still yours."

"It's ours," Steve said.

"So you're just going to go back?"

She wore a knit fleece top today, the color of sunset, an uncomfortable contrast to the spring day with wetness curling at the edges. Steve knew—really *knew*—that what she wore was not a concern. If she wanted to, Brooke could breathe on Mars. Humidity, in any measure, was a stone in an ocean.

"No."

The papers removed from the porch; the job was done, and he returned to the bike.

"It's different now," he called back to her.

"I don't see it that way."

"It has to be."

"You're right," Brooke said now in front of him, her hands flung opposite to his over the bars. The left ring finger shimmered with the wedding set she wore this time. "But all I see is two brothers, twenty minutes from now, beer on each side, a box of Andy's between them, and the TV on. There's nothing different."

"Brooke . . ."

"Make it matter."

Her grip tightened against his. Blotches from the squeeze left a constellation of pink and white.

"You have to let all of this go, all of it. Start by moving back in or selling it I don't care."

"Brooke, I've already left so much behind, I just can't—"

"Left behind?" Her breath was cold on his cheek when she spoke. "What have you left? You haven't even said goodbye to me yet. Steve, you have a choice. You have to choose one path or the other. I think that's what scares you the most."

"It's because I don't do anything right!"

"No," Brooke countered. "It's because you don't do anything at all."

"I should have just let it end."

"No, that's not how this goes. I was behind you that day at the sink and all the other times," Brooke said.

"I know."

"I didn't let go then, and I won't now. Not yet."

"But I can't . . ."

"You can," she pleaded and then gathered herself. "We both know that if I let go of your bike, you'll fall."

Her hands took a grip in a steel vice that was beyond her. "So I won't. I won't let go, but you have to be the one in control."

"Okay."

"Not okay forever," she answered. "But for now."

From a distance, he was a man, alone on a bike in a red nylon jacket. His feet against the pavement held the bike in place, and with a breath that expanded his chest, then another that spaced his ribs and his back, he rolled away from the empty house as late afternoon welcomed the dusk.

"Where have you been?" Marty asked. His head was a half moon over the rear of the sofa, his body crumpled, fixed toward the television.

Steve wrestled the bike and two brown grease-spotted bags into the apartment.

"We're never going there again."

The rodeo-like entrance was settled as the bike was placed against the closet and the bags were tossed on the table.

"Where?"

"Andy's," Steve said. "All the staff is new. Took forty minutes just to order. It's a wonder they're still there at all."

"What'd you get?" Marty asked.

"Seven Eleven dogs and sodas. Take it or leave it."

"I'll keep my soda for later," Marty said, arriving to claim his share from the bags. "This will do for now."

He placed a bottle of beer on the tabletop.

"You know, I'm only a few hours in here, bud," Steve said and took half of his contents and all the condiment packs to the counter. "That is not helping me."

"I don't know how to help you. I've done everything I can."

"You can start by not having that around."

"I'm around, it's around," Marty said. his mouth full of bun and hot dog. "Deal with it. Are you really just going to stop drinking? Really?"

"I thought that's what . . . this was all about," Steve started. "I thought that's what you wanted. What everyone wanted."

"I don't care anymore," Marty said. "I have nothing left. No horse in the race. I don't care what you do."

"But what if I care?"

"When did you ever give a shit?"

In a fluid spin that shocked them both and would register a complaint to both knees later, Steve wheeled to the refrigerator and pulled a beer from the neck and held it toward Marty as if holding a dagger waiting to be driven into a tree.

Marty didn't know the velocity at which another bottle had been launched at the far wall in January. His defense, a raised bun, would not have slowed the impact on his face if Steve had let it fly this time.

"You know what, keep it." Steve holstered the beer back in the cardboard slot and shut the fridge behind him. "Have it all. I gotta go to work tomorrow."

"Yeah, I'm sure Cleo will have some pretend jobs for you," Marty said.

"He said he had something."

"Sure, something to keep you distracted." Marty turned his back and went an end of the sofa. "Instead of wasting away here, you can do it there."

"Don't talk to me like that!"

Marty stormed back to the kitchen, his sack dinner held aloft in front like a shield.

"I'll talk to you any way I want! I have earned that." He set his wares at the table again in undecided rage. "You wrecked my in-law's car, destroyed birthdays, holidays, weekends, and that spectacle at Mom and Dad's. Don't you think I had a reputation to protect?"

"Seems you did a good job on that one by yourself."

"Steve, we've been knocking back beers together since I've been fifteen." To emphasize, Marty took a king-sized gulp. Steve swallowed along with him and tasted saliva the flavor of baked air.

"You were the only one—the only one—who had an issue with it. I will speak to you any goddamn way I want. You are the most selfish person I'll ever know."

"I don't really want you here that long," Steve said into the space Marty had left behind.

"It won't be, believe me." Marty pulled out a kitchen chair and sat. "I just need to sort a few things out."

"You? You need to sort some things out." Steve laughed and pulled a chair as well. He didn't know what was more comical, Marty's statement or the fact that he wanted to sit across a table from his brother. "When do you leave for work tomorrow?"

"Guys who have soon-to-be ex-wives who call their bosses and tell them they may have been taking money to cover off the record wagering don't go to work anymore. Especially at law firms."

"Jesus, Marty."

"Administrative leave," Marty added with air quotes. "We both know that's fancy talk for 'does he really have a problem or was he acting of his own accord?'"

"Well, I'm sorry about your job."

"Yeah," Marty said; a long look away followed. "Figured she would have left the office part alone, seeing she liked the money so much. I guess you're the second most selfish person I know."

"You're surrounded by us."

"Yeah, I'm surrounded by shit." Marty drained the beer and pressed his fingers into his temple. "Does that damn train ever stop?"

"No." Steve dragged soda through his straw.

"I just need to hide out here for a bit."

"It's a good place to hide," Steve said. "Everybody knows you're here, but no one's coming."

34

A stutter of three or four basketballs conversed with the hollow gym in a fractured drum solo. Judgement seemed an afterthought as shots from the boys were taken from loose footwork and improbable three-point angles from the corners. The rim clanged like a gong as a line drive rebounded off the underside of the metal.

"Okay," Steve said to Troy. "Get on out there and warm up a bit. Stretch so you don't hurt anything."

"I don't know how to do that," the boy said with a nervous glance to the other players.

Five boys in shorts and generic playing tops gathered at the free throw line while another boy in long shorts and long socks fired miss after miss from the three-point area.

"I'll show you all some stretches later," Steve said. "Now go out there and shoot some. Cleo's waving at me."

Steve held a palm up to the far corner of the gym.

"I haven't shot since that day with you." Concern morphed to alarm across the bags of Troy's eyes.

"You'll be fine." Another miss in the background hit the rim with the sound of a fist hitting a heavy bag. The ball dropped in a vertical line instead of the expected angle. "You can't do any worse."

Steve put his hands on his knees. It was a kind of homecoming where the sounds churned on like an old song, but just because you knew the tune—each note and the lyrics free-formed in perfect recall from the vaults of your mind—didn't mean the dance was for you anymore. He strode toward Cleo who had since taken a defensive crossed-arms-over-chest pose. Cleo was thinner than Steve had remembered. His head stood atop a spring that had replaced his neck. His dark skin walked about on his arms and rolled up in wrinkles. On the walk to the gym this morning, Steve counted six as the number of basketball games he had played in or watched where he had been sober.

"You all right?" Cleo's words were deep, rubbed with sandpaper and concern.

"Yeah, just a little tight. Went jogging this morning."

"Jogging's good."

"It stinks."

"You know what else stink?" Cleo asked. "You got twenty that paid, about ten more than that show up. Only fifteen can make the travel team for summer league."

"Travel team? Wait—"

"Only fifteen," Cleo started right where he felt Steve stopped listening, "can make the travel team. But the others can stay on your practice squad. Good for scrimmages, injuries, and other disappearing acts that are sure to show."

"Travel team?"

"Yes," Cleo said, enunciating the words with a harsh space. "The team that represents the gym in competition."

"How long have you been working with these guys?" Steve asked.

"Twelve weeks." Cleo's hollow eyes were an eight ball on a snowbank and looked past Steve instead of at him. "These parents— they know they kids ain't the best, but like I told you, this is where they can play and they got nothing else to do over spring break, nothing to do after school. We ain't got no fancy shirts, no sponsors, but if we play against those teams that have all that, some of our boys may get noticed, earn their way up. We work against better teams we get better."

"And then they move on."

"Of course," Cleo said. "Who the hell would stay here?"

"I'm here."

"Point noted." Cleo wrung his hands. "Now I've got paperwork. Grown-up leagues starting. Summer, two months away. Some lockers to clean and some folks prob'ly wanna come in and start working out."

"Cleo," Steve said, "I'll get the lockers later, don't worry about . . ."

"I'll get 'em." Cleo looked over to the groups of boys that cordoned off into cliques and expanded from half court to full. "They yours fo' a little while."

"Hey, Cleo," Steve called back to him. "You heard from Freddie?"

"His mother-in-law," Cleo said. "She took ill. He in Kansas City for a while. That's the story at least."

"Oh," Steve said. "He didn't call."

"Sudden thing. Been having some trouble. Guess he didn't know when you gettin' out an all."

"Thanks, Cleo," Steve said. "And seriously, thank you, Cleo."

Game 7, Steve repeated on the way back to the players. *Game 7. The seventh time you have been on a court not under a hex of liquid or a pill or several of each.*

He scratched at his chest for a whistle, found none, and hoped basketball looked the same in Technicolor as it did through lenses sick with inebriation.

"Hey!" he yelled ahead to no response.

The only other adult in the room approached him. He wore a purple sweatsuit last seen in the late seventies with "COACH DARRELL" sewn at the left pocket in block letters.

"I'm Darrell, your assistant." He handed Steve one of the clipboards he was holding and the second whistle from his neck. "You might need this."

"Right. Thanks, Darrell," Steve said to the man he had last seen at the gym cleaning the locker room in between play in two late-night leagues.

Steve placed his lips firm to the whistle and made the sound of a soft bird. The second attempt was the same soft bird that now retreated under the safety of a pillow. Steve looked to Darrell who nodded encouragement. Steve inhaled and blasted air into the whistle as if inflating a tire. The soft ringing moaned into a crescendo that hit a sonic peak in the confines of the gym, and the players shuffled in and out of a malleable half circle around the coaches.

Steve studied the group. Broken-in and borrowed shoes clawed at the gym floor. Some had socks that were not washed, some unmatched, and some had none. Most of the shirts were torn, and others were fresh white from a man's package of Haines. A group of three were pointing at Troy who was on one knee hunched over as if a weight were behind him.

"You have something to share?" Steve asked toward the group.

"We was just wondering, what was he gonna do? Block?" A smattering of laughter gurgled.

"Yeah, he's gonna block." Steve went to Troy. "You all right?"

"Yes," Troy wheezed.

"He's going to block or pick, and when the guy defending you loses the step and you're open, you'll shoot."

"Man, I'll shoot when I'm open, when I'm covered—"

"When you're covered, you'll pass."

The young man looked away, but Steve pressed on.

"Basketball is an architecture of the complex. A paradox of infinite possibilities that can never escape the confines of physics and angular logic." Steve took the ball from the player and rolled it across the gym. He did the same with another. "It's about motion and mismatches. It's five on five until one of theirs is cut off. Then it's five on four, and then we'll shoot."

Steve took the last ball he could see and rolled it away.

"Basketball is more than you think, you know. But we'll start simple," Steve said, now at the center of the players. "It's a funny name for a game, basketball. Funny because most of it is played without the ball. And today, we work without the ball."

There was a collective groan.

"So line up at the backline." Steve directed the boys with his arms and a more deliberate finger point for Troy and some others. "We run the court, end to end, ten times and then again. And we'll do this until every last one of you can beat me."

35

Steve was flat on his back, forcing himself to exhale, each one arriving with a slice of tongue. An arm went to his side, hooked over the lower shelf of a rolling ball cart. Troy stood over and shrugged to the old man when he appeared.

"Tried to outrun 'em on the first day," Cleo observed more than asked with a wink toward Troy.

Steve replied in a heaving pant.

"Practice has been over for a while, sir." Troy stood between the men as an uncertain messenger.

"I'll take it from here," Cleo said. "Why don't you run up to the desk and grab us some waters."

"Yes, sir." Troy's version of a run was a walk-skip with feet like hooves.

Cleo strained to sit next to Steve and then grimaced, setting a plane on a moving airstrip. His legs were worn-out poles of rust with hinges he no longer trusted.

"Why don't I try and assist my assistant tomorrow."

"That," Steve spoke for the first time in twenty minutes, "would be helpful."

"Who knows, we may even get to use the ball."

"Yeah," Steve said. "I just thought we'd see what kind of shape they're in."

"Well, now you know," Cleo said. "These kids run a lot. From stuff not to it. Bursts of speed with no endurance." He shared a glance to the illuminated celling with Steve. "Let's teach 'em some basketball now. Show 'em what we know—or at least used to know. And maybe we'll learn something in the process."

"Cleo, can I ask you something?"

It was rhetorical, but Steve was going to ask anyway.

"When I was . . . at that place . . . you kept coming to visit. The rules, though, they said only family was allowed. How'd you keep getting in?"

"Guess they thought I was your long lost uncle."

"Come on, Cleo, no one believes that bullshit."

"They never turn away a former guest," Cleo said and rose like a younger man. "Now get your ass home. We got practice tomorrow."

* * * * *

```
     St. Charles in and out-patient treatment
facility.
     Intake Survey, (partial) January 20xx
     Please   respond   to   the   following
statements:

     8. I am preoccupied by the thought of
the next drink and become irritable if I
am unable to drink as planned.
     Answer: Not certain.
     9. I modify my schedule to drink or
abstain from certain activities altogether
if they interfere with my drinking.
     Answer: Not certain.
```

* * * * *

Melinda Berecki–Coleman did not opine on much. Her lane was wide, but the sharing was defined by the procession to which her days conformed, keeping personally aloof but remaining in cordial step with followers and those she followed after. Her contribution to the silent dialogue and emojis kept pace with the generalities of the other moms, both single and married, but added little substance to the claims of success at having roused the kids and delivered them safely to school, comments on the weather and the news, and new recipe achievements and disasters, both of which elicited the most annotation and exchange.

At a more granular level, she kept pace with a geographically widespread but still connected group of college friends, the school parent source, Marty's firm, and a local dog rescue shelter. She liked photos of puppies; Adam Levine; triumphs of others' kids, even when the update was tinted with hubris or pinched at her with envy; and most things associated with Springfield, Illinois, where she grew up. She even sent a like and a two-word push of encouragement to a nearby suburban mom who was a month into her DIY cookbook project fashioned from the pages of her grandmother's books that she had found after a move into a new house. But what she liked most of all was seeing her maiden name in the scroll.

To the world around her, Berecki—and Springfield, for that matter—were places to be from, icons of the past that had not packed up and traveled ahead. They had both been left behind at the altar, by her option, but still, no matter how phony a digital social life was, it provided evidence of a time in her life before the Coleman became stapled to the end. The mail, even the junk, neither carried the reminder nor did, when she bothered to look—the mortgage papers, the insurance policies, or the bank accounts.

It was the bank accounts that were troubling today. The savings balance was lower than she would have liked, but that did not signal an alarm on its own, without context. But she felt it. Like an itch in the corner of your eye that could be tamed with a blink or semiconscious dab of a finger. It's only when you realize the discomfort is caused by a shard of glass that has weaseled under your cornea, and the more you scratch, the more it itches until the wizard-sharp fragment is driven deep enough into your eye to remove any myth you once had of sight.

An out-of-balance savings account was a fact of living. A part of adulthood continually present but not routinely shared outside of musings from Cathy Warner-Simpson, friend of a friend of a friend who had merged a link—*shared?*—to Melinda's page called the Coffee Click—or was it *Chick?*—who had a habitual post every other Thursday in the neighborhood of "Woohoo! Payday tomorrow! Good thing, bank says I need a refill." The traffic on the joint savings account was "a fish out of water," as Melinda's mother would say. Which reminded her to check her mom's feed and saw that Mom was currently enjoying aqua aerobics at Springfield Fitness and Tennis Club just off Sangamon and Coulter, a hundred miles and then some to the south yet right in the palm of her hand.

She would ask Marty but not tonight. Admittedly, her own traffic had been flowing in and out of the account as well. No big moves, a spot here, a spot there—nothing that could not be explained by her saying that the kids needed something for school or she needed something for the kitchen. But Marty had not asked, and the surprise that she had planned for tonight, Friday night, two days before Valentine's Day, remained undiscovered.

If Marty wanted to buy a boat, fine. He didn't have to hide it; and if he thought he did, well, then that was partially her fault. Marriage was a two-way street, she told herself, and if he's more willing to sandbag money for something he wants rather than telling her, that is not his issue alone. Besides, somewhere in the near west suburban shopping malls, there was a two-piece suit she could find that would still flatter her. It may cost a small fortune, combined with the bag and wrap to match, but she would just have to *have* it. And that would be that. She would even promise to try it on for him after the kids had gone to bed. Marty, a big fan of shoes and stockings, was an equal fan of behind closed doors fashion shows.

If he instead wanted to sell the Mercedes and upgrade, Porsche was the next step she just knew it. She might resist at first, but it would be a rebellion of play, capitulation served with a fine dinner (his treat), a fine evening (her treat), and the agreement that she could drive it whenever she wanted.

She closed the laptop and went into the master bathroom. The bank could wait. She had been wrapped in the towel since dropping the girls at Taryn's after school, who agreed to keep watch over them tonight if she and Marty would watch their house starting Sunday— the real Valentine's Day—when the neighbor's midwinter vacation would be underway. A service to which Melinda volunteered, and she was certain Marty would be agreeable to.

Taryn said, courtesy of Cosmo, to "be present and in the mood for your man, you had to make yourself available and elevate toward the occasion." It had to be inhaled—deep—like the tender smoke from a joint, if you wanted to feel the impact. The boredom of the bedroom, the routine, had to be allowed to erode under wave after wave of eagerness. The top recommendation was just to be naked. Melinda stopped short of acting upon the reminder of Taryn's advice, which was to combine nakedness and a bout of self-exploration, but naked was good for now. Taryn even offered a DVD, but for Melinda, the anticipation of Marty in charge of the voyage later would be enough to set the sails with the wind, tear back the sheets, and attack the sex with a lustful return to craving and need that normalcy had furloughed.

Yes, a boat would be great, she thought.

Summer weekends on the road, maybe Lake Michigan but more likely Wisconsin. Definitely Wisconsin. Away from the traffic and out of the city. A small lake or inlet where other families went with family-sized vessels meant for sun worship, a light swim off the side, and water ski instructions for the novice. They did not need to be among the display of Lake Michigan wealth or in the way of perilous passage through drunken millennial contests of speed in boats too large to control and too small to survive a crash. The girls in life jackets—pink, if that's even a choice—seated in the captain's chair, a grip on the steering wheel in faux pilot mode, or along the port and starboard drenched in the spray of the wake, awakened by screeches of the solstice just under the rattle of the motor.

The soft oversized towel dropped, slid down her torso and snaked at her feet. The mother of two stood, bared under the stage lighting that strode across the top of the mirror, and she studied— imperfect, yes, but not depreciated to where the triumph of age was forgone. The boat would assist with the winter paleness embedded along her skin. It was the cocoon of motherhood, stretched over a body of wear but not neglect. A suit she found herself at peace growing older in where she shrewdly dealt with unwanted folds and welcomed tautness in areas that still surprised her.

She cupped and ran her hands down her chest and to her hips. Her nipples, never striving to keep up with the rest of her, were the flick of the tongue pinprick variety, the cherry on top of the sundae her college roommate Elise Blatt had said. Melinda was mindful that despite their supposed averageness, they had been the destination of six boys and one man, who each fumbled through the maze of her bra strap and were allowed to caress, twist, bite, or pinch, dependent upon the mood she found herself in, and had enough breast left in them to serve as the nursing station for two daughters. Elise, on the other hand, had been adorned with thick, swollen mounds that swayed in time, even when her body was still, with an eastern Mediterranean melody only they could hear—a chant that was surreal and exotic like her olive-tanned skin that screamed in contrast to the lily-white Midwestern music Melinda found herself surrounded with. Natural circles of flesh, each with a center that looked hand painted by a rag, were proudly on display most evenings in the small dorm they shared.

A sip of bitter wine chased the image. Wine was also part of the mood enhancer but not enough to keep her from driving to Marty's office and securing his release earlier than the five o'clock he expected. She checked the bottle and saw the purple line was less than halfway down the opaque green.

Still good, she thought.

It was a beneficial, gentle use of wine—an aphrodisiac for once—instead of earmuffs that she called upon to block out the girls after school while she made dinner. And lately, it had not been wine but brandy; and if brandy got away from you, like a car with no brakes, a car that was designed without brakes, she ended up too tired to be conversant with Marty, much less make love to him night after night like he wanted. But his was coming. Departure in an hour, maybe a touch longer, reported the block amber numbers from the clock on the bathroom counter.

Lingerie too, her inner voice called out as if making a shopping list—with some sort of lace, jet black or a luscious red but not white. Something naughty, Taryn had suggested, with mischievous strings and a bow to unwrap like a gift, but Melinda had nothing left that fit that description or fit in the way the catalogue said it should. Marty though had been asking for some lately, and he may have just bought some on his own for her during lunch this week. No matter what he chose, she'd have it on for him later in the privacy and blessed low lighting of the room she booked at the Giorgio.

She turned and looked at her ass reflected back in the mirror. Springy dimples had been replaced by two long U-shaped grins. She lifted a cheek to where she estimated it once had been and let it drop. Across the top, Melinda could still see where she had wanted the ink. She wondered whether the Chinese letters, after two decades of contraction and expansion, would have still held the same meaning now as they did then or if the mark would have become a source of compunction. That answer, she could not know. What she did know is that in any phrasing, the second letter had a line that would have been a permanent directional arrow over the crack of her ass, which created a problem because she always thought the next man back there would have been distracted under the compass of where the previous guy had been directed to go. Her forty-year-old self was thankful most, if not every day, that her eighteen-year-old self had made the decision to walk away at the last minute, especially knowing that Marty would have been at most timid and, at worst, flaccid at work under a tramp stamp.

Marty had been convinced by a biology major acquaintance that the prior guy's junk would survive for seven years, much like swallowed gum in a stomach. So even if the last knight had been vanquished, swords were continually being crossed. Convincing Marty that this information was not accurate—Melinda thought (hoped) it wasn't—and that he would be the only one from then on had been a chore in itself. The eighty-year-old Melinda would also be thankful that she never had to see what "live, dream, believe" looked like in Mandarin, under the rolled parchment of maturing skin that would grapple with but eventually come to terms with the aging process in her lower back.

Her legs were in need of a quick shave, a rub of the organic salve that had been delivered today, and, maybe in the long term, a recommitment to the gym membership that was deducted from the account monthly—the account that she would be forced to ask about later. For now, there were some dry spots on her knees that needed to be calmed down and maybe a curve or two that could be beat back by some Spanx. She'd wear wedges to go with the dress, the ones with the soft instep and thick ends for support, not the spiny heels that left you to balance on a nail. The nude style with the cork underlay she had purchased would be a perfect match and was better for walking to and from the car. It also calmed her fear of poking Marty in the chest or legs when he insisted that she keep her shoes on for the first little bit.

Melinda relieved the last of the wine from the glass and went to the shower.

36

Seventy to thirty-eight—the square red numbers over the entrance to the gym, the team ledger, and Steve's journal would all report the same result. The end of the game, the part that others took with them, was often so much different than the beginning. The optimism of the start, the attrition at the center and the tangible take-away at the finish. The first game, much like the measure of a life, felt divided by years instead of minutes.

The quiet at the end weighed heavy, unlike the light anticipation of the moments before when Steve sat alone in the first row of bleachers. The clipboard and notebook he had been using were silent partners to his side. Unaware strains of "anything can happen" scrolled in his mind's eye like a rolling dataflow that charted the markets, and like the markets, predictions were fossils when the final bell rang.

The week of spring break camp gave way to thrice-weekly practices where the players phased in and out, ballooning to thirty-three at one point and contracted to seven on the last day of school. The constants were the neighbor Troy, who had nowhere else he wanted to go, and the outside shooter Austin, who would not give up a shot if the Hancock Tower stood in front of him. The team that gelled in spite of the absences and selfishness had size, a quality that could not be taught, but were slow, a feature that could not be undone. There was aggression that led to fouls—too many too soon—and laziness that made dribbling an adventure where it was second nature to other teams.

"You early," Cleo's voice bounced from the corners of the empty gymnasium before the game.

"This was always my favorite part," Steve said.

Cleo's movements were stiff, as if his joints fought against glue. As he walked, his fingers pointed downward in the perfect ten digits of a skeleton.

"I used to just sit here going through all the plays, every option. Sometimes I could play the whole game in my mind."

"You know," Cleo said, "there are grand masters of chess who can do that."

"Do what?"

"Play an entire match right there behind their eyes. The pieces may as well be on another planet." Cleo rubbed his fingers into the sides of his head. "Most of them have lost their minds."

"We don't have to worry about that," Steve countered.

"What do we have to worry about?" Cleo eased onto the seat next to Steve.

There was a vague memory of a younger Cleo who long ago paced the sidelines like a caged panther. A tweed sport coat would spend more time over a chair or on the floor than it would draped over the coach's small shoulders. There was regret there, like a child who looked back upon his parents and only saw the time passed by under the shroud of routine or disagreement. Steve knew there was more there behind him, other than the fog of days and nights that overlapped, where he would turn to the bench and see the gestures of his coach. Where he would venture a peek into the stands and see his parents. Acid, which he volunteered for, had taken what it wanted from the memories and burned black holes into photographs and movies that could never be recovered.

There was some solace that those around him remembered what he used to be. That was not to worry over. The moments that were gone would stay gone. The old man who had replaced the vibrant young coach was of concern, but Steve was sure that Cleo was not asking for a diagnostic assessment.

"Their confidence," Steve said.

"Maybe if it goes bad, they'll start to pay more attention."

"Or," Steve said, picking up the clipboard, "they'll climb back in their shell and never come out."

"Nah," Cleo said. "These kids are fighters, you should know that by now."

"I don't," Steve said. "I can't get 'em to show up. When they do, they're already worn out. Big Macs and Cokes are not a practice snack."

"These kids, they don't have a choice," Cleo said. "You want them to be that kind of fit you gotta show 'em how. You want them to pass their classes and do their schoolwork, you need to give them a reason. You want them to have a better snack at practice you need to bring it in."

"Why are you just telling me this now?"

"Because you need to figure these things out by yourself."

"Who are you, Socrates all of a sudden? Jesus, Cleo." Steve watched the old man stand. There was a grin on the creases of his face even as he bent so his hands could find his knees. "And I'll never know why you'd schedule us against the best legion team the first time out. You're at practice too. You see what I see."

"Cause when they get their ass kicked," Cleo leaned into Steve, "they gonna reach to you for advice. Like a thirsty man in the desert searching for the oasis."

"They're going to get they're ass kicked, aren't they?"

"Yeah." Cleo took a long breath. "But that don't mean this ain't worth it. These kids are like a forest fire burning out of control. Not because it wants to but because it has no other option." Cleo's index finger drove the last three words into Steve's arm. "We'll give 'em an option."

"How long you been holding out on me, Cleo?"

"Twelve weeks, you dummy," Cleo said.

"What in the hell is a matter with you?"

"I needed to know if you could do it."

"Needed to—"

"Now I know. Besides, you a grown man, you get options too. Just because you make shitty choices don't mean you ain't allowed to make 'em. I ain't gonna stand over you 'n' tell you what to do."

Steve's eyes welled, and a hand was quick to hold back what was brewing.

"What's wrong now?"

"You were the best coach I ever had," Steve struggled to say.

"I know that." Cleo winked. "We could have done better. The both of us. I just wish you could remember how good you actually were."

"Why didn't you tell me?"

"We did," Cleo said. "It's all we ever told you, though."

"My parents and the school . . . what we could have built," Steve said. "I turned it all to garbage."

"But it's time now," Cleo said.

"Yeah, I know, but—"

"No." Cleo placed his hand on Steve's shoulder. "It's time now, your team is here."

The opponent from Olympia Fields had a warmup that crackled with the precision of a military drill. Complicated weaves of dribbling and passing snaked along a grain of bright blue uniforms. Every rebound was accounted for, and sideline two-on-two drills were run as written, lorded over by assistants in crisp, pressed suits. The head coach—bald, slim beard, with wire glasses who in another context could be mistaken for a professor—waved in Steve's direction.

On the home half of the court, Darrell chased a loud miss into the half-empty stands, and Cleo demonstrated for what may be the tenth time a pick in the corner to release a bigger player inside. He had to explain again that the contact was only allowed if the player who set the pick was motionless.

"But how can I not be moving if I'm moving?" Steve heard the player ask Cleo.

The player who grasped the concept best was Troy who was behind the basket with his mother Lisa adjusting the jersey that had drawn out from his shorts again and flapped like a flag in the wind.

"Hey," Marty called from behind him.

"Hey, man, you came!" Steve said. "What are you doing here?"

"What the hell else have I got to do?"

Marty continued up the bleachers, and Steve followed.

"I don't know," Steve said. "It's just good you came is all."

"Yeah, well . . ."

"Hey, no wagering."

"You think that's funny?" Marty stopped halfway and hung in an unseen chair.

"No," Steve said with a quick focus back to the floor below. "I don't think any of this is funny. It's just who we are, and what we have to live through."

"You know," Marty called after Steve, wearing what had become his new suit, khaki shorts, and a gray T-shirt, finished by untied high-top shoes. "I hate being your roommate."

Steve was suddenly conscious of the black slacks and white dress shirt that he wore.

"Good. I don't like having a roommate," Steve said. "You cramp my style."

Steve drifted back down the bleachers, not hearing his name called from the side. The horn sounded, and the clock on the scoreboard counted down from five minutes. Cleo brought the thirteen members of today's team to a circle under the basket. The professor at the other end of the court hauled his team back toward the locker room.

"Yo, Steve," Freddie called again.

"Hey, man, how've you been?"

"I just got back a few days ago." Freddie held his palms up.

"Yeah, I heard. Dani's mom, huh?"

"Yeah," Freddie said. "Busted hip. Dani's sisters in Seattle, you know, so..."

"You guys doing okay?"

"Yeah. Dani—she comes home this weekend. Not sure for how long." Freddie let his eyes wander. "I think we'll be all right, you know. Some things are kind of in the air. Might put in for a security job out there. Maybe leave the force at the end of the year."

"Really, man?"

"Yeah, maybe. You know. I'll tell you all about it sometime," Freddie said.

"Yeah, that'd be great. It'd be good to hang out again."

"So I hear you're doing great, right?" Freddie asked, but he knew there was no time to visit. "Team's looking sharp."

"Well, we're all wearing the same color, so it's better than yesterday."

"I think it's great."

"Thanks for coming, Fred." Steve felt the need for his hand to move so he pushed his hair back. "And thanks . . . you know . . . for the other thing."

"Just my job, man." Freddie pushed his palms down near his waist against an invisible weight in a reminder to Steve to keep some things to himself. "We got a new league starting up this fall."

"No," Steve countered before there was a concrete invitation.

"Come on," Freddie pressed on. "Five cops, three fire, two out-of-work finance guys. and a gym teacher. You'd fit right in."

"Maybe."

"Hey, Coleman!"

"Hey, Petrelli." Steve shook hands with the uniformed man who was climbing up the bleachers. "You out busting chops today?"

"Yeah, some chumps too." Petrelli cupped his hand over his eyes and scanned the court with mock binoculars. "Those guys out there look like the fucking Bulls."

"Yeah, thanks for noticing."

"So what will you do when they got you down by thirty?"

Two officers behind Petrelli laughed as well.

"Something I'm not so good at," Steve answered.

"Oh yeah, what's that?" Petrelli asked.

"Get back up."

37

The buoyancy peaked at 7–2. An immobile pick set by Troy allowed a shooter to get free and find the net. A predictable response from the opponent followed. From there, Austin shook his defender but passed the ball, which left his teammate as shocked as it did the defense. The mishandled pass drew the attention of three and a pass back out, in panic more than strategy, found Austin behind the three point line who would not miss an uncontested attempt from there.

"There you go!" Steve yelled from bench.

The rushed inbounds pass was deflected right to Troy who deferred to Austin and an easy layup. There was a scattered applause from the small crowd, not enough to drown the shriek of a time-out from the opposite bench. The professor coach looked to Steve with an air of disregard to which Steve replied with Michael Jordan's shrug.

"You know," Cleo said with a pass of the clipboard to Steve, "they still gonna kick our ass."

"Yeah I know," Steve said. "But it's something."

"Yeah, it's something," Cleo agreed.

"All right, guys."

The five starters took a seat, and the rest stood around Steve in a captive circle. Over the top of those who encircled him, a movement stole his vision. The tail of a long coat, a season or two removed from necessity, escaped the latch of the closing door. A black flame snuffed out as the wearer went out of sight.

"Hey, coach," Austin said. "We down here."

Steve handed the clipboard to Darrell as the Tilt-A-Whirl started.

"Draw something up."

And then you really were no longer at the game, were you? You went through the same door that should have led you to the hall beyond the gym, but you may as well have stumbled into the wrong side of a vault. The door sealed behind you. The air you breathed was water, your lungs stuffed to their limits. Sound was extinct. You stepped against an incline, each step forward led back to where you were. You and your brother had always dared each other to attempt an escalator in reverse—you no longer need to try.

Pressed into the pillow of thick air was a voice—no, two voices, clearer now. An older one chided a younger one on a phone message from a New Year's placed under a stone in your mind. It was like—no, it was . . . it just was . . . the long coat did not go through the door. It was force . . . it was pulled . . . just as there was a pull now . . . shaking, waking you at the sleeve.

"Steve, Steve!" Cleo said. "Steve, you in there?"

She asked for help.

"Yeah," Steve said to Cleo, pressing against the wall.

The hall spun like a top losing velocity. The wall behind him gave way and he went to his knees.

"Are you all right?" Cleo demanded.

"If you're asking if I've been drinking, the answer is no," Steve said. "I'm okay. I just got warm in there. I felt like passing out."

"It is warm in there," Cleo agreed. "Ain't no damn air. Still blows so they won't replace it. Colder air down in hell than what comes outta there."

A woman walked by with a girl, both in workout clothes.

"It was just them."

"What?"

"Never mind," Steve said. "Let's get back inside."

The sharp horn called an end to the time out. Steve waved his hand to an official and sipped on his water bottle.

"Here." Cleo handed Steve an open sports drink. "Sorry I asked."

"Cleo," Steve said, feeling a rush of lemon-lime complete his return. "You get a free pass. Now come on, we've got a game to lose."

The pressure at his back abated the longer he sat on the bleacher. Steve looked up, and the four numbers still looked back with the one-sided conclusion. After the first seven, the points were diamonds under coal.

"They're wrong," Steve said to the empty gym.

"Who's wrong?" Coach Darrell said, his hand on the exit door across the court.

His hand pressed forward in agreement with the look of concern on his face.

"Everyone." Steve went to the center of the gym and took the ball that had been left behind. "We're going to win one of these, Darrell."

"Well, that would prove everyone wrong."

"Have you ever done that?" Steve rolled the ball between his hands.

His thumbs caroused familiar territory for the grip he needed. "Done what?"

"Proved somebody wrong." A snare drum snapped from his hands below. "When it really counted."

"I don't know," Darrell said. "Have you?"

"No," Steve gave a firm reply. "I've fulfilled expectations. That's all I've ever done."

"Well, good night, Steve."

"Darrell?"

"Yeah?"

"Are you parked under that AC unit?"

"No." Darrell looked to the dorm fridge-sized unit that intruded halfway up the far wall.

"Good." Steve dribbled to the free throw line. "Cause I'm gonna knock it out of the window. It's too hot in here. We need a new one."

38

Fred Hagen waited.

The apartment stunk like a used tomb. The scented candles of his wife's closet would be a futile stand against an essence that bit with a mouth of stale corn. A stain of spattered liquid sliced along the living room wall. Fingers of the explosion opened like a peacock around a center design that could have been painted.

He wasn't sure where the bike should go but it wouldn't survive the night unattended in the park lot. He set it inside against the closet doors after a debate about leaving it in the hall that may have been as secure as the exterior. Fred knew any interference in the landing would be heard, and he needed the space between the doors unencumbered.

Despite the friendship, Fred had not been to the apartment in the months that Steve had lived here. The built-in pantry had more dust than provisions, and the items that were inside had more miscellany than logic. There were oyster crackers but no cans of soup and candied sprinkles with no staples for baking. There was bread with no evident toaster, and nothing in the refrigerator could be placed on the bread. Two dozen beer bottles lined the walls of the fridge. The door light beamed brown from the reflection. A leftover sack from Andy's Pizza was the edible outcast.

An equally impressive display of liquor was kept under the sink. Unopened wines and a well-stocked dram shop worth of rarities like Pernod and Ouzo rested at the rear, caged in by the galvanized plumbing while well-used spirit bottles patrolled the front. Fred pulled out a Canadian whiskey. A ring of crust had formed under

190

the cap. Permanent marker across masking tape read "Thanksgiving or Christmas." The Kentucky bourbon next to it had a section of tape with "May and June" written on it.

"Well, you're an organized drunk," Fred said.

He took a tumbler from the nearby shelf, blew into the bottom, and covered it with a pour of the Kentucky. A bitter massage washed over his throat, and he added more to the cup.

"Well," he said with a sip, "this won't be around for the summer, bud."

During Fred's fifteen years on the force, Steve had never asked for a favor. Until today. They would have been given anytime within reason, but there were neither parking or moving violations to be waived anymore nor ride-alongs ever requested. Moreover, it seemed Marty had the big needs covered.

It had been Marty on his own, behind everyone's back, who persuaded the court to dispose of the impaired driving charge as he cited the negligible distance driven and the obvious first offense. The citation that survived was the loss of driving privileges and behavioral probation for one year. And it was Marty today when he caught wind of the woman's hesitation in further pursuit of criminal charges, who cleared the air and talked her back when they swapped stories about the great home she owned in a safe neighborhood. He assured her that the perseverance of the police would not allow something like this to happen again. Marty's entrenched, prudent debate skills of capture and retraction would not prevail over an official report but would avoid a worse punishment.

The wait drew longer. For Steve, it had been worth the mention; so for Fred, it was worth the few hours. Steve—shuffled off to court-ordered rehab, shaken, angry, and still drunk—asked if Fred could check on the neighbor in unit 3. Fred's mistake was not asking enough questions, so the unofficial stakeout crept into and then took over his off-duty hours. Hours he could be home with Dani where the repair of the marriage had taken precedence over the actual marriage.

Fred whisked back another ounce of Steve's summer selection. He could not find one source other than time itself that undid the foundation. Neither infidelity nor money issues creeping around every corner to rot the core. Dani married a cop and she knew what that meant. He had told her. He wouldn't always take the form of the handsome, strong protector who was the envy of friends at backyard cookouts, weddings, and reunions. In the true, played-out line of work, long hours bled into longer hours; and shifts, though scheduled, were frequently inconsistent. Downtime in fraternization with partners and colleagues at the expense of time at home. Nights he worked were hours she was sleepless. which impacted her career and a failed startup he had no energy or time to support. Children, which had been a goal—or at least on the matrimonial radar—were now less likely by the day.

A crack of settling in the frame sounded like a giant cracking a knuckle overhead. A half hour, Fred thought. I'll give him that. He pulled a chair from the table but had no mind to sit so he traversed the small unit.

One bedroom with truncated walls held what was maybe a full-sized bed. Dani would know for sure. The comforter was without wrinkle, secure like a lid over Tupperware. There were no pillows at the top, and a gym bag rested at the foot.

The small bathroom was a throwabout with lights on the low yellow end of an invisible dimmer switch. There were towels bunched on the floor, and two more draped over the shower rod. Boxes of bar soap, stacked in front of and over more boxes, were the backsplash to the chipped vanity sink. The medicine cabinet was sparse, its contents just a toothbrush, paste, and deodorant on the top shelf. A half-empty—or half-full?—bottle of nighttime cold support with smeared medicinal green across the label was on the lower.

There was a yellow number 2 pencil on the floor. It was an item out of place as no magazine or journal were in attendance. This was the kind of pencil that drove into Fred's neck when he was ten. In his hand—point to the humid blue sky like a short sword of ignorance— the pencil pressed between hand and the coarse rubber grip of his dirt bike. The skid that turned into a crash made his hand let go and the pencil charged, lead up. It had been Steve's dad who was there.

Not a special man, just a dad in the right place who held the pencil by the eraser, so the point would have adjacency to but was not permitted to slice the jugular. Steve's dad, Warren Coleman, held the pencil in place, like an instrument of surgery, until the ambulance arrived and kept it in his fingers until the doctor in attendance at the hospital pried his locked fingers away. Had the pencil skipped a centimeter in either direction, Fred's last visual function would have recorded a grown man's dress shoes crossing a street.

The boy across the hall who sat with his legs crossed was older than Fred had been that summer but looked as frightened and defeated as Fred may have then. The boy sat with his back to but not on the wall, and his face was driven, lunge after lunge into his hands. The boy's eyes were red, and his elongated shirt collar had finger-sized holes of Swiss cheese. Muted shouts were behind the door to unit 3, which meant they were near the bedroom.

Fred bent to the boy's eye level.

"Is it open?" he asked.

There was a head nod in affirmation.

"I'm going to end this."

Fred lifted his shirttail to show the badge pinned underneath. He slunk through the door like a thief and plotted direction from the barrage of language that settled at the rear of the apartment. There was a tipped chair in the kitchen, a half-eaten plate of pasta, and a Hamm's beer can in witness. Animated figures were in sight, voices not at a yell but close. Two fingers pointed in a joust, extended like lances. He'd have to wait and offered a silent apology. Still invisible, he slid a hand to the small of his back and patted the outline of his backup plan.

From lifelong fandom of boxing and his share of dustups from days of assholery and nights of patrol, Fred knew the velocity of the fist that had connected at the side of the woman's face. Her momentum carried her back to the living room and a contortionist's collision with the cheap sofa.

"Go on," the man growled at her. "Go see your boyfriend now. Maybe he's back."

"Hey!" Fred used his voice, leaving the gun tucked in the waistband for now.

"What the hell are you doing in here?" It was a question from the man in the red flannel shirt, but there was no inflection. "Baby, call the cops."

"I am the cops, idiot," Fred said, the words parceled between gritted teeth.

The woman Lisa, Fred figured, groped at the couch like a downed pugilist in need of the ropes.

"Son," Fred said and looked back to the open door, "close it."

Troy complied in reply.

"Now look you," the man said at Fred, "I don't know what you think . . ."

"I think this." Fred looked at the man for giveaways, but his hands remained at his front. If he had anything, it would have been drawn by now. "There's two witnesses in this room. One a battered woman and the other a cop with no blemish on his record. We'll say it was self-defense, and no one will know any different." Fred was fast enough to know his firearm could be reached and discharged if the man moved forward and was smart enough to have put the switchblade in a ziplocked sandwich bag, which he tossed at the man's puffy bare feet. "You have fifteen minutes to pack whatever garbage in here is yours and never come back."

"You can't do this!"

The man shuffled one then two steps toward Fred.

"I don't have to let you walk out of here," Fred said, his voice straddled the steady line of calm and hypnosis.

"Just get out!" Lisa wept into her shirt.

"Baby," the man said. "I messed up real bad. You need to know . . ."

"Get out!"

A banshee shriek, and she charged him, fists like battering rams on springs, slammed against his chest.

"You hit back, I guarantee I won't miss." Fred held his sidearm down to the floor and pulled Lisa back in a side embrace but only after a few punches were allowed to connect. "Fifteen minutes."

The man lowered his gaze toward the ziplock bag.

"Go ahead then. This is easy," Fred said.

"Crooked bastard."

The apartment had the possessions of a beggar's cave, but the man took all of his quarter hour to fill a duffel. Empty dresser drawers were tossed at the walls, and Lisa's items were thrown on the floor.

"You'll want to get some ice on that," Fred said.

"He'll come back," Lisa said.

"A good friend of mine just starting his shift and in a very bad mood today is at the end of the street." Fred went to the refrigerator and got the ice himself. "He's gonna tail him a bit. Put a good scare into him. He won't be back here."

"They always come back."

"You know, I don't believe in restraining orders," Fred said.

Take shared the kitchen with Lisa for the last time.

"If I ever see you here again, I'll put your face through the floor."

The man grunted. He slammed his hand into the side of the pasta plate. It flipped from the table to the ground. Whispers of red sauce dredged from the overturned edges.

"You'll rot in here," he said to Lisa.

"You'd rot anywhere." Lisa finally attacked her now beet-colored bruise with the ice bag.

"It's still self-defense," Fred said evenly. "Time to go. You so much as brush that boy on your way out, I'll make sure and aim for your front."

"Thank you," Lisa said, her hands trembling an uncertain dance from her face to Fred's arm.

"Thank your neighbor."

39

I hadn't thought about the accident. The words that I wrote in the spring but did not let Marty see, played the role of a cleanser, and a hole the size of the event was left in my conscious mind. It was not the total darkness left behind by alcoholic blackouts like the others, just a scratchy space I could—would—no longer see.

The day it returned, rung in by another collision, was almost like a welcome of an old friend who was determined to reappear but never said exactly when that would be. A moment of "oh, you're back" but no real surprise and no reaction other than rediscovery. After it happened, I had replayed every recoverable moment to myself daily just after waking: A mental cassette tape on a loop of play and rewind. The thrust forward of my car into his. The angry, bulged eyes of the old man and his nonnegotiable but silent mask of fury. The panic, busy with confusion and neighborhood chaos, which overtook the afternoon.

That summer day had been a part of me for so long, the memory crept back into the black spot it had left behind and turned about like a cat looking for a spot to settle. And like a tired back that treasured a soft chair after a long day, it sat.

Our shopping cars butted one another. A crash of pliable metal in a duel for the unavoidable blind corner, due both to plastic wheels that would not follow orders and basic distraction. Hers not a phone but a handheld notepad, mine the need to be off aisle 10, no questions asked.

The fluorescent rectangle under the ten held what I wanted most—craft beer stacked halfway to the ceiling. Maybe something to enjoy in moderation for the taste, not effect. We'd get the cheap ones for later. Today, high-end something, was the true elite watermark of the gold, blue, or green label. Just think how long a four-hundred-dollar bottle of Scotch would last. About three days. But no one would know. You're still able to work, you're present—but present in a life that missed so much.

Since the television was relocated to the room he is using—I refuse to say his room—it's beyond no interaction; it's like he's not even there. About three days I repeated. We wouldn't just sip at it and pretend it's not there. We would be the parched man who crawled the Sahara and landed at the well, dried out like a raisin by an incorrigible sun.

Speaking of what cannot be cured . . . here, it's the Spanish Red you had always wanted to try with the dinner you are making tonight. No. It stays on the shelf. The man on Cleo's fork in the road is not made for the other path. Not yet.

* * * * *

"Oh! I'm so sorry," she said and looked up. "Hey . . ."

"Hey . . ." Steve extracted from the aisle as precise as a driver leaves pit row. His eyes drifted over her. A familiar face out of context due to her appearance, and then it came to him. "Cindy Lancaster?"

"Yep."

A thick moment of recognition spilled, and together they felt the red rush of embarrassment erupt under their skin.

"Look," Steve said, "I'm really sorry."

"No. No worries." Cindy patted the cart. "Not a scratch."

"No, Cindy." Steve straightened from the slouch he had worked into over the cart. "About last winter."

"Oh?"

"We met," Steve said, "and I acted like I didn't remember you. And I did . . . I do."

"No, that's all right."

"No it's not. It was really rude, and I truly apologize."

Steve left the handle of his cart and moved toward her.

"If it was December, last December, I probably wasn't worth a second thought." She wore a rose-shaded high-necked top over knee-length cargo shorts. Her strappy heels were replaced by jogging shoes and ankle socks. A good-sized mess of blonde hair waved from the fringes of her classic blue Cubs hat.

"Still, it was rude."

"I'm sure I wasn't very, um, pleasant either. End of the year kind of sucks sometimes," she said.

A swirl of discomfort found its way between them and sat.

"Yeah. It can."

"You know, when I think about it," Cindy said, "a lot about last year kind of sucked."

"Well, the Cubs did make the playoffs."

"There's that." Cindy noticed him a step further away than he had been, and his eyes dove into assessment. "Look, I'm sorry I shouldn't have . . ."

"No," Steve said. "I was just thinking I haven't been to a game up there in a while. It'd be fun to go. We should do that."

"Sure, but that would be next summer. Probably."

"Right."

"Well, maybe before that," she started, "you'd like to go get a drink sometime?"

"I'd love to," Steve said. He knew aisle 10 was not going anywhere. Best to wait until next time we're here he thought as the placard winked down at him. "Coffee would be better though."

"Okay, coffee then." She arranged candy bags in the part where the child would go. "Where's your Halloween stash?"

"There's not many kids in my neighborhood," Steve said. "And the one I know of, I'm trying to keep off of the stuff."

"Who am I kidding," she jested. "I know it's still a month away. I just can't get enough of these."

"There's worse things that could chase you," Steve said. "Those actually look pretty safe."

"For sure. Here." She tore a sheet from her notepad. "Old-school, I guess. Call me, okay? If you want."

"I will." Steve folded the sheet into his shirt pocket. "It will have to be the Oaks though."

"Huh?"

"For coffee," Steve said. "The chain place is overrated, and the shop with the deer on the door up and closed."

"Yeah I saw that."

Another pair who could not figure out a discrete pass around them split the center with their carts, a short two-car freight delay.

"No problem, I like the Oaks."

"Great," Steve said. "I'll call you. It was really good seeing you."

"Steve?"

"Yeah."

"Thanks for remembering me. Not a lot of people do."

* * * * *

Steve let the phone ring one more time, the burr from the tone fluttered against his ear. He turned the phone to the side and made sure his own ringer was on. If there were a way to wear out the slide that changed the ringer from silent to audible and test if the function was covered under the warranty, Steve would find it. He tried to play out the conversation with the phone man or woman that wouldn't end with his explanation of an obsessive need to have the phone with him at all times but have the ringer off. And when he went across the room, the sound needed to be clipped back on, but not all the time because he still wasn't sure if he could handle what may follow if the phone actually made a sound that requested a response.

"You know," Cleo said. "You have an office."

"It's your desk with a second chair." Steve placed the phone, screen side down, on the chair next to him. "Besides, I'm more comfortable in here."

"Seems about right. Don't even need the new AC today." Cleo noticed the rear doors of the gym were propped, and the cool fall air could trespass when it chose. The breeze mulled in stillness for now, and the open gym smelled of rubber. Steve turned the phone again so the screen faced upward. "You call her again?"

"Cleo, I know what I saw," Steve said. "Long wool coat in the summer . . . her running out like she was leaving a burning house."

"That was months ago. She hasn't returned a single call, and she said she didn't want to see you. I read the letter, remember?"

"Then why show up like that at all? Just to make sure I see her and then leave?"

"She's a woman, right?"

"Cleo."

"You know," Cleo said and took a free chair. "When I quit, I would see things—shapes, colors, people, a mess of things I knew really weren't there. Why, one time, I saw a white wolf, another a neighborhood cat from when I was a kid . . ."

"Cleo, I see things all the time. I know the difference."

"Ain't no difference."

"And her phone messages," Steve said. "I know they're from before New Year's and all, but . . . they sound like they're from two different people."

"Aren't you two different people?" Cleo asked. "The one we see now and the one we hope we never see again. He ain't dead you know."

"Cleo, don't you think I know that? Are you here for any reason or just for some words of wisdom?"

"Matter of fact," Cleo took a folded envelope from a pocket, "we got it."

"We qualified?"

"Well," Cleo said with his voice in a fade and handed the envelope to Steve. "The three in front of us turned it down. Guess they didn't want to log the miles just to be lambs at the slaughter."

Steve undid the trifolded letter.

"Yeah, no kidding," he said. "These are the best teams downstate."

"And some from the suburbs." Cleo stood. "We the lowest seed."

"That means Roosevelt."

"Or Carbondale. Still a month out."

"Yeah," Steve said. He had a giddy bounce when he stood to match Cleo. "But still, Thanksgiving tourney. This is a big chance for these kids."

"They played their way in."

"You," Steve said, his hands on Cleo's arms, "you deserve this."

"I ain't going."

"What do you mean you're not going?"

"You and Darrell got this."

"Cleo, this is every bit yours. We can't do this without you. You've seen how these kids respond to you."

"We got time to get ready."

"Cleo."

"The doctor says I can't travel on a bus for more than two hours," Cleo said. "I can't sit like that."

"We just went to Park Ridge and back."

"And how did I feel? After we won."

"Shitty."

"Okay then." Cleo put his hands on his hips.

The old coach, *swimming in* rather than *wearing* the running pants and top, had the eyes of authority but a body of use. His hands were cheap leather gloves left in the rain. His neck, a series of bars and lines, shook as he spoke.

"Besides, you get to a time in your life where you may not want to spend too many more Thanksgivings away from your family. These tournaments—they a young man's game."

"Cleo."

"You got this. You earned it too."

A pickup game opened in the far court with the reverb of canvass against the floor.

"And not just with basketball."

40

The visual that Melinda could not disburse was the one of her husband's cotton, dry-clean-only dress shirt camped over his bony ass. The fleshy white bottom that was centered between two raised legs. His hands held her legs aloft and apart, a perfect, experienced angle at the edge of the desk. The thrusts were methodical and silent. A performance much like at home with no extra potency or vigor as if this act was habitual as well.

She expected affair sex to appear different in some way, more cinematic, at least better lit than it was under the muted platinum from the closed blinds and shimmer of office luminaries. It should be passionate or ribald with sweat and language she didn't recognize and would only pretend to understand. Each movement of the hidden act she surmised should have been accented by a deep moan of verboten pleasure from the taste of an exotic sample instead of an entrée that could have been ordered with "oh, just the usual." It looked like everything Marty was and what she had become— practiced, scheduled, and routine.

Melinda thought, at some level, maybe the mind overrides the body and deadens the near audible precum buzz once the fucking starts. The thrill that led to this moment—this moment she was seeing, born of the id—is defeated by the ethos when the brain realizes that the animal is getting what he wanted, but the animal was wrong and simply should not be able to enjoy the act to its fullest potential. Like how electric make-out sessions of youth, that riptide over feels, licks, fingers, and rubs become manna. But once the V card is played, the kissing and touching are buried in a very loud interrogation, an internal press conference that keeps perseverating, "Is this just kissing now or do we fuck? Is this leading to fucking? Will it always? Does it have to? Do I let him unbutton me? Do I unbutton him?"

And then you're there just getting laid. The blaze of magic has gone cold. Once the end of the tunnel was discovered, there was nowhere else to go—for some, a satisfactory conclusion; for others, there were of course, always more tunnels.

The watch that could withstand hundreds of cubic feet of oceanic pressure winked a reflection with each deliberate push forward. From each calf, her high heels swayed like out of control puppets, the straps still fastened at the ankle. Melinda had a comical intrusion at that moment that almost released a wave of laughter. Had that been Melinda on the desk, the dangling shoes with the tiny spikes for sure would have caught Marty across his face or arms. As it was, the woman seemed to have a line or two scratched into the skin that was visible. Maybe she was not a deft as her spread eagle on a desktop behavior presented.

She had captioned under the photo of her in the new dress "Surprising Hubby Early," and by the time she arrived at the office, she realized Marty could have seen the post by now and the jig of the unknown start to their night away was given up. No matter, she figured. If he saw it, he could finish what pulled him into the office at seven that morning or leave it and pack up until Monday. She delayed with a stop in the lobby powder room.

A tile floor below her had the look of wet polish, and the air a scent somewhere between flushed shit and roses. There was a quick, nervous—*why nervous?*—walk around the atrium before a return to the bank of elevators and a bypass of building security with the badge Marty had given her some time ago. The wink to the security guard didn't hurt either because surely he knew the ruse but didn't mind the attention.

"I think they all left for the day," navy polo and khaki Friday casual pants said as she passed Melinda on the way to the AIMS Mortgage office that shared the seventh floor. "Loud bunch over there."

"I was just returning a file," the unconscious words escaped from Melinda.

"Cool."

The woman disappeared behind the door that responded to her badge swipe with a beep and harsh click.

A crack opened inside Melinda. Not the pit in the stomach but a crack—a hairline, really. Just a rip along a seam. A split along the fold that had potential like a run in a nylon. Marty had planned something on his own and was at home or on his way. The worst of that was the hotel. They could arrive a little later than expected or maybe not at all. The reservation lost because Marty was not at home. His Mercedes was downstairs. The unknown woman from the shared seventh floor only *thought* they had all left. She didn't know…she thought.

Melinda waved the security card like a wand at the panel. Her door beeped too, but the clack of the lock was subdued like a real key lock and not a hammer-hitting one. The office foyer was unlit. The screensaver from the receptionist's cube ran a darkened cinema-like blue over the back wall that divided the lawyers from the receiving area.

I should wait here, she thought. *Or, better yet, go back to the car. Let him finish. Pick him up as planned.*

Melinda badged into the office area. The conference rooms to her left and right waited for their next moments. The panels of office glass were polished and looked like water. She rubbed a hand along one to be sure it was a window. The best part about this weekend— her internal monologue went on without input—is that Steve cannot mess this up. He's inaccessible, as they say. He can't call. He can't show up, and even if he slithered his way out of that place, he'd never find the hotel. The hotel that she had doubts about ever showing up at herself. But still, no Steve.

Even if the absence were temporary, she would accept the prize. There was a pinch of disappointment, though, wasn't there? It lingered like a spice from an unpleasant meal. She would have appreciated being the one who let the dogs run out the front door. She knew she had some involvement in leaving the door ajar, but the taste of being the one who held it open would have been the better remnant. To have him vanish of his own accord was still acceptable and gave a desired salutation of good riddance.

Her hand slid from glass to the textured wall. The ripples from sight should have felt like silk, but the ridges were stiff under her manicured fingers. She stopped in the office hallway. For once, Melinda felt—more than thought—no one else is *here*. She took a delicate step toward her husband's office. No one else knew where she was. A long-lost feeling and a unique vacuum to find herself in. There was liberation in that. She felt for a moment as if she were still under her hot shower.

The past months—hell, *years*—of motherhood and wifedom washed off under a moment of deliverance like used soap down the drain. Obligation was cast away unlike an old shirt not all at once but in stages like the end phase of a long cold. Not that she didn't want those things. Of course she did. But they were so present, and there was so much more. Tonight, right now, it was the man she married and her, alone, against the world. The used shirts of battle could wait. They would be back—she and Marty—to wear the clothes of routine again. Tonight, there might not be any need for clothes at all.

D

Wake up.

I just fell asleep.

You've been here all night.

It's still night?

It's time to work.

I need a minute.

You don't have a minute!

Christ on a stick, I sound just like her.

Like who?

Never mind.

Hysterical, that's what she was. Like a tourniquet that unraveled but a spew of words exploded instead of blood. She was a fountain of voice. At least he didn't say that it wasn't what it looked like. I would have puked if his apprehension would have sunk to a level of laziness that an amateur could write.

He didn't say what?

Never . . . mind.

If I've been here as long as you say, why am I so tired?

She actually was surprised.

Who?

Oh my god, Alphabet Girl. Shut up and get your sorry ass out of that bed! Goddammit, she wailed over and over again. She pillaged. A boisterous tart dressed as a pirate in a mauve dress and clodhopper shoes. She ripped a book from a shelf to the floor, and she pawed into a stack of folders like the destruction of a snowman by mitten-covered hands, layer by layer. Her lame script set in: How could you? Why? God, she defined *pathetic*.

She was shocked as if her years of careless put offs, fake ailments, and outright neglect didn't have a summation and end game. Did she skip the first day of girl school? Lesson one, ladies, if you don't provide it for him, someone else will! We've known that for a long time, haven't we, Alpha? Did she think every time had to be perfect? Not like it was her first stallion. I'm not even sure it was the second. Just enjoy the ride, sweetie, protect and reclaim what is yours.

God gave you one, two, three ways to serve and defend—four and more if you felt inclined to do a little research and take a creative stand. Oh, right. Like every guy before him always found you on the perfect day with a clean shave, minty-fresh breath, and just the right amount of man musk to get your fire burning? You don't think I know. He told me. Everything. Sometimes even in your bed. Which I liked, by the way. The haters can claim it's a high-priced air mattress, but I enjoyed fucking on it. How can you be angry at him? Or me? At least I say what I am and act the part. You—you won't even use your own body to keep domain over what you have. No woman wants it that much, even if they say they do. Just bitch up.

Seriously, every time before Marty—or *with* Marty—you wanted it? Every cock, every finger. Did you make sure he washed his hands and brushed the lunch off his teeth? Don't lie to a sister. You're either a whore or you're Little Orphan Annie. You can't be both.

Abby, who in the hell are you talking about? Are you still here?

I'm not talking, I'm . . . making up a story for your drawing book. Graphic novel. Whatever.

You are a wart. If ever I could peel you away and somehow . . .

Well, it didn't sound like a very good story.

Well, it wasn't. It had a terrible ending. A man shamed for, well, acting like a man and a woman who was astonished and angry about something she created. The lesson of Mary Shelley's monster never took hold there, I guess. Don't create that which you have no chance of controlling. I was fortunate to have still had my trench coat on. An easy escape.

You're not wearing a coat.

Well, of course I'm not. She—yes, *she*—had a coat on, and . . . oh, never mind.

Abby, you said you weren't going to hide things anymore.

And I'm not.

Well, I don't trust you.

Well, too bad.

Abby, do you have any other stories?

Sure. We'll tell one. Let's make it about the thing she hates the most.

Nope. No more questions.

I'll create, you draw.

A SORT OF DEPARTURE

41

"Mr. Coleman." Mrs. Chambliss's platform shoes clicked against the wood with a defined snap in defiance of the soft wood underfoot. Her words were a demand, neither a question nor a statement.

"Mrs. Chambliss." Below Steve's steps, the sound was the usual defeated groan. They met in the center as if on two separate staircases. "Happy Halloween."

"I thought we had that conversation already."

"We did," Steve said. "How's your family?"

"Distant," Mrs. Chambliss replied with the same snip of her shoes. "So you've been keeping something from me?"

"I don't think so."

"Your brother?" Her pencil-drawn eyebrows reached into her smooth forehead and gave a stiff underline to her pulled back hair.

"Oh, yeah," Steve said. "He's been here a few weeks."

"A few weeks?" she asked with resonance. "He said he's been up in there since before summer. You know there's no unauthorized residents allowed here. It's in your lease."

"Right." Steve drew in closer as if to share a secret. The landlady smelled of burnt wax. "Mrs. Chambliss, my brother just got out of rehab. He doesn't like saying where he's been, so he tells everyone he's been here."

"Mmhmm." There was sound, but her pink lips were still. "So if I ask your neighbor Lisa about this, she'll say the same thing?"

"Pretty sure she would."

"As do I." She straightened from the conspiratorial lean in. "Make sure he's gone by the end of the year."

"I will." Steve hugged the wall as she passed. "He's looking at a place on Elm. It's nice. One story, basement. Detached garage. Been empty a while."

"I don't care." Her back was toward Steve. "Either add him to the lease so I can amend your bill or get him out."

The glass door below closed in exclamation to her directive.

Steve noticed that Lisa had taped the same paper cutout on his door that stared at him from across the landing—a plump orange pumpkin with an even chubbier ghost oozing past the uncarved center. Against the foot of the door, a small, black cauldron held two small plastic bags of hard candy.

We used to trick or treat for beer, he reminded himself. *Me and Marty, Melinda and you.*

Steve unwrapped the purple one that stood out on top—grape. It tasted as all grape candies did, like the creators had never eaten or heard of a grape and invented a unique flavor to match the deep purple that resulted from just the right mix of red and blue dye. The sugary saliva also had no reminder of wine, another perversion of the grape but a vast improvement.

"Hey, Marty," Steve called into the apartment. "Heard you met the landlord," he said to the back of the couch, and Marty's head and had a pristine moment of de ja vu but played back through a mirror.

"Yeah, she's a piece, walking in here like she owns the place."

"Well, she kind of does."

Steve took a protein shake from the refrigerator. If his brother had replaced the beer, Steve couldn't tell. There were as many now as before but in different locations. He felt a bit of infringement on his idea of bottle replacement and repositioning which had been part of the wool Steve used on his parents and on his wife when one turned into two, into six, and then into a quick trip to the 7-Eleven to recreate the original twelve in a different shape.

"I don't think she can just walk in." Marty wore a blue T-shirt that stretched from shoulder to shoulder over his gray shorts with paint stains along the thighs. "There's laws about that." He had a beer in his hand.

"I'm sure she knocked," Steve said. "So what have you been up to?"

"Nothing," Marty replied. "Walked around a bit. Came back."

"All right." Steve put the tournament envelope on top of the mail that Marty must have left on the table after his walk. "So, Marty, what are you thinking about for Thanksgiving?"

"What!" Marty snapped. "Are you kidding me right now?"

"Marty?"

"Some kind of damn joke?"

"Man, what the hell?"

Marty dispelled Steve with a pointed exhale and a deep tug of beer.

"I'm actually asking what you were thinking of doing."

"What do you care?" Marty set the empty bottle on the counter and approached fast.

"I honestly don't," Steve said. "I was wondering if maybe you'd want to help me out with something."

"Help you?" Marty asked. "With what? Carving Cindy Lancaster's turkey and licking her pie?"

"No, we haven't even talked about…"

"Good. Cause that shit's rancid." Marty wiped his lips with a forearm. "Do you know she blew Brendan Roscoe so many times in high school, her throat must have taken the shape of his dick?"

"I don't know anything about that." A chug of vanilla slid down Steve's throat thick with a chalk outline and his own bottle was set down in opposition.

"Well, you should," Marty said. "Knowledge is power, you know."

"That was a long time ago, Marty."

Steve shuffled the junk mail into the ads and pulled two bills and another envelope that he laid on his side of the counter.

"Still," Marty said. "Bring some hand sanitizer or something."

"Come on, Marty."

"Help you. That what you say?" Marty lurched at the kitchen chair nearest him. He hovered over the seat as if lowered by a crane that was unsure of where to leave the load. "All I've done is help you."

An estimate of the number of beers that Marty drank was formulated based on his stunted movements and the slime under his voice. A looser phlegm than dairy but more persistent wore each word.

"Forget it," Steve said and finished his shake.

"I'm not sure what else I could do to possibly help you."

"I was just wondering if you'd want to help out with the team, that's all." Steve fingered the edges of some forms he would need to complete later. "We were invited to a Thanksgiving tournament, a pretty big one, and we could use an extra coach."

"Is that how you see yourself, coach?" Marty's voice turned lower. "Some kind of savior to those kids just because someone handed you a clipboard and a whistle?"

"No."

"The coach," Marty mocked. If sitting had been a question, Marty's aggressive exit from the chair was an answer that resounded with purpose. "All better now, right? Spend some time at the Holiday Inn with the padded cells. All fixed up!"

"Fixed?" Steve matched Marty on his feet.

They were two opponents across the table circling the arena for the next move.

"I fucking dare you, I dare you to fix me! You and everyone else who can walk into a food store, go to a restaurant, Christ, a gas station and not have to talk yourself out of . . . shit, scream at yourself so you don't walk out with an arm full of the only things you want. The only thing that that has made your life bearable for as long as you can remember!"

"Well, you've been making the right choices now," Marty said. "It's all a choice, right?"

"You think I chose this?"

"Most of the time, yeah, I do."

"You know who I feel sorry for?" Steve asked himself out loud. "Yourself?"

"No. All of you who've had to be around this . . . who wasted their time standing in the watchtower."

Steve knew the trail, the path that started with Brooke. She may stand at the front of the line out of importance, but in any chronology, she was the median.

"Mom, Dad, you…Cleo, who lets me come to the gym every day so I have a reason to get up and place to go. Lisa, who drops by here after dinner every night to make sure I came back. And yeah, Cindy who makes sure we stay with the coffee. Abs the only one with any sense. She disappeared."

"Who?"

"You didn't know her." Steve considered this and fought against a smile that would have taken the weight off of the late afternoon. "I didn't know her. Being me is easy, Marty."

The weight of the counter was heavy behind him, and he spoke like a seer at the end of a lesson.

"When I don't feel like fighting anymore, I'll just go up to the liquor store. Not just any one, not the Walgreens, not the quick mart, but the nice one south of the bank. The one Dad would go to and get the holiday wine and the anniversary champagne. They had those plastic fruit drink bottles we used to get when we were kids from those long coolers up front, with the ice on the inside. Had every color, you could squeeze 'em, and they'd never break, you remember? They had that little tin foil lid you could peel back."

"Yeah."

"I'd get the good stuff Marty," Steve continued. "Something they'd have to check the back for or unlock. But I'd wait. And when I was done, there wouldn't be a drop left. Everyone—*every voice*—would have their final say and would just go away. I'd wash 'em all gone. Then I'd climb that hill right outside of here and sit on those tracks and wait. I'd never have to hear another train again. Joke's on all of you."

"Nah," Marty said. "It's on me. It's always been squarely on me." He pushed his hair from his face, and his words were an oven set to broil. "You screwed up, all the time, on stage, in front of everybody. And then, you did it again! Crawling around through our backyard like some kind of vagrant. I always left you alone. Couldn't you have just done the same? Was that too much to ask? Now you, you've got a new job, a new friend," Marty said with the addition of air quotes where he felt necessary. "I screw up once—*one time*—I lose my wife, my career, I can't see my kids!" The back of Marty's fist met the table, and he tossed a folded envelope from his pocket across to Steve.

"What about your kids?" Steve scanned the letter inside with the tacit approval provided.

"Apparently," Marty said, "the court agrees with Melinda, her non–law school background, that due to my association with known criminals, I create an environment unsafe for children."

"Petition for supervised visits accepted the first Monday of January," Steve read aloud.

"They're gamblers, Steve, not killers."

"Marital dissolution with regard to serial infidelity," Steve kept reading. "Marty, what the hell?"

"So"—Marty grabbed the letter with a hand Steve didn't see coming—"I deserve this now?"

"I didn't say that."

"You don't have to." Marty tore at the letter with each word and dusted the floor with the pieces. "I'm so glad for you, that you're better now. Back and better than ever."

"I told you . . ."

"I hate you." Marty's eyes bulged like a frog been wronged. "I wouldn't throw garbage at you if you were homeless in the street."

Marty's open hands hit Steve's chest as if fired from a catapult. If his right knee had been planted, the outcome may have been different than a bruised back that just missed the pointed corner of the counter behind him. Steve was able to brace his neck so there was no impact to his head, and he saw with clarity the smooth, youthful arm that reached for him.

"So," Troy said from overhead, "I guess were not going trick or treating, Coach?"

"Just . . . yeah we're still going." Steve reached for the young boy's hand. "Help up." He took a breath with his hands on his knees, thankful the right one still felt useful. The dairy shake changed directions under his midsection but still held in place. "You need to get out," he said in Marty's direction.

"After all I've done for you?"

"You've done enough." Steve put his keys in his pocket.

The nails-on-chalkboard grimace they would make against the Mercedes was not to be heard outside of Steve's imagination. The fabricated sound itself was sweet revenge. The boy next to him did not need yet another example of how men behave. The boy needed to know there was a man who would give up this night and a hundred others to look for houses with the porch light on in search of candy, even if Mom would throw most of it out.

"You want to be left alone," Steve said at Marty. "You win."

Steve left with Troy, his arm still across the boy's shoulders.

"You okay?" Lisa asked, filling the frame of her open doorway.

"Just another day," Steve said.

42

St. Charles in and out-patient treatment facility.

Intake Survey, (partial) January 20xx

Please respond to the following statements:

10. I have in my life a family member or friend who I can count on for support upon my exit from this treatment center.

Answer: ~~Not certain~~. My brother, Marty Coleman.

Marty was the best man at the wedding. He was the first to arrive, the last to leave, and punctuated the bookends with a rousing toast that summarized the glossy, kind, and visible moments of Steve's life, from childhood onward in three garrulous, drunken minutes. Marty's face puffed with sweat he wiped with a sleeve of bowered polyester and sweated some more. Two family members laid a silent glass of cold beer on the lectern beside him, but he ignored both.

The summer day was oppressive like calculus. You knew what was coming, showed up anyway, and were beaten back by arcane formulas of relative heat ratings that were indifferent to the kind of clothing you wore or the amount of water you drank. Astute midwestern preparedness and a church air conditioner at the top of its game did nothing to erase the dense cloak of drowned atmosphere that seemed to land at sunrise and clung to life until dusk.

"Here you go." Marty pinched the top back into place but left the flask on the table. Steve took the half-filled solo cup and set it down, caught between another indecisive removal and put back on of his tuxedo coat.

"Leave it on," Marty said. "You're going out in ten minutes."

"It's just hot, dude," Steve said. "I'm sautéing in here."

"You're going to wrinkle the back," Marty said, pulling Steve's jacket forward onto the shoulders. "Drink this." Marty handed Steve back the cup and sipped on his own.

"You were supposed to bring back water."

"This is more interesting," Marty said. "Scotch. Twelve-year age on this bitch. Christ, why do you smell like an old man."

"I used Dad's aftershave this morning. You should have stayed over last night."

"I couldn't."

Steve took a long sip from the solo cup. "Brooke said she didn't want us drinking before the wedding. I've been good for three days."

"Well, that's three days better than me." Marty finished his drink in a flourish and put the cup back next to the flask. "First tenet of marriage…what the wife doesn't see . . . doesn't happen."

"All right, all right." Steve placed his empty cup on the other side of the flask and felt the alcohol churn across his lips and drip down to his stomach. Its carnal relief was like a professional masseuse had taken over the care of his insides. "So that's your big wedding-day advice, little brother?"

"Yeah." Marty finished his second and filled each cup again. He returned the flask to the inner James Bond pocket of his tux.

"Marty . . ." Steve took the cup anyway.

"What? It's not the first time we ever had a drink down here," Marty said. "One of the perks to being the youth group leader was having the keys to the basement."

"The Cavallini sisters?"

"Yeah, that's right. Over there, where there used to be a couch."

The lower narthex had been modernized and expanded from what Marty had remembered. Sunday school classes once divided by heavy curtains that refused to be pulled cleanly about their runners had been replaced by popup half walls that were in ironic contrast to locking doors on each room. The meeting area, designated for teenagers where the Coleman side of the wedding party had been directed to set up camp, was now painted a strained white and was devoid of furniture, save for eight or ten desks with C-shaped legs and attached seats.

Each station was equipped with a quartet of device charging squares and a flat screen television gripped to the ceiling above like a climber on a dangerous cliffside. The paltry, almost closet looking room with two long couches, folding chairs and a cabinet stereo in constant need of repair that once served as a getaway in younger days, was erased by the improvement.

"I watched," Steve said. "There was a lot going on."

"You thought there was a mess of hair on top of them," Marty laughed. "It was like feeling around for the sweet spot on a Chia Pet."

"You don't have to remind me. I can still see it from here." Steve drained another cup and under the lost tally of the second, third, or fourth, he allowed the blip of bachelor party that sat astride the coattails of the nuptial to play on. "You always did end up with the easy ones."

"Hey, I offered you a trade," Marty said. "Thirty seconds before, we could have switched."

"What, and deprive myself of the world's most uncomfortable hand job?"

"Right." Marty downed another. "I fucking remember she didn't even take your shorts off. Went right up the leg and gave it a tug."

"Several hundred tugs," Steve said. "I guess she figured her eyes were still pure that way, but that hand . . ."

Marty was in a full disheveled upheaval now.

"When you got home, you had to keep that book across your crotch. It looked like you sat on a carton of eggs."

"Wrong night for khaki shorts."

"Man, those were good days," Marty slapped Steve on the shoulders.

"They're long over now."

"Just wish there could have been more."

"At least we had them, right? Some brothers don't get any."

"Yeah."

"You know," Marty said, "I always thought it would be you and—"

"I know, I know." Absently, Steve twisted the sides of his bow tie. "But it's not."

In another room, a much more pleasant space was filled with the subdued matrimonial countdown of hair, makeup, dresses, and shoes.

"Didn't we toast to her some night?" Marty continued in the groomsmen's cove.

"Yeah, like a thousand years ago."

"I don't even know where the hell we were," Marty said. "Future sister-in-law."

"Yeah, it just didn't work out," Steve said. "But this, this is good."

There was a rap at the door, and it opened without invitation.

"Hey, guys!" Freddie entered. Trailing, as if in position to climb aboard his back was a dark woman in a dress so yellow, the color beamed outside the fabric. Her hair was taut to the point of looking painful, and a jade emblem was a submarine deep beneath her cleavage.

"Hey!" a duplicate reply greeted Freddie and his guest.

"You guys remember Paula."

"Couldn't forget."

Steve and Marty volleyed their surprise between them, eye-speak that only brothers had.

"Sorry we couldn't make it to the rehearsal," Paula said.

"No," Steve replied. "Just glad you guys are here."

"My wife Melinda is up front on the left," Marty offered. "You should sit with her."

"Thank you." Paula kissed Freddie on the cheek and sent him forward with a nudge against his rump. "Well, I'll leave you to your groomsmen duties."

"Looking good there, Frederick," Steve said. "Where's Dani?"

"Ah, just needed a change of pace this weekend."

"Want a little warm-up?" Marty drew the flask, a blade from a sheath, and took another solo cup from the top of the overturned stack.

"You know it." Freddie emptied the cup as soon as it was full. "Paula and her sisters are training for a half marathon. She's on her third detox in the last six weeks."

"You don't live with her," Marty chided. "Just do what you want, man."

"Trying to be supportive, you know." Freddie waved his already-drained cup at Marty for another.

"Yeah, that." Marty obliged the empty cup. "And she looks like a porn star."

"Probably bangs like one too," Steve added.

"Got that right." Freddie finished another. "She makes spaghetti squash and pesto sauce worth it. You guys ever had that?"

There was a dual negative.

"It tastes like dishwater rung through an old sock. Stevie, I know it's your wedding and all, but if you could blow through the formalities and get us to that buffet dinner, I'd really appreciate it."

"And don't forget the open bar," Steve said.

You really didn't say that did you? You had no reason to because . . .

"Hey," Marty, now with two pencil-thin glass flutes, said, "I'll probably be drunk later or just mess it up anyway, so before all of that . . ."

Marty passed one empty glass to Steve and lifted his own.

"Everybody full?"

Steve, Freddie, and a small crowd of others agreed that they were with a unified nodding of similar empty glasses.

"I just wanted to say, to my brother, congratulations and the best of everything."

Steve drove a cautious look to his left and right, uninvited at an event he knew by heart.

"And a thousand curses on Frederick Hagen who gets to walk down the aisle with the hot sister," Marty said behind yet another solo cup full of Scotch. The shake of the nearly drained flask from his other hand sounded like a wet cowbell.

"Hey, isn't your hot *pregnant* wife out there?" Freddie tossed his cup in the nearby trash can. "What are you looking around for?"

Marty laughed under the gush of yet another drink.

"Yeah," Steve said. "Marty gets a free pass on that one."

Steve conceded the point at this juncture, as usual, allowing Marty to continue the ruse. His boisterous fantasy a cover for his very public and pronounced fear of sharing the same saddle with long-ago trespassers.

"Why's that?" Freddie asked.

"He has a little thing for single moms," Steve lied. "Both the sisters have a kid."

A sudden urge to check his pockets overcame Steve, and he frisked along his trousers. Keys and wallet were accounted for. As suspected, his phone was missing. He spoke in spurts, as he patted his body up to and through his suit coat and distracted himself with another thought. "Brooke is the best of the lot. Says she comes from a long line of afterthoughts."

"Into single moms, huh, Marty?" Freddie asked.

"True story."

"Bud, if they have enough kids, you won't even hit the sides."

"But still, you have to consider them if they're cute, lonely, and, hey, there's a track record that says they put out."

A cloud the size of the sky covered the sun. The miniature windows along the top basement walls flashed to black like an overhead light bulb had reached a sudden end.

"We almost forgot. We need to toast Mom and Dad."

"Okay, but we can do that later," Steve said. "We need to get going."

And Marty was no longer in his tuxedo, size 42 regular that had been rented like a prom suit from the formal wear shop in town. He stood frozen, a stone with open eyes still lingering in the direction of the escaped medusa, a satisfied grin of booze etched across his lips. His stiff fingers gripped the red plastic cup left behind from the church picnic.

Steve's cup hit the floor, and it rang hollow with an empty false bounce. He studied the odd roll that circular items have as the cup traced its circle but could not veer from the heavier center.

"You're not going to want to look under there."

Steve looked up at the voice that belonged to Brooke's father, coming from a man who could have passed for a smaller, younger

John Candy. A week before, it had been Larry from the Three Stooges and before that former Bears quarterback Jim McMahon.

"But you always do." The figure stepped aside and allowed Brooke to climb the short, felt-looking steps at the church altar. The steps were correct, firm green, like the shorn edges of a billiard table, and the enamel-satin ballerina slippers she didn't wear that day glided across the top as if she no longer had to take steps to move.

But the dress was wrong. That was how you know, every time— the dress.

The moment she was there, you look for the top of the dream. The ladder that must be left behind so you can be extracted from the pit. The narthex was empty, and you had a clear view down each side and the center. The left and right aisles, abandoned and dark, where childhood Easter and Christmas processionals were once made in blousy choir robes, white with red trim, Steve on one side and Marty always on the other. But the center filled in where not John Candy, not Larry, and not McMahon escorted Brooke in a sheer white bridal gown that floated just over the top of her knees. When she appeared like she was doing now, in the long shawl with the opaque veil over her face, you looked behind you for the reverend who was never there and each side door would shut into place with the crash of an anvil that you knew would take a hundred men to push open.

"Don't go," Brooke says. The veil caught a draft, a draft because it couldn't have been a breath and it floated upon waves at the underside.

Steve thumped into the communion rail behind him. It was wood again today but had been barbed wire before.

"You're the one who left." These were not the words Steve would have chosen, but they were next in the loop. Some of the setting would change, but the script would never deviate.

"It will be different this time." Brook passed a burdensome corsage, with roots suctioned on the stems to her left, as if she could see someone on the periphery, but single-mom sister, maid or matron, was never there. The flowers fell into the floor and like small snakes, the ends of each flower searched for the earth. Dirty fingers tore at the bottom of the veil. Small reflexes—jittery like they would rather pull down or scratch at the cloth instead of lifting it so it could be removed *right now* from a tight-fitting scab.

"Brooke, you don't have to."

"I do," Brooke would say then. It would be the last sound she would make.

43

There was a scene near the end of the first *Indiana Jones* film that Steve had not ever forgotten and would partially relive for the rest of his life. He wondered if the movie still meant as much to Marty as it did to him. It was one of three times he and Marty would be at the theater with both their mother and father. The first was the original *Star Wars*, which he had been too young to fully embrace and the last was the much maligned *Rocky V* when he was older and could still feel reverberations of his mother's slurred speech, de-fucking-manding that they take her to see a movie that day.

Her mother had died two weeks before, and when she half recovered from a bout of grief steeped like a tea bag in a vat of Jack Daniels, Dad relented after she promised to not serve Frosted Flakes for dinner the next week and drove them to the show in Orchard Park—fucking Orchard Park.

"Don't let them take it from me, Stevie," their mother would say. "Remember all those times I helped you hide and protected you."

The new era of their family began right there—Mom at the left next to Steve, Dad at the right next to Marty—beneath the afternoon matinee glow, sharing in the dissolution of a family and a film franchise that were both once considered hopeful.

The moment near the end of the Jones film, where the angel rises from the dust, only to drip into the form of a lich, was Brooke slowly emerging from under her veil. The cloth peeled back as she shed the cotton skin. But the nightmares and dreamscapes skipped the first part and went right to the skull. Instead of glowing with the magic of Spielberg's mesmerizing angel, Brooke stood there as if someone had dug her from the ground and did not trouble themselves with removing the mud, grass, and earthworms that still believed they were alive.

Fingers more bone than flesh held the veil like a used handkerchief, the tricky silk made the grip ambiguous. Sometimes she would wave it like the white flag of surrender that gave the monster acquiescence to eat her from the inside. Her jaw had rounded edges where it pretended parts of her face must still be attached.

Her bones reached forward for his arm, but it was his legs that were afire. Steel wool rubbed the front and backsides. A thousand mosquitoes all at once in voracious descent.

* * * * *

Steve woke with a scream. In waking recovery, on the couch, from the first afternoon nap he had taken in nearly half a year, his first thought was a hope that the shout was not as loud as it sounded behind his eyes. His legs were propped across, feet still with athletic shoes, on top of the coffee table. He moved, but even when his legs were back on the floor or as sure as he could be, he still felt as if his shoes had been replaced by stilts and his bones by chipped ice.

"No!"

He lashed out for the red plastic cup that was also on the table. He smelled it but couldn't decipher. A taste reminded him—iced tea. The same stand-in directors used to replicate whiskey on camera and the same kind that had been part of his own ruse from time to time in the past, whispering against his lips. Tepid, room temperature, but sill a relief.

He felt the blood escape back into his legs as he stood and drifted into a waddle. The muscles, tendons, and whatever was left inside jockeyed for position as his legs reclaimed the correct shape in a massage of invisible fingers and the tea found the bottom of the sink. No cars in the park lot below. A train that would have been a godsend five minutes prior rolled another strike into the brick-and-wood frame of the exterior.

"Marty!" The green digits on the countertop microwave were at two thirty. "You sick, sorry bastard, I'm going to the gym."

227

Steve's voice bounced against the dry wall.

The release of tension in the weeks since Marty had been gone made the apartment larger as if stress and angst alone possessed the power to suck air from the corners of the rooms, which Steve supposed on some level, they did. Each expansive and contractive whack from the whines of building settlement were like the sound of a wood bat against a ball that beat the place back into shape. It was a reminder that sometimes—*things*—which should have no right to express the way they felt about certain choices you made, did reach up and have an opinion.

Was that a paradox? Irony? Steve tossed the ideas around, a sphere of flour crust in his mind. Like when someone tells you that silence has become deafening. Like a house that cares if you sell it or not. Did the house do this to Steve and Marty? *No* was his answer.

Steve looked again at the folder of permission slips on the table, where he did not leave them, before the nap he never intended to take. His mind rolled in unspoken words. The old apartment is not really engaged in knocking back at the corners that Steve and his brother eroded, the house did not tip an axis that it did not know existed. Things happened, good and bad, *to* and *at* the house and in this very apartment. Nothing occurred *because* of them. Corrosion is just present and will be a part of these rooms long after Steve is gone.

No, it won't be. The room is just a room, and it does not care who or what is in it. It is a box in a larger box with a roof. The rooms of our lives neither feel nor think, and neither do they act with nor in deference to us. Just like the folder of permission slips that Steve needed to take to gym. They did not care if they ever were turned in. And the folder did not have—though Steve could see and could have felt them if he dared—two small lines of dirt in the shape of fingers across the top. The thumbprint of the hand that laid it on the table would be on the underside.

That the folder had been out of sight for the past few days did not concern Steve. It just needed to be taken to the gym and placed with the team equipment now that it had been found/returned.

A walk was chosen over the bike. Steve withdrew from this constant companion gradually instead of the sudden break that was garnered for the other. At first, it was every other day until the summer when it became every third day, and as fall phased in and out of the approaching winter, riding everywhere was a memory. The bike would be back in the garage like a relic, but the exchange would not have to be made tonight.

The old bike had a look about it like a dog that wanted a walk, another object that cared if it still belonged or not. A pat against the seat gave credence to the exchange of regret between the two.

"All right, old friend," he almost said as he closed the door. "Some other time."

The sound of the other door, a second or two behind his, gave the noise an odd and equal echo.

"Hey." Steve adjusted the backpack he had already put into place.

"Hey, you," Lisa said. She accepted the gesture from Steve and went ahead of him down the stairs.

"Lisa, listen," Steve said from behind. "I'm sorry again that Troy didn't make the travel roster."

"Steve . . ."

"It's just that as good as he got and as hard as he worked, the other kids came along too."

"Don't you think I know that? I've seen the games." Lisa held the lower door for him. "It will just make him work harder. What you've done for him, it can't be undone."

The brisk November air added a twine of vapor to her words, and her glasses fogged against the shift from false heat to real cold.

"He's more confident in school than he's ever been. I told you last week this is the first year I haven't had to bail him out of PE class with a pretend doctor's note or a last-minute phone call."

"I know, but . . ."

"Not everybody can make the team," she said. "Sometimes a no is better gift than a yes, especially for a boy. Makes the yeses more valuable."

Her glasses returned from a wipe down, and she pulled her gloves on.

"Look, I have the four to midnight today . . ."

"Don't worry, I'll keep an eye on him when I get back. I shouldn't be long."

"Thank you, but," Lisa said with a gloved hand on the breast of his jacket, "what I was going to say is that Thanksgiving at my place starts at one, and if you're still up and want to come over for some cider after the late shift, feel free."

"That sounds good," Steve said. "Can we have it in a wine glass this time?"

"I'll think about it." A thin wafer smile reached for more but withdrew in deference to teeth that still rooted part of her to the past. "And thanks. Troy will appreciate the company."

"If you need anything between now and then, just let me—"

"Steve?" She stopped mid-step as if her legs had quit but did not consult with the rest of her. "Did you ever shake? I mean, have the . . . shakes . . . when you would, you know . . ."

Never are the power of words more relevant as when they remind with bouts of silence the depths from which you were dragged.

"Yeah." The admission galloped upon the stream of his exhale.

"So did I," Lisa said, her eyes bored to the pavement below. "Like a frozen ragdoll whenever he—whoever *he* was—was gone. I couldn't . . . I wouldn't be alone. I would . . . my body would . . . rage with fear and anger and revulsion until he got back. And I didn't care what he did with me . . . to me."

"Lisa . . ."

"Night after night, fist after fist. It was an addiction. Nobody gets that. It's not that I didn't want to, it's that I couldn't. And it didn't matter what was keeping me from being alone, as long as somebody—*anybody*—was touching me, kissing me, or punching me, keeping a larger darkness at bay. What you must think of me."

He placed his hands under her elbows and lowered her hands, holding her at first like a brother would a sister and them around her back like a partner who was clinging to the last song.

"You don't ever have to say that," he whispered. He steadied himself against her and believed his own voice for the first time in nearly thirty years. "Night after night, drink after drink—it was an addiction. Nobody gets that. It didn't matter that everyone was mad and begging at me, as long as something—*anything*—was keeping the larger darkness away. You never have to worry about what I think of you."

* * * * *

I made peace with you, wherever in this world you ended up. I don't mean ended up like where you are at the moment. In our age of connectedness, I can estimate your location is within the reaches one or two distant metropolitan areas, which is of itself surprising, as I never figured you would land anywhere other than under the shadow of the city where we grew up and eventually met. A city that would have carried us on its broad shoulders if we would have let it. But I don't know what became of you.

Your small hands that interlocked with mine. Your face, the cradle of your lips that kissed me, and your eyes that knew me. Your body that you said I earned and you were willing to give. And your mind, the parts that you would share, so beautiful and kind. What became of that? Were passions fulfilled? Were your goals unlocked? Were heartbreaks requited? I can assure you here, no matter how much you thought you had wanted it—wanted us to persist—you would have been disappointed.

I know now what you were. There is a reason why first love, the domain of the poets and songsmiths, never runs dry. It is not because it was real or was meant to be, but the opposite. First love lingers because it has the role of remainder, the leftovers from an equation that cannot be balanced—a nagging small piece from behind that inoculates us from the pursuit of what we do not want.

We met, like most young loves do, in medias res, at the center of the web. We were studying, friending the old-fashioned way, experimenting, growing, playing with the same fervor as we were trying to love. The flame that rages is as quick to die as the one that stumbles out of the gate. The fire that smolders is the one that will last. The fire that is consistent, tended to, looked after, fed, compromised with—that is the one that brings the ships back to harbor. It's also what makes first love both a cherished novelty and a beast of burden. An invasion of a space that has already been pillaged and conquered.

At first, the new shape is carried about, introduced to holes in the maze into which it was never meant to fit. It spends time in the boxes marked as Family, School, Friends, Hobbies, *craving purchase. But even the most astute peddler cannot close the sale. The new shape permeates the others but cannot find a home. Two choices arise—the other shapes can all conform to the new or the unique one changes into all of them. Neither one works because you don't choose your new man or woman over your friends, family, school, work. And the new shape— with its own needs, wants, and goals—is beyond being included with the others. "I'm the new man or woman, she or he should want to spend more time with me rather than with friends, family, school, work."*

So the decision is clear. You take neither path and just love. And burn. And we loved and loved.

My memories of you have been filled for so long with anger, vitriol misdirected at a person I forgot I knew, extended from a person that I wish I never became. You did not deserve those thoughts, the bastardization of our moments together. I know why we break up. Funny how when I think about it now, I place it in the future-present tense as if I see it still ahead of me rather than behind. Like I know what is coming and not seeing what had passed.

The reflections of school dances, summer fireworks, trips to the beach, and dinners out or in that freeze-frame us in a still, just off the past, are crooked to me—benign thoughts of you, forever jaded with the madness that was around the next turn. There were times when I was alone, and I'll admit it, when I was married too, that I went looking for those two kids. In the alleyways of dreams, in fits of morning wakefulness, I'd tell them to fight through, become that which is predictable, routine, and real. Survive! But those two, much like us, dared the monster in the corner because we could outrun it, we would outlast it.

We'd look up and see the danger had vanished in our wake, and I looked at you and you looked at me, and we had become perfect mirrors. Even as the monster gazed back at its own reflection, we never told each other what we really saw.

"Hey, Darrell," Steve called ahead into the empty gym.

The retracted rims and backboards were stretched into impossible yoga positions high above at each end. From their view, Steve looked like a merchant versus an angry sack as he pulled a lopsided net full of basketballs across the court.

"Hey, Steve." Darrell locked a cabinet and tossed Steve the set of keys. "You find them forms yet?"

"Yeah," Steve said. "Just scanned and sent them. Hiding in plain sight, I guess."

"Funny how things do that."

"Speaking of hiding," Steve found the locker room key among the others on the bracelet-sized ring. "Have you seen Cleo?"

"He's not up front?"

"Nah. He could be out back. I'll see him before I go." Steve ended the struggle and let the bag fall on the floor. He walked toward the locker rooms, the key extended like a short staff. "So you ready for the weekend?"

"I will be," Darrell said. "Good news for me is that Thanksgiving dinner at my aunt's is tonight."

"Early, huh?"

"Yeah. The family is mostly split working retail or in hospitals." Darrell looked at his phone that flashed a message. "I understand folks getting sick and needing help and all, but who wants to buy socks or a TV on Thanksgiving afternoon?"

"Got me," Steve said.

"I mean *in* my socks and in front of a TV, I'll take that."

"Yeah that sounds better," Steve said. "I hope it's great."

"My aunt's the best cook in the family. No matter if its Thanksgiving, Christmas, or Tuesday like tomorrow."

"Well, all right."

"You ready?"

"Yeah," Steve said. "Just need to pick up a few things at home. I'll see you tomorrow afternoon then?"

"I'll be here."

Steve pulled the heavy door closed. Cleo's snub-nosed sedan was the lone car in the tar-and-gravel lot. The car was black with entrails of winter spit along the lower panels and tires. The dented grillwork at the front, dental braces with missing teeth, was a frozen grimace that hung between the headlights. The early winter evening was at the crossroad of day and night, the uncertain sky in a shift from burgeoning rain to snow.

"Come on, Cleo, you can drive me home," Steve said to no one as he went back to the locker room.

He patrolled the rows and tossed a towel into a hamper. Steve hadn't seen Cleo on the first pass through the lobby as he turned for the basketball courts instead of the front desk. The locker room door opened into the rear of the reception area, behind the desk, and Cleo was out of sight from the other side on the floor below. He looked crumpled as if he had been a toy played with and forgotten about.

"Cleo, shit." Steve held a finger under the man's nose and felt a faraway breath. "Shit, shit, shit, Darrell!"

He knew his assistant coach had left but filled the seconds between his drop to the floor to cradle Cleo's head in his lap and calling the appropriate three numbers on his phone with the loud shout.

"Does he have family nearby?" an ambulance driver unknown to Steve asked him.

Cleo's head was a fixed beacon against the pale white sheets of the stretcher. Two other members of the medical team secured Cleo with a slight bounce into the back end.

"Yeah," Steve said. "A daughter . . . somewhere. Maybe it's in his emergency contacts. I'll go see."

"You know where his phone is?" the driver asked.

"Don't have one."

"All right, look," the driver said to Steve, "we'll be at Memorial West. If you find something, bring it."

"Just wait a minute, I don't drive."

Later, Steve remembered he said *don't* instead of *can't*.

"I'll be right back!"

"Sir, we can't wait, we need to take him now." The driver rushed to the front side. "Memorial West. Just follow behind, however you can, if you want."

The taillights contracted into a perspective point, and the screech of the siren followed like fumes into the night.

Cleo had left his personal keys at the front desk next to the house phone. The message light flashed in a steady three-beat pulse, but whoever had left word at the gym for someone about something would have to wait. Drawers held gum, mints, pencils, and day passes to the fitness center. Clipboards of league roster sheets were stacked in threes across the desk like homework waiting to be organized. A snow globe of dust recirculated from the heating vent overhead, swarmed like flies around Steve.

"Really?" Steve asked the locked steel two-drawer filing cabinet where the employee files would be.

"How long have I known this guy?" Steve quizzed the hollow lobby. "I should just know."

He turned back to the desk for Cleo's car keys. An index card with deliberate male handwriting showed an edge from under the calendar—"Felicia Turner," with a number underneath. Steve quickly thought if Cleo had ever mentioned his daughter's name and found a resounding no; and he was even more surprised that if that was her, they had never met. They had a good chance at being around the same age. He kicked again at his memory, which replied with a blank stare. He folded the card anyway and put it in his pocket where the keys to Cleo's car now were.

"*You have to go,*" a voice not his said as he shook the keys forth.

He wished it didn't, but the main door from the street opened and closed. In his haste, Steve had neither turned the welcome sign around nor had put the lights out behind him.

"Hey, we have to close," Steve said to the empty space ahead of him.

"*You were always a shitty driver anyway,*" Brooke said.

She was next to him but transparent. Her voice was chopped liked a distant radio signal.

"All right." This was not the first drive he had planned for, but he bolted from the gym as if late for an interview. "Make sure nothing happens," he called toward the closing door.

"*I can't,*" Now it was Brooke who spoke to the empty lobby. "*Oh, never mind.*"

Steve sprinted from the gym lobby to Cleo's car, but once seated inside, slow and then stop motion took hold.

The keys achieved entry into the ignition, and the click toward idiot lights was made then retracted. He pounded a fist into the steering wheel.

"Damn."

He looked into the rearview. Nothing but the night. Not the back end of Marty's driveway in the summer, not Melinda and a concealed jar of strawberry jam ready to break across the pavement as Steve dropped the car into reverse.

"*You're just going to have to go.*" Brooke placed her hand over the floor shift on tops of Steve's.

"I can't." Steve eased the ignition off. "This isn't the way I wanted to drive again or where I wanted to go."

"*Not everything is delivered the way we want.*"

"Brooke, don't you think I know . . ."

"*Sometimes, things and people are taken from us so we can focus on what we need to do, no matter how hard it hurts.*" She put her hands into her coat pockets as if searching for gloves. "*This is not that moment. But your friend might need you to be there.*"

"That's where they took you." Steve's eyes drilled ahead as if already on the road. "That hospital."

"*Because we lived ten minutes from there. Not because everything in life has some grand need to be connected.*" She knocked on the driver-side window with a gloved hand.

Steve pushed the key enough so the window could be pushed down.

"But this isn't about me, and it's not so much about you."

"Can you make sure everything is all right?" Steve asked.

"*No,*" Brooke said. "*But you can. I'll see you later, just like we planned, okay?*"

"Yeah."

The sedan's engine whirred into a high-pitched life.

"I'm gonna back up now."

"*Ooh,*" she laughed. "*I better get out of the way.*"

"Brooke . . ."

"*Sorry,*" she said. "*Couldn't resist. Go!*"

45

You're going to try and pretend you don't remember the automatic doors that sounded faster than they parted. It was almost as if the whoosh was programmed to distract the entrant from the languid procession of the wheel and pulley. The atrium had a Vegas-style carpet that kept your sight trained up and forward toward posters with healthy multicultural models under block letters that reminded us what not to do and end up back here for treatment of some sort—the familiar and expected display about smoking was next to the one of the family with the crop-haired adolescent off to the side in a hazy field of violet (the meth warning), and further down was the suggestive one of the young couple reminding us to be safe while they pressed their noses together, both with a concealed pack of condoms behind their backs like bouquets.

Potted plants—there were fifty, one from each state—lined the visible halls in three directions, and a piece of high art made of pipes twisted and overlapped over one another called *Free* stood center about thirty feet in front of a main desk. You don't need the information desk because you know how to take the third hallway through the double doors and hope you can close your mind's eye as it dares you to look into the first room on the left once inside and not see Brooke in a bed that you know was not hers.

It looks like she's sleeping your mother would say, but it was not rest. It was decay. Her body was flaking like a peel of a sunburn, but instead of refurbishing under the wasted skin, the cavities were left unattended. Clear tubes from her arms made evil marionettes of the slim poles around her bed. Knowing looks and pats on the back from doctors and nurses degenerated just as Brooke did. They had a pitch of comfort at the start, but near the end just reconfirmed that everyone else had already accepted what was coming and were waiting on you to jump aboard.

"Sir, can I help you?"

No, you can't help me. My wife, you see, was in here. But she's gone now. She was released after a round of treatment that turned out to be more devastating than the disease. On the couch at home, she told me she was anticipating a return in seven days to have yet another dunk into a pool of toxins masquerading as respite, but her body had not been willing to pursue the irony any further, and the travesty expired in the hallway between our couch and the bathroom.

"Sir?" The round nurse in a pink overlay repeated.

"Yes?" Steve uttered.

Her head caromed against the woodwork that we meant to refinish or remove someday. She bled. Did you know a corpse could bleed? I found the first aid kit under the sink, cleaned and tended the wound, and thought she may need a thicker bandage at one point but then—

"Do you need something?"

I moved her to the bed and had a drink. Right next to her. I stepped into a void, an orison to stop the day or set into rewind what could not be reversed. On television, there would be baseball. Outside, there would be family picnics. A distant lawn mower called with a steady roar. It was a bourbon with little ice, then another, then no ice, then no glass. That had hit the closet door in our—now my—room an hour or so ago. Brooke, me, and a bottle of booze on the bed. See, nothing has changed.

"Cleo," Steve said. "Cleo Washington. I need to see him."

"He was just admitted."

Steep manicured nails ticked on a keyboard below her.

"What you'll need to do is have a seat." She pointed with a nodded head to a bank of cloth and plastic chairs.

"Oh, here." Steve pushed the folded index card toward the nurse. "Paramedics were looking for a daughter's name and number. I think this is it."

"We'll check it out."

"Thanks." Steve added his hands back to his pockets. He felt the foreign keys next to the apartment's. "When I can see him, just let me know."

"That's what we do."

Steve found a corner with the least amount of company and grabbed the top magazine.

"You mind if the game's on?" a man in a paint-spotted forest-green work uniform asked as he directed the remote at the television. "Bulls got Cleveland tonight. That's where I'm from."

A young woman in jeans and canvas Vans shoes worked her crossed leg like the handle on a water pump in the chair opposite from Steve. Her red stained eyes were set forward, and her hands rubbed upward against her chin. Her greasy hair, the color of a latte, folded at the ends over her shirt collar.

"Just like Chicago, you know," the man in the work uniform rolled on like play had been pushed, "got a lakefront, a skyline. Maybe I'll go back there some day."

The television was on but muted.

The woman's jeans chafed in the background as she switched legs again, but most of the noise in the waiting room came from a police officer rolling the top of a fast food bag as he strolled from one entry door to the other across the emergency room. A radio chattered from his shoulder.

"Mr. Washington," a nurse said from the desk and waved.

It took her two tries to bring Steve forward.

"Coleman," Steve said. "It's Coleman."

"You here for Washington?"

"Yeah."

"Daughter's on her way." She passed the folded card over the desk. "Thanks for passing this along. No wallet no phone—she'd been hard to find. Good thing you was there."

"Is he okay?"

"He's slowing down." The nurse folder her hands. "You want to go back and see him?"

"Sure."

"Number 6." She stood and pointed.

Behind Steve, the young woman in the jeans had been joined by two men in patched leather jackets. Her fingers sprayed venom into whatever text message she was sending. The man in the work uniform was gone.

"Thank you." Steve slid the index card back into his pocket. "Oh, here." As if in exchange or barter, he passed Cleo's keys to the nurse. "These are his."

"I'll see that she gets them."

The same beep that chimed for Brooke bounced over Cleo. The pulse of the heart monitor was offset from the key and rhythm of the patient behind the curtain for number 5. One tube ran from an IV bag to his arm. Wires that seemed plugged into his chest connected his body to a computer.

"Hey." Steve stood at an angle near the foot of the bed.

"I told you I didn't want to go to the tournament."

"It's all right. Just like you said, we got this," Steve said. "You'll go next year."

"Two years in a row? With that team?" Cleo cleared his throat. "Now I know you still ain't right."

"Your daughter is on her way."

Steve considered the dimensions of the room with his eyes and noticed Cleo doing the same. A bent index finger tapped to the absent drone of his heart monitor, reaching up after each down stroke in hopes of the next to follow.

"Spend Thanksgiving talking about heart surgery and recovery options." Cleo's gnarled voice had returned. "Don't seem fair."

"Could be worse."

"She's just reached the point where she doesn't have to take care of her kids every day." Cleo strained against an elbow to lift but thought better of it. "Now her old man might be moving in."

"If she's anything like her old man, she won't mind."

Steve pulled the tissue-thin gown from under Cleo's side, but it didn't seem to provide any comfort.

"How does that figure?"

"Cause her old man never passes up an opportunity to care about someone else."

"You know I'm not one of those . . ." Cleo stopped like he had fallen in a hole.

Steve looked to the small screen for visual evidence that Cleo was still present in spite of the nagging chirp that had become the sound of raindrops during a storm.

"Drunks." The old man's voice returned with a vengeance. "I won't be all preachy up on you and telling anyone who will listen about my recovery and how I've never had another drop. I've had my drops. We all do. Just 'cause you visit the mistress don't mean you sleep over."

Steve's thoughts drifted to Marty and Melinda and how fucked their Thanksgiving might be in comparison before the deep voice below him pulled him back.

"But I've had good days," Cleo continued. "Hell, good years. Even started to kick the fried food habit last couple of 'em. I guess at the end, it's too late. Could I have some water?" A productive cough erupted.

It took Steve some seconds to realize Cleo was asking him.

"Sure." Steve filled a small paper cup from the pitcher behind him.

"You know, they say youth is wasted on the young." The few sips slayed the loose hacking for now. "More like, moderation, thoughtfulness, and logic are wasted on the old. Guess it don't really matter what I do now."

"It all matters, Cleo."

"Come here."

Steve could only shuffle a half step closer until his knees felt the edge of the bed, but he obeyed.

"There's a box, a cigar box just like your picturing," Cleo said, "in my locker at the gym. There's enough in it for all the boy's families to come down with the team, stay in that nice hotel, have dinner . . . I was gonna give it to you tonight."

"Cleo," Steve said, stopping him. "Come on, you're going to need that. I should bring it here."

"For what?" Cleo asked. "So I can go golfing in my retirement? Ride on in some damn hot air balloon? Maybe I'll fly to Paris and sip wine or, better yet, pick up the trombone and play in one of those noisy elderly jazz quartets? No one is going to applaud for me out of pity. Maybe now that my kids are grown, I can finally learn to skydive? You think I'm gonna do any of that?"

"No, sir."

"Then you buy them gas, food, clothes—anything they need. I'm doing do my part," Cleo said. "Don't matter how late it is. You call each and every one of them families starting with the ones who can't afford to go the most, and you make sure that those kids don't spend Thanksgiving on the road alone. You hear me?"

Steve nodded in agreement.

"You know," Steve said. "You were wrong about something."

"Oh, was I?"

"Yeah."

Steve adjusted the blanket again and took the empty cup from Cleo's grip.

"You weren't the best coach I had growing up. I needed someone better, someone stronger." Steve fought for the words over a flow of tears that were waiting. "You were the one I needed now. And that's how I know you can't die tonight."

"Go do your job." Cleo's lids hobbled into place and shut over yellow where there should be white, and black where there should be a color. "I've done mine."

The first person Steve noticed in the waiting area was the young woman in the jeans. Her canvas shoes had joined her in the chair, and she held her knees as if clutching a stuffed bear in her sleep. The leather-clad near twins were gone, but one of the jackets was draped over her like a cape. The second person in the room called out to him.

"Steve!"

"Freddie?"

"I was out in the Heights," Freddie said, silencing his side radio. "I came as soon as I could. What happened?"

"Heart attack or something." Steve rubbed his shirt over where his teachers had said his heart was.

"Is he all right?"

"Yeah," Steve said. "He is. I think he fell asleep. His daughter is on the way. You could probably go back and see him. You're uniform and all. They'd let you through."

"Nah, if he's resting," Freddie said. "I'm good here. Shit."

"Yeah."

"You bring him?"

"No," Steve said. "Ambulance. I followed behind."

"How'd that go?"

"Strange."

The woman in the waiting area tossed the jacket to the next chair and beat against it as if she snared a rat and trapped it underneath.

"You need a ride back?"

"No, man, I can grab a bus." Steve zipped his jacket. "If I have to, I can walk."

"You're not walking from Harvey to Deerwood, and I'd lose my badge if I let you hop public transit from here." Freddie finger-saluted a slim security officer as she walked past. Steve noticed the gold band was absent from the ring finger. "Besides I have to get back anyway."

46

"See, it's better up here in front," Steve said.

"Glad you can joke about it." At a traffic signal, Freddie checked the plate of the car ahead of them on his dash computer.

"You do that all the time?"

"Yeah," Freddie said. "We all do. We're like teenage chicks checking their phones with these things."

"Hey, can you take the second right?"

"Thought I was taking you home."

"You are."

The one-story home on Elm with a basement foundation and an elfish detached garage at the right rear was a rook. It held the periphery while the king and queen muddled about and stood, no matter the abuse or loneliness it suffered, at the ready when called to duty again. The queen was lost and mourned; the king in a tumble somewhere between lost and found. The cement stairs at front were a trap seen from the car window and may buckle when the first attempt was taken, but the drawbridge would give in and steady the way to the front door.

"Are you sure?" Freddie asked.

"Yeah, I am."

"I can wait for you out front."

Freddie had been there the day Steve and Brooke had moved in and had come back the next weekend with Marty to paint the living room, drink beer, secure some insulation in the attic, and drink beer.

There are easier days behind us than ahead. If only we could have kept them. If only we could have been allowed to.

"No really," Steve said.

We'll do the second coat, you guys have done so much. Well, if you brought beer and the rum and the Coke, I guess you could stay.

"I've got to get some stuff for the trip downstate. A lot of its still here."

"Remember when I dropped that box of dishes?" Freddie asked. "Good thing Brooke was in the garage. I don't think she ever knew."

"She does—*did*," Steve corrected.

He wondered if Freddie saw the front sheer move like a kitten had brushed against it. He also wondered if the neighbors had taken note of the squad car running out front of the empty house.

"She found the receipt from Macy's."

"Shit," Freddie laughed. "Wasn't it Fields back then?"

"I can't remember."

Steve knew Freddie well enough and brought the reminisce in for a landing before the past coated the present.

"Hey, you and, uh, Dani doing okay?"

"Just hard, you know? Sometimes?" Freddie's hand and eyes were poised as if the car were moving. Perhaps to a someplace in drive or reverse that he would rather be. "You get married and you think it's the last piece, only to find out it wasn't. It's not that she's not the same person you married, but you're not the person that married her."

Steve let his friend settle into his own stream of words.

"Or maybe you're both the same," Freddie continued. "And all that baggage you thought you were leaving along the aisle as you walked down it never really went away. Not a vow in the world that could have kept it away."

"You know," Steve said. "I'm not the best source or anything but if I can . . . if you need . . ."

"You mean a lot to me, Steve. I've stopped thinking I owed you something a long time ago. I'm just glad to be your friend."

"You're better than a brother."

"Well, considering."

They both laughed.

Steve's phone lit up in his hand.

"Oh, geez."

"What?" Freddie wanted to reach over and answer himself. "Is it Cleo? The hospital?"

"No," Steve reassured. "No, Cindy. Lancaster."

"Oh." Freddie pulled back into his seat. "How's that going?"

"She's a little bent that I won't be around for Thanksgiving and a little more bent that I'm not in too much of a hurry to get back." Steve sent the call to voicemail with his thumb. "Said she'd hold off on dinner until Saturday but not Sunday."

"That's a bit odd."

"Well, you remember Cindy. Possession mixed with passion."

"Not much has changed, huh?"

"No." Steve did know some of her had though. "Not at the core, I guess."

"From what I do recall, that's not all bad."

"There's that."

"Happy Thanksgiving, man," Freddie said. "Maybe one of these years we can spend it together again."

"Yeah."

And those would be difficult days that would only look simple.

"Seems were working in that direction."

Steve pushed against the front door, and it fought like a refrigerator when the seal needs further persuading. He thought of that old *Jones* movie again where the Egyptians lift the top of the chamber away and the sides belch with ancient smoke. Here at the old house, there was no smoke but dust. The lungs of the house exhaled a plume of recycled air that landed like sawdust along the waist-high cabinet just beyond the door. He drew a finger path across the top.

He edged in along the back of the sofa with the interchangeable footing of both a hesitant thief rummaging over new turf and the confident return of old shoes that had found a familiar road. His hands stayed active in the light, as if any moment either he would go blind or the house decided it preferred the darkness. The suits he needed would be where he left them; there was no need to check the closets yet. His car keys were still claimed by the right peg on an interior framing wall that divided the living room from the kitchen.

The left peg thrusted at the same angle, but the glossy wood there was bare.

Under the television on a shelf was a cake-pan-sized DVD player, longer than it was wide. Video cassettes with permanent marker reminders of days past were slanted as if napping into a small stack of DVDs. The bottom three were smalltime horror fare; the top, an old comedy with stills of wide mouths on faces that promised ninety minutes of hilarity you could hide in.

"This one used to make us laugh." Steve sat in the orange cloth chair with the "I know they're plastic, but they look wicker" side arms. The chair croaked a melody of stiff, tentative wood. "We didn't laugh enough."

"*We laughed plenty.*" Brooke sat cross-legged on the small sofa next to the chair, silver-blue wool socks tucked under each knee, an overdone sweater hid her slacks. "*It was some of the other things we missed on.*"

She reached for him and discarded the DVD box. She took his hands into hers.

"*It's good to see you. Good to see the man I met.*"

"I don't think I was ever this good." Under Steve's fingers, Brooke's hands morphed from a kind touch he remembered to the sensation of holding air. "I kept a lot of things from you. Even when you asked, I kept them. Drawer full of those airline-sized bottles. The decanter in the cabinet that you never saw. Even after you asked me to . . ."

"*Who says I didn't know?*"

"I say you didn't."

"*So you really believed that my favorite cologne of yours not only had a woodsy, masculine smell but also masked the scent? Coffee or that menthol mouthwash you use doesn't work either? Newsflash, we weren't perfect. We didn't invent that. I kept things from you too,*" Brooke said.

Steve saw her again in the hospital bed, bald with a blood-stained scalp and a body run through like a pincushion. Liquids pulsated in and out of her, chugging through transparent tubes—the decimation of a living disease in a dying host.

"*Now we both know that.*"

"It would have been so different." Steve studied the table in front of him—the table with four finely tuned ninety-degree points that they always said would have to be replaced the minute a future child would have found mobility. Somewhere in the breaths the house held on to, a much-used Scrabble board favoring Brooke rested on the tabletop between two cold beers—relics that were done in by the next blink.

"If I stepped left instead of right, that one night. If I'd have been more aware of my knees, took better care of things, I could have played out that scholarship, been what everybody wanted. Maybe even played pro, you know, not a first-round draft or anything but a short solid career. I could have done that. It would have been better."

"*You're forgetting . . .*"

"No I'm not."

"*Yes.*" He could feel her hands peel away. "*You are.*"

The real Brooke would not have made this about her, but the understudy leaned in other direction sometimes. It was best to hold all tickets until there was an official result as to which way the process would break.

"*Cleo,*" the real Brooke said. "*Without you being there tonight and everything that led up to you being there, Cleo doesn't have much of a chance to get to a hospital, and those kids would have no one. From what I can see, it turned out very well. We always end up right where were needed, but the path is often mighty different than expected.*"

"Someone would have been there," Steve said. "There's always someone. It's why you don't jump to the front of the line when the teacher asks for volunteers. Always someone."

"*That kind of thinking*"—she paused as if having a sip of her drink—"*stops most intentions from turning into actions. Absolves a lot of responsibility, if you ask me.*"

"I wouldn't have traded my time with you for anything."

He reached for her again. With a finger like a paintbrush, he drew along the high cheek bone, the curve of her jaw, and her feathery lips.

"You were the shelter in the storm."

"*But that means there was still a storm,*" Brooke said.

"Always a storm." He stood.

Strained steps sought their way to their bedroom—short in distance, miles of memory.

"*Mostly the ones we make for ourselves.*" She waited now by the front door, hands folded in front of her. Her posture was of one who stood by while the last guest scrambled for their coat and stumbled to the door. "*This next part . . . make it matter,*" she said when Steve returned. "*You no longer have to live in the past. You are free to go. Sell this house or move back in. All that you have left behind is behind you to stay. Life is so short, Steve.*"

"No," he said. "No it's not. It's enduring. It's painful. A treadmill over a minefield, filled with mornings I have to drag myself from bed and nights I can't summon the energy to sleep through. It's just a waiting room with an unclear destination. I've lost the all the things that I love. I've even lost the things that hurt me."

"*Then while you're waiting, make it matter.*"

"Speaking of Cleo," Steve said and brought the house key forward. Suit bags were slung from a shoulder. "Maybe you could keep a watch on him while I'm gone?"

"*You know I would, but . . .*" she said. "*It doesn't work that way.*"

"Oh."

"*Yeah, I was surprised too. I thought there would be more purpose, more haunting.*" She opened the door for him. "*Cindy Lancaster, though, really?*" Brooke asked. She had a wiry, sarcastic grin and a tone that could have asked "is that what you're wearing?"—a rhetorical beep she would often utter as he neared this very door in days long past.

"I though you just said it didn't work that way."

"*Well, some things do.*"

"Goodbye, Brooke." Steve stepped back into the night.

The deadbolt was encouraged back into place, and it sounded like it always did—like the key needed to remind it to go. Steve had examined the lock almost every month for the first year he and Brooke lived on Elm Street. It looked like it should fit into the hole that was designed on the doorframe. There were no rough edges, no scars in the metal, but the turn of the house key was a struggle of wills in both the warm, humid summer and dry, frigid winter. The side door nearer the garage was an exit of habit borne of surrender.

"It's not goodbye."

Brooke stood on the lowest front step. From the side of the house, she heard the garage door open. The rails scraped against the wheel's dry gears against the balustrade, in resistance to the cold and time. She waited through the pauses of the car door closing, the car starting, tires in a slow roll on the driveway, the door opening, the garage door being put back into place, the car door closing again, and the car now in gear trekking in reverse. It was the song of stops and starts that was owned by non–garage door-opener people.

"Not this time."

"What are you looking at?" Steve adjusted the rearview just over the sight of the back seat so his eyes were a vivid Kilroy above the rim of the mirror. The car bounced onto the street behind him. It was the same thick roll of the curb that had been there every time the car left the driveway and felt like an old shirt returned to its owner, familiar but a part of you that had been donated and not meant to return.

The steering wheel was frozen rubber and the size of a pipe cleaner, much too small in his hands—too small to control a ton or so of metal and plastic through these streets that were meant for a bike. Too powerful of a machine to drive the ten blocks to the apartment. The dash was alive with video-game lights and square numbers that belonged on the space shuttle, not a midsized Chevrolet.

He stopped parallel to the house, the house that was now dark as the night outside of the car and as still as a last breath. The house on Elm that he once shared with a woman named Brooke who had died a painful death from a disease and treatment that were as old as one another.

We can just put the car back. We should take the bus anyway with the team. No, Steve thought. *Cleo said I could have some time after the tournament, time to go up and see for myself.*

Marty's neglect of the mail left him to overlook the missing piece, a piece that would not bring anything or anyone back and, years later, would still not be—what had Marty said, closure? No, it was none of that. It was the one step that Marty could not take and could not be asked to, not now. He needed the illusion, just as Steve needed his.

47

"Isn't it beautiful?"

The man wore a light gray suit with a white shirt sealed by a striped tie still knotted but asking for relief under every breath. Steve had undone his own knot and retired his tie to an inner pocket just after the welcome dinner.

"The Taj Mahal," Steve replied.

He had been looking up at the flat screen perched over the bar, but he knew what the man had meant.

"Emerald city."

And the man was right. Under the golden lights of a stage, the ziggurat at the open center had the blistered blue-green of Midori at the apex closely guarded by the liquors that were mulled over but rarely tried—the Frangelico, Tia Maria, Drambuie, and others like the tempting rocket-shaped bottle of liquid yellow treasure that Steve had often wondered about and now guessed he always would. The level where the real business was done; the bourbons, the United Nations of American, Canadian, Scotch, and Irish whiskeys that parleyed with rum, gin, and vodka ran across the lower tiers; half bottles in a fading color wheel from dark to light, set just ahead of sealed ones that waited to take the field. A four-hosed beer tap sat at each end, domestics to the left, IPAs and seasonals to the right. The display was a market of magnets, in this and any other place like it, meant for you to stay if you'd like, with the option of always being there when you cared to return.

"Errol Richardson," the man in the suit said. He had the professional toastmaster's handshake, the one with the overdone eye contact and the near five-second pump that lingered like a snapped rubber glove after the release.

"Steve Coleman." He fought the urge to over flex his fingers from the pressure.

"Yeah, I saw the name tag," Errol said. "Forgive the intrusion, but I think my dad used to coach against you. He was up at New Trier. Tony Richardson?"

"Oh, Richardson, sure, I remember." Steve studied the man next to him, conscious of the still-worn "Hello, my name is" tag and the fact that he was at a bar and now at a bar with someone else. "That was a long time ago."

"Yeah," the man said. "Yeah it was. Three years in a row. I think they just tanked on the playoffs the last time around so it wouldn't have to be four."

"No," Steve said. "Those were good teams and some good games."

"He finally retired," Errol added. "I've been in his chair five years now, but it still feels like he never left. Watches every game on YouTube. Sends me a summary of things I missed, what I should have done more of or less of."

"So he's still the same?"

"Yeah," Errol conceded. "Down in Myrtle Beach most of the winter these days—living the dream, I guess. Retired and still coaching the game. Maybe like all of us someday, right?"

"Can I get you something?" the bartender, resplendent in a tuxedo shirt and bow tie, leaned in to ask.

His coifed-and-pressed guise added to the appeal of the pyramid behind him. He was the carnival master dressed to the nines with a slicked back coif of vampiric hair on top. He was the host who would allow you to choose from the big board and distribute with no judgement rendered. You could tell your best story over the potion you requested, and the secrets would be sealed in honor—a time-tested code stronger that patient-doctor confidence or attorney-client privilege.

"I'll have a Coke," Steve said.

"A Coke?"

There was a groan of conversation in the hotel bar and space that expanded beyond but not enough of a roar for the timber of the question.

"You can put a lime in it if that makes you feel better," Steve replied.

"And for you?"

The formal airs were put back on for Steve's suited seat neighbor.

"Club soda with ice," Errol answered. "No fruit." The request of the tie was finally granted with a tug.

"So how long you been a member?"

"Member of what?"

Errol had a knowing look but a look of comfort and counsel when he spoke.

"The 'coffee, water, or soda' club?"

"Not long enough," Steve replied. "And you?"

"Probably could give you the same answer."

The bartender placed the sodas at their fronts with a bowl of bar snacks in a rush and left as if there were a window to close ahead of a hurricane.

"Two marriages gone. Kids I don't recognize. Bills I shouldn't still be paying. Hangs on you like the flu—and a determined one too."

The men raised their glasses to each other as more of a crowd moved in.

"To the simple game," Steve offered.

"Made complicated by men like us. Pass to the open man," Errol said.

"I think I've used that before."

"Then you know more than most." Errol sipped, and the sour club soda bit down on his taste buds. He squinted and swallowed—a premium tank filled by regular fuel. "Which reminds me," Errol said. "Word is you've done a real good job with a club team. Handled some of the big boys already."

"Some," Steve agreed. "Of the ones who will play us."

"Well, you must have done something right to get here," Errol laughed. "Lots of opportunity on the North Side, you know. Chairs being vacated right and left," he said. "Some retiring like my dad, but for others, it just wasn't big enough. For some, it's too big. I'd bet you'd fit right in."

"Well, I'm not looking to—"

"Don't matter if you're looking to or not," Errol interrupted. "I'm still gonna pass your name along. Wouldn't hurt to talk to somebody—they might know somebody. You know how it goes."

"I think." Steve pushed the lime into his Coke with the slim straw. "Thank you."

"People still remember you, Steve."

"Errol, have you noticed?" Steve pulled at the edge of his welcome tag but left it in place.

"Yeah," came the answer. "I thought we'd be the best dressed in here."

Steve raised his hand in the direction of the bar staff.

The secret weapon answered—peroxide blonde, eyes like gems, and a body of taut curves that disputed the need for straight lines.

"Gentlemen?" she had a husk of a voice that roared with confidence as she embraced her passing years and she looked like all women do when they wore a man's dress shirt—clothed in the afterglow of fucking and on a saturnalia for more. "Change your minds?"

"Not yet," Errol answered in a start as if released from sleep by a teacher and was now on display for the class.

"We were just wondering," Steve said. "Why are Batman, a Stormtrooper, and a crew of Hobbits in here?"

"Oh," she said. "Central Illinois Comic Convention. Every year the night before Thanksgiving."

"Ah."

"Yep." She took a towel from the underside and wiped the area behind Steve's glass. "Convention center is just across the freeway, but we have the better bar. And let me tell you"—she leaned in to *tell* them—"those nerds drink more, tip better, and stare less than you sports guys."

The swath from hips to ass, a pied piper, visible and audible behind the snug polyester slacks swayed as she left.

"Thank goodness, I thought I was back to seeing shit," Errol said.

"Yeah, and I was thinking I just started." Steve ran the gamut with his eyes.

For every person dressed for travel, business, or pleasure, there was one from a comic, fantasy world, or film. There weren't many gatherings like this, but when there was, most of them showed up. Maybe they all did.

"Errol, it was a pleasure meeting you."

"You as well."

"And thank you again."

"Hey, I'm serious." Errol remained seated, a former monarch on a missing throne, while Steve stood. "Somebody will be in touch with you. I know they will."

Steve delayed just out of hope that Errol would leave his seat.

"Well, see you tomorrow, I guess. Take it easy on us, just in case, you know."

"You'll be fine," Errol said.

But Steve heard it as "I'll be fine," which had nothing to do with basketball and usually meant the entire edifice that we spent the last weeks or years building was threads away from becoming porcelain to the preordained earthquake. Lesson learned—you don't tell yourself you're fine, talented, or beautiful, always let somebody else tell you. That way, it counts. But it was not Steve's field to tend.

"Hey!" Darrell held the door as Steve passed through from bar to lobby. "We're meeting at eight, right?"

"No." Steve checked his silent phone for the time. "I think we'll be good. Enjoy your night, okay?"

"Sure, you're the boss." Darrell looked for the signs with uncertainty as if he had been warned but was unsure of how to use the instruction manual. Or if he should.

"Honestly," Steve said and moved himself and Darrell out of the doorway back into the hotel lobby. "It's not what you think, and it's all right that you're thinking it. There's an old friend of mine across the street. At least, there's a chance she's there—a small one—but I'd just like to see her."

"Okay," Darrell said. "Go get her. I'll bring the schedule up to your room later then."

"Yeah, thank you. And thank you for understanding."

"I get you man, no worries." Darrell stepped aside for an Iron Man trailed by a zombie.

"Good luck in there."

"Hey, you're the guy with name tag."

48

It was one of those times where "across the street" meant "directly across the street but nowhere close to being easy to get to"—like when a child in the next room tells a parent they'll be *there* in a minute. Exit ramps where there would be a paved road were out of sight on both the north and south ends of the street, but a drive still felt pointless.

It's right fucking there.

The convention center and the Hilton were the only buildings in sight over the flat Midwestern Highway, and from some angles, there appeared the possibility of leaping from one to the other.

His loafers were no match for the slick grass decline on the side of the expressway until he turned sideways and lurched hard into each step as if wearing snowshoes. Near the bottom, his shuffle turned into quick eighth-note steps to fight the decreasing angle and crescendoed into a live-action *Frogger* against the early evening traffic.

His dark suit, a welcome cloaking device in a room full of coaches, was a risky proposition for a pedestrian. But crossing the interstate on foot had not entered his mind when he dressed in his hotel room. The side opposite had an incline at the same degree as the downside which could be conquered, he found, only by testing a knee that had not been pushed past the boundaries of contractual obligation for more than a decade.

The fence placed in prevention of egress was frail. Intentional, Steve thought. It kept anyone from walking up the freeway and having access to the hotels both by being present and looking as if one good pull would rip it from the ground and send you back to the pavement below, holding a piece of the gate as a shield versus a truck.

Steve wrapped his hands into the chain link for the moment, to prevent a fall not to start a climb.

"Well, I'm just not used to having a car," he said aloud in reply to a question that tapped against him. "Shit."

The tip of his shoe lay against rather than allowed for an insert into the diamond that was the logical first step.

His hands and arms were the anchors as his legs and shoes with no traction discarded their use. The top had no wire but found a ready replacement in pliability, which forced the end of the ascent to be parallel to the ground and the hope that one hand and a focus on balance would hold him as the other tossed his shoes over to the landing side. The shoes made a chore of going up and would have made a slide going down.

"There." Steve landed on his socks, disappointed in a mixture of more gravel than sod. "I did it. You didn't think I could, but I made it. I'm going to make it."

He brushed each sock and found his shoes.

"You're right, Brooke. We're right where we are supposed to be."

From his new view, the presence of a walkway below the freeway was fully visible but was only earned a quick glance. Had his venture taken him south instead of suddenly across, he would have arrived on the comfort of cold but dry asphalt, had enough light to read by, and had the probability of dry socks and insoles that had not been exchanged for sponges.

"Even if we take the long way."

"Hi there, hello, my name is Steve Coleman." The man who provided Steve his last handshake of a long day had a grip that was thin and soggy like a wet sheet of newspaper. "Your tag, it's from Dr. Who, right?"

"Oh, this," Steve said and removed the name tag from his breast pocket. "No. It's forgetfulness from the hotel across the street."

"I see."

The man moved in jerks behind the small table as if his body wanted to break the confines of the booth and was reined in by an electric field when he reached the edges. The tail of his untucked black shirt followed at his waist like a trained dog. Character buttons and lapel pins competed for fabric along each front side.

"Well, I'm Merlin. No name tag, though."

"I don't think it would fit."

"What?"

"Never mind," Steve said. "This artwork is amazing."

"She's really great."

"She?"

Steve was at his ninth table visit now, three-quarters around the horseshoe of the converted meeting room. The convention held more spaces for collectable toys, books, and cult films that it did for its namesake. Though several women abounded in costumes—some scanty and others downright terrifying—none were, at the moment, perched in the cube to mind and celebrate their wares.

Merlin, with fingers long and wiry like bristles on a broom tied together, brushed the large placard at the front of the table.

"I'm a little biased, but she is the best," Merlin said as he pointed.

"I think I agree."

"My girlfriend." In winding calligraphy, "A Reynolds" was slanted just under the drawing and title. "The artist not the creature. Abby. She calls him the Mender."

"The Mender?" Steve looked up at another presentation of her concept, a foot or more above him.

From rings of fire, a horned demon broke free. One clawed hand held a frayed chain that had lost the struggle. The other hand tempted any opposition with a bright ball of light that had stripes like a basketball would. There were shreds of clothing that revealed red muscle to rival a space-age prizefighter. Intricate body ink trailed outward from its pectorals. Golden eyes that made you believe in something lurking behind you shone from an executioner's hood. The face itself was not visible, buried in swirls of black ruin, but Steve did not have to see it to know and was glad she had hidden it.

"Best-selling independent urban comic series of the year," Merlin announced more than said. "She's at a panel now but should be back in ten minutes or so it you want to meet her."

"No." Steve took one more look at the Mender. "I've got to get back."

"Well, here then." Merlin reached into a milk crate. "First edition, issues 1, 2, and 3 each signed, package never opened, with a letter from the artist. If you like the work, that is."

"Yeah," Steve said. "I'll take those. Let's get two. I have a neighbor who may like to read through them."

E

Abby? Abby, can you come out? I want to draw.

So draw.

No. I mean the real way. Like we used to do.

Oh, okay.

Why do I feel so dizzy?

I'm going to have trouble sleeping again tonight so I took something.

Oh.

If we're drawing, why do you want to go to sleep?

You mean later.

All right then.

If we're drawing, what are we doing in here?

I'm just putting the pills away, Abby.

I'm so much more attractive than you are. Look at yourself, it's such a shame how you've let yourself deteriorate to this.

I know, Abby.

You know what we should get you? A tattoo. Yes, that's what we should do. Like a token. A permanent reminder of all you've accomplished.

Yes.

Yeah? Here, let me do it. At least let me try. You've done so much for me. We could draw him right here on this arm so you'd always remember. You can't even draw a straight line without *me*. I should be the one who . . . why is my head spinning like that? How many of those did you take?

I told you, just enough to sleep.

262

The door is locked! How are we supposed to get out there and draw? Come on, Alphabet Girl, unlock the door. A straight line, you want to see a straight line? There! Let's start it right there.

Well, we haven't done this in a while. I must admit, that is comforting.

Guess it's back to the long sleeves, but hey, you're going a bit deep, that kind of hurt.

What? Put your top back on.

Well, he may want to look at your body later, but I'm not sure I do, you pasty white shrew.

What?

Your name, yes, I know your . . . never call you by it.

What do you mean?

Yes, I see. It's staring right back at me. Reversed but in the mirror, I can see it, like the word ambulance in the rearview when you drive.

But why would you?

For all the world to see so they will forget who died and remember who lived.

What do you mean? Why is the door still locked? What do you mean they were dead before the fire!

He gave you this idea.

No, he is not doing this to us. Open the door! Now! Whyisthefuckingdoorlocked?

Another straight line?

No, I don't think I can take another . . . straight . . . line . . . that now I know you can draw without *me* . . . how beautiful that line is . . . so . . . relieving. I don't think that is paint in the sink . . . he's going to have to clean . . . just like we did . . . the cleansing, the cutting . . . Alphabet Girl?

No, no more. No more name calling or shoving me out of the way. No more lying.

Honesty—you want me to be honest? I was the one who let you live.

Abcde? No . . .

See, there, I said it. I said it, I know your name. I will, from now on. Don't make it be too late.

No, it's already late . . . dawn to ashes or is it ashes to dust? Midnight, twilight, some light that I don't know.

Sunlight? Look, it's the light of the next day.

No, just the lights from in here in front of the mirror. The mirror never lies. I was so beautiful, how could you? They all wanted *me*, you just had to watch.

So it's a turnabout, the devil's dance, and now, I want you to watch.

Goodbye, Abby.

COMING HOME

ONE FAREWELL

The ringtone pierced like a cold arrow to the throat. He allowed for a breath to take shape, aware of the vapor it made, and he chased back the hot oil that gathered from his neck to just under his eyes.

Steve had made a new selection as he did every week; but the tone, buzz, bell, sound, or song were irrelevant. A small victory was registered with the phone, audible now for three straight weeks. But spells of anxiety persisted with each call and reminded him, at the macro level, defeat had high hopes of returning.

"Hello," he answered.

"Steve. Hi, it's Ab."

The two unspoken syllables were a phantom limb in Steve's mind.

"Hi, I was just about to tear into volume one here." His fingers traced the cellophane. "Your drawings are just beautiful."

"Thank you," she said.

Her voice—at word six, the change was as apparent as a red stain on a white shirt. It was no longer wind through a flute.

"What are you doing here? And where exactly are you?" She was the confident bellow of a bass drum interested not in his proximity but concerned he would be close enough to meddle.

"At the hotel across the freeway." He strode to the window where the view was the side opposite but looked out anyway. "You know how hard it is to cross an interstate on foot?"

"No."

"Good. Take it from me, it's harder than it should be," he said. "I'm here with the team. We're kind of passing through." Back at the desk, he slid a finger down the plastic wrapping of her books. The drawings had no dimension, but he could feel each sharp bend of Abcde's pen. Black, leaden fences erected to separate color from color and bring to life the secrets of her mind. "Thanksgiving tournament in Centerville this weekend. The turkey shoot."

"That doesn't sound too fun for the turkeys." The crisp riff of her new instrument again. "Are you coaching?"

"Well, me and Cleo are, but he's not feeling too good at the moment."

"Is Cleo all right?" Abcde asked. "I remember him."

She met him?

"Yeah, he's going to be fine. I talked to him earlier. Just thought it best if he stayed back this time."

A knock took him from the desk to the door.

"Hey, you know, since you're not too far away, maybe we could run into each other or something tonight. I know it's been a while, but there's a nice place here . . . on my side of the street."

Steve took the papers from Darrell and, with a wink, reclosed the door.

"I'm not so sure we should." Her voice a reluctant thud but a thud nonetheless. "It's kind of complicated right now, with Merlin and all."

"Yeah."

"I mean we're kind of at that new place, you know?" She paused to make sure he did. "Where every guy on the street is a threat but the exes and used-to-be's are a sure poison."

"Yeah, I know, but I'm not exactly an—" Steve stopped to consider and acknowledge her point. "He seems nice. Different but nice. So what are you doing for Thanksgiving?"

The question was quick, as if a lifeboat to a conversation he would rather have stay afloat for a long as the night would allow.

"We'll be at Merlin's parents. They're up in Peoria."

"Oh," he said. "That's not such a bad drive."

"No."

He heard the grating of a sliding door from her end of the call and a breezy hum of the interstate below.

"And you, what are you doing?" she asked from what Steve saw as a small balcony.

"I'll be here with the team," he said. "Most of the parents came down, so you know, dinner and such. Maybe a quick practice." He set the team papers out of sight. "So the Mender, huh? Former basketball player, possible toxic accident, keeping the city streets safe from madness and mayhem?"

"And other stories. Just like the title says."

"Well, I can't wait to read them."

"Steve," she said, with one word her tone muted—an indication that her side of the conversation no longer had an audience. She was a reed with a hollow center. "It's good that you're doing better."

"There is no better."

"I know. I shouldn't have said that."

"You know," Steve said, "I never thought that I'd ever be at the point in my life where convincing the right foot to follow the left out in the morning is the hardest thing I do all day." He sipped from the water bottle at his side with only a quick second's desire that it would be something else. Something that was in full flow just five floors below him, the call of the mermaid to the lost sailor ready to seduce, indulge, and pull you under. "After that, it's easy. But I have to choose it. Every day."

"It's good to know you're doing something that you like."

He could not see her but knew she was leaning, lifted on the pointed ends of soft shoes, the thin railing a metal restrain across her middle.

"I hear it helps." She wasn't going to give him any more space.

Steve reached for the remainder of the time he had with her and found a memory, one like a child peeking from a corner found at hide-and-seek. "Didn't we do this last Thanksgiving?"

"I think we did," she said. "Just like us to drive a hundred miles further and still be standing a few blocks from each other."

"Maybe this could be our tradition. Every Thanksgiving, the night before, you know, we check in."

"Now that's a tradition I could be in to."

"Be better than stuffing a turkey or boiling cranberries."

"Yeah, screw all that. No visiting, no . . . nothing."

"You ever notice that bad stuffing has the consistency of a hair ball?"

The silent space spoke to both of them. It carried the reminder that they had ended up back in—or maybe had never left a place— where Thanksgiving would always be turkey, dressing, cranberries, and visiting. And maybe, *maybe*, one late-night phone call that others, as they came and eventually went, would have to grow to understand or learn to ignore.

"Congratulations on your success," Steve told her.

"Thank you." The woodwind and percussion wove together. "It's been a hard year. Maybe . . . there is some light after all."

"There's always light," he said. "Sometimes you just have to open your eyes and make sure they stay that way."

"Good night, Steve," she said and closed her eyes.

She welcomed the night breeze, a drift of soft cotton over her face. Part of her imagined the wind a caress of a gentle lover she would never know or one she had just pushed away. He would have been gentle, accepting to a fault and understanding when she needed to stay in or break out. Despite her pretend, she knew the breeze was the flames of a tornado winding up for one last strike at her frame of wood and ill-conceived but well-intentioned nails, the outcome all but certain.

"Goodnight, Ab—." He never knew why he stopped. "Talk with you soon, okay?"

"Soon."

SECOND FAREWELL

And there was a Thanksgiving a year or some years later. The trick of memory made the exact moment unclear. She wove her way down the stairs and through the hall, avoidance of her Casper the Ghost–like fondness for entrance through the wall and found you—you, standing at the picture window in your home office, the optional fourth bedroom. There are three of them now looking back at you from the small expanse of land that abuts the new house. *Your* new house.

"Your brother is here," she says from beside you. She shares the view, seeing what you see, quite sure her use of the doorway was intentional.

The static from her skin to yours true as her breath you swore you could see and not the gooseflesh from an all-too-real illusion.

"I figured it was about that time," you say to Brooke. "I was just . . ." You start but you can't deceive her. Not anymore. Not before. "I just thought I saw something."

"It's okay," she says, slender, gentle hands entwining your arm. "It's all right to remember, as long as we remember to let go. They need that too sometimes. Even more than we do."

You turn now, face to face. She is at once the girl you chased, the woman you loved, and a shimmer, maybe more, of the woman she was not allowed to become. Her eyes, a pool of time, radiate a life passing by. There would have been a solid grace in that aging.

"You know," you say, "I have a feeling that this is the last Thanksgiving I get to spend with you."

"I think it is," she answers. "All things end. If you wait long enough."

Some of what you left behind was a walk through quicksand that had no intent of letting go. This was a sudden pull at the bandage of an old wound.

"Then thank you," you say, your tone level, dagger-sharp like a wedding vow. "Thank you for every last moment."

You look again, through and then past the window. The woman next to your parents removes her wool hat and holds it at her side. The broken smiley hangs from her left coat pocket. Her hair, longer than you remember, runs in layers of color from bleach to coral. She smiles, but it's her expression just beyond that will stay with you—a broken record pining to hurdle the scratch and find the next groove suddenly free to share the song she had to give.

"I'm so sorry about her," Brooke says. "She was so scared. She learned to control everything outside of her—or keep it away—but never thought she deserved to control the inside. It's why she could never be with you. You would have given her peace, and she didn't want to know that road. She was a cage but only allowed herself one key."

Brooke looks back to you. Her face awakens in anguish. She no longer knows where she is. This space was not hers, but she came anyway.

"Steve?"

In a motion of suffocation, her hands levitate to her throat. But you reach and hold them back, hold them as if they were still part of yours, which you imagine they always will be.

"You can go now."

She calms at the elixir of your words that are painted with the tones of "suffer no more."

Sounds of muffled greetings pulse from somewhere in the house. You hesitate. This room, this view, has become a dock where you are safe from the peril that may lie ahead.

"You know," Brooke says to you, "some time ago, your brother opened his home to you on Thanksgiving. You don't know it, but you needed him then, just like he needs you now."

She looks to the doorway of your office needing to go but first showing you the way.

Setting in, you privately count from three, two . . .

"Thank you, Brooke. You were priceless."

With that, she's gone.

A look into the window, and there are now four.

Nodding in perceived agreement, they walk—*float*—to a space behind the trees and vanish from a world that can no longer hold them. As if on a moving walkway, you shift more than arrive in the kitchen. The old Bears jersey you remember wearing once on a day like this long ago has been replaced by a gray man-about-the-house cardigan. One that Lisa picked out for you. The first gift she had ever bought for a man that was not thrown back at her or used to steal more of her. You believed her when she told you this and feel it in every fiber of the familiar wool.

Marty is there, holding a six-pack of bottles. Dark green. Imported. Marty of *ago*, for better or worse, was almost back. He had left enough behind where once a month he had a weekend with the girls—this fall, so far, unsupervised.

"Hey," he says, lifting the beer almost in admission. "It's okay, right? You said it was, but . . ."

"Yeah, it's fine. Get them to the fridge, man," you say.

"All right!" A mock celebration in his voice surrounded a puzzle-frame of relief. "Hey, just in time we got the Bears and Lions, finally."

"You know," you were saying with an arm draped around him. "I remember a Bears–Lions game when . . ."

And yes, you do remember. Remembering certain days based on a series of numbers was benign, but it was still a spur—a small hurt that panged when you tripped over the peripheral presence of days where most memories were gone. Some parts die harder than others in all of us like the gesture of sincere gratitude from Lisa when you looked back upon turning away from the bustling kitchen with your brother. Never had a man asked permission to vacate the kitchen in order to escape to a football game in the next room.

"Go," Lisa says. "He needs to be here. He needs you. I'll need you later."

"I also remember," Marty says when you and he are clear of the crowd. "I owe you this."

He worked a folded envelope from his back pocket into your hand.

"Marty, you don't have to."

"Yeah, I do," he says. "You're just too nice or too dumb to ask about it. I know you didn't forget, and I didn't either."

You take the passed envelope, still sealed, and lean it against a photo on the mantle.

"It's not everything, but it's some."

"You really didn't . . ."

"Yeah. Yes I did." Marty glances at the photo now. "Mom and Dad would have wanted it that way."

And you realized then that the only way Marty would ever see your parents—ever feel them again—was through that photo and others like it. A photo taken long before the end, shortly after Marty and Melinda had married. Mom and Dad in dark, pampered clothing bought for church services they no longer attended and dinners out that would define them.

They showed age but were still young. Young, based on the moving target of old, as measured by growing and now older incomplete children.

"We're older, Marty," you would tell your brother one day. "Not grown, just older."

There would have still been time that day, the day squared off by a ten-dollar frame. Back when they placed hands on smalls of backs as ordered to, not because they provided any comfort and were told to look at the camera and—*Mrs. Coleman, could you tilt your head just a touch? There, that's right.*

The picture, like all pictures, was a cover for the words unspoken, the words just off to the side. Blasphemy to expect a picture is worth a thousand words because pictures speak their own language, far more elegant and removed from a tired swath of nouns and verbs. They only hold the moment the photographer asks for and the one the participant wanted. What happened before or after is of no matter to the photographer or the observer, and in that, there is perfection.

He didn't have to know—may not ever have to—what the investigator from the hotel told you. You look at your brother and see him, almost childlike, watching another Thanksgiving Day game unfold in front of his eyes, his lips ready for what may not be his first beer of the day. That was all he needed to see today like another stranger you once knew so many years ago.

Later, if anyone was watching, they would see the oval table complete, overdone with well-worn shades of pumpkin and six chairs, like the plates and glasses in front of them—full. This moment neither erases the past nor defines the future. Even behind closed eyes, you have the impression of Lisa and her son to your left. You and Lisa together from a distance, pressed into proximity from circumstance and not a true need to be with each other.

"I give it four months," Freddie said four months earlier over the phone.

And he was right, even if he misread the actual expiration date. With Lisa, there was passion but in moments, not a deluge like with Brooke. It was the kindness that was the crutch, which was reciprocated as well as the allowance, without payback, for the space and silence you both needed. It was a relationship at best defined by the nonchalance of those who cling to one another after a shared truth or the logistical simplicity of being stuck at the same school of office together.

Cleo Washington—older now but always wiser—to your right. Further down, Marty. Still someone you don't recognize but a touch closer to the one you grew up with. Mrs. Chambliss, who insisted on Esther but will always be Mrs. Chambliss, despite her loss this past spring, was at the opposite end from you. A call out of the blue to her so she could have the Thanksgiving she always missed was made, and the invitation accepted. The other invitation was declined by a faraway voice of an old friend that sounded full of doubt upon a return to Illinois anytime soon.

The table holds around it what remains. As the days pass, the gap will close, you are sure of that, stitch by stitch and thread by thread. The nightmares will also come. Some, when expected, as if called home by their old master. Other times, they will be furtive like a sunburn on a cloudy day. Those moments will push, will make you want to push back against the mend, splitting it but just a crack. Just enough.

And you may look—indeed, you will. You have that right, the right of freewill to take the wrong path every damn time. Your reality is that the seam could part, almost as if the weaver designed it that way. Runners stumble, and we all know airlocks rupture. Your hope is that what remains with you will be gravity when called upon.